"Dangling participle: A participle with no clear grammatical relationship to the subject of the sentence."
—*American Heritage Book of English Usage*

DEATH
Dangles a Participle

By | E. E. Kennedy

Elkhart, Indiana
46514 USA

Praise for E. E. Kennedy

"Mystery writer E. E. Kennedy brings back her plucky sleuth, teacher Amelia Prentice, in *Death Dangles a Participle*. Newly married Amelia is plunged into a mystery involving a frozen body discovered on Lake Champlain, site of the rumored Lake Champlain monster. This time however, the monster is human. Will Amelia discover his identity before it's too late? Kennedy delights and satisfies lovers of cozy mystery with her newest offering."

—Nancy Mehl, author of The Ivy Towers Mysteries, the Curl Up and Dye Mysteries, and The Road to Kingdom Series,

"*Death Dangles a Participle* is a mystery lover's dream. Just when you think you've found the truth, someone walks in and blurts out the unthinkable. With laughter hiding in unexpected places, and clues hidden in plain sight, *Death Dangles a Participle* will cause you to guess and second guess what it truly means to do the right thing and to speak the truth in love."

—June Felix, scriptwriter, executive producer for Life of Prayer Ministries, Trans World Radio, and host for Moody Radio, WGNB

"E. E. Kennedy has 'dunnit' again! I loved her first book, *Irregardless of Murder*, and her second book in the Miss Prentice Cozy Mystery Series, *Death Dangles a Participle*, is another A+! [Kennedy] skillfully pulls you into the story from the very beginning, and you don't want to leave Amelia Prentice's rustic, historic, and quaint hometown in northern New York State. I love the journey, the descriptive language that creates a cozy ambiance and paints pictures with words. You meet memorable characters of every type, age, and stage experiencing the complexities of human relationships, not to mention references to the Lake Champlain monster (cousin to the Loch Ness). . . .

"I found with *Death Dangles a Participle*, there came a point of no return and you simply had to read it to the very thrilling conclusion. If you like a heartwarming, humorous, and thoroughly satisfying mystery, you'll love this story!"

———Ann Ault, actress, singer, screenwriter, and author of
Hi From the Sky: On the Road to Happily Ever After

"E. E. Kennedy has done it again! *Death Dangles a Participle* is a cozy continuation in the witty and brilliant Miss Prentice Cozy Mystery Series. The characters feel real . . . and make me wish they were flesh and blood. This is a who-dunnit with heart— and I can't wait for the next installment."

—Donna Earnhardt, author of *Being Frank* and blogger
at *wordwranglernc.wordpress.com*

"E. E. Kennedy has written an endearing story sure to entertain cozy mystery lovers everywhere!"

—Pamela Thibodeaux, author, speaker, editor of
TheWordsmithJournalMagazine.com

Dedicated to the memory of a sweet and talented young woman: Kelsey Spann, who designed this book's cover.

Other books
by E. E. Kennedy

Irregardless of Murder
Book 1 of the Miss Prentice Cozy Mystery Series

"*The Applesauce War*"
in the anthology *The Farmer's Bride*,
from Barbour Publishing

Prologue

Christmas vacation was coming to an end, and the Rousseau brothers were determined to savor every second of freedom before the public school system once more took them prisoner.

"Two more days, man, that's all we got left," sixteen-year-old J.T. complained as they drove along the lakeshore road in the elderly Volkswagen beetle that they had lovingly painted a garish, glowing purple.

Dustin, the elder by eighteen months, agreed. "Yeah, so what do we do?"

It was a brilliant, sunny day, and each new turn in the road revealed a different sparkling view of a frozen Lake Champlain, but the brothers noticed none of this beauty as they chugged aimlessly along.

"We gotta do something, man," J.T. said. "We gotta make a name for ourselves. Maybe get our picture in the paper."

He spoke aloud of glory, but in his mind he envisioned a pair of twins, Crystal and Courtney, pink of cheek and sleek of limb in their identical ski pants. The brothers' perpetual quest was to persuade the Gervais sisters to go on a double date.

But how? The Brothers Rousseau lacked the self-discipline for athletics and were not particularly studious. Their looks, while agreeably masculine, lacked the definition that would come with maturity. Their jobs, J.T. working part time at a service station and Dustin at a sporting goods store, barely covered the basic necessity of gasoline for the car and CDs for their battered boom box. To make matters worse, Dustin had just been laid off. They were now reduced to buying used CDs wherever they could find them. IPods were financially out of the question.

The one currency they had in abundance, however, was their utter, wonton recklessness. This they had spent eagerly and in public at every opportunity, taking ridiculous dares, usually involving height: climbing goalposts, water towers, and once last summer, a ranger fire tower. The resulting attention from the police had put a temporary hold on their adventures, but the fire inside them remained unquenched.

"We can't climb anything. Dad'll take away the car if we climb anything again," Dustin reminded his brother. He gazed across the expanse of frozen lake to the Vermont shore. "That ice festival coming up in February? There's a fishing contest. Dad said we could enter with him," he proposed halfheartedly.

"Don't be stupid. Girls don't care about fish. Besides, if I'm going to take Crystal to that dance, I'm gonna have to ask her early. We gotta do something now."

J.T. squinted at the windshield. The sun could be blinding when it reflected off the snowdrifts.

The Volkswagen skidded on an icy curve in the road, and Dustin struggled to return to the right-hand lane. "Stupid car! It's too light to drive on this ice. No traction. Now if we only had a Hummer."

With difficulty and an abrupt jolt, he navigated over an icy ridge. The door of the battered glove compartment flopped open.

"This thing is falling apart!" Dustin reached over and slammed it shut.

"Wait a minute!" J.T. grabbed his brother's elbow.

"Cut it out!" Dustin, startled, accelerated and narrowly avoided sliding into a snow bank.

The glove compartment door bounced open again. With a curse, Dustin leaned over and slammed it shut once more.

"You're gonna get us stuck out here!"

"No, I'm not. I'm gonna get us famous." The wild light of bravado was once more in J.T.'s eye. He pointed to the lake. "How thick d'you think that ice is right now?"

Minutes later, Dustin had driven the Volkswagen down a path that led to the edge of the lake. Both boys climbed out and sheltered their eyes with gloved hands as they gazed at the level, white plain that stretched to the snow-covered Vermont shore. The Green Mountains were a blue shadow beyond. The thumping from their ever-present boom box on the floor of the passenger seat shook the little car and caused gut-wrenching bass thumps to run along the ground.

"I'm telling ya, man, if we make it across, we'll be in the paper. Guaranteed! Maybe on TV too!"

"Yeah, if. I don't know, J.T. It's kind of dangerous."

"I know!" J.T. took a flying leap into a nearby snowdrift. "It'll be great!" He formed a hasty snowball and hit his brother squarely on the shoulder with it. "Don't be a wuss!"

Dustin took no notice of the horseplay. His eyes were still on the lake. "How long do you think it'd take?"

Sensing victory, J.T. scrambled to his feet. He flung out his arm. "Look over there! You can see the other side. It can't be more'n a mile. Two, tops. How long does it take you to drive two miles?"

Five minutes later, the VW had traveled one hundred yards across the ice in an eastwardly direction.

"Come on," J.T. complained as he slid another CD into the boom box on the floor and turned up the volume. "We can go faster than this."

"Who's drivin'? Shut up, okay?" Dustin hunched over the steering wheel and squinted into the distance.

"Whatever." J.T. bobbed his head to the beat of the music and beat a fingertip tattoo on the dashboard.

Another five minutes, and another hundred yards had passed beneath their wheels.

J.T. sighed and slumped in his seat. "This is boring. The speed you're going, it'll be night before we get there. I wanna see people's faces when we pull up on the other side."

He rolled down the window and stuck his head out. "Hey, wait a minute. What's that? Some kind of tent?"

Reverting to his driver's ed training, Dustin was tightly gripping the steering wheel at the ten and two position. He glanced to his right.

"Just somebody ice fishing."

"Wonder who it is. Wait here a minute." J.T. scrambled out of the slow-moving car and slammed the door.

Muttering curses, Dustin braked carefully and went after his brother. Sliding a little on the ice, he quickly overtook J.T. and grabbed the back of his jacket.

"Get back in the car!"

But J.T. was already at the threshold of the tent. He pulled aside the door flap and stuck his head inside.

"There's nobody here!" he called over his shoulder. "But they're fishing, all right. There's the hole. He pointed. "What's that round thing?"

Dustin sighed and peered over his brother's shoulder. "That's called a tip-up. Keeps hold of your fishing line. That's a Frabill, top of the line. When I worked at the store, we sold a lot of 'em. This tent is one of those NIB fishing huts. I bet they bought it at Shea's. But where's all the other stuff, like stools and ice chests? What kind of a guy goes ice fishing without food?"

J.T. shrugged. "Maybe they're off somewhere, makin' yellow snow." He snorted at his own joke.

Dustin glanced back at the car that still throbbed with the hip-hop beat. He pulled at his brother's coat again.

"Come on! Let's get out of here."

J.T. moved further inside. "Wonder if he's caught anything."

"Cut it out! Come on back to the car." Dustin's voice cracked with anxiety.

But his brother wasn't hearing him. J.T. squatted next to the hole in the ice and pulled aside the round plastic disc that stoppered it.

"Look! The ice's got to be more'n a foot thick," he called.

"Better be, or we're dead meat," Dustin muttered, "frozen dead meat."

"Look, over there, Dus, they at least brought some lunch."

J.T. pointed to a metallic lunchbox resting on the ice off to one side. He abandoned his examination of the fishing gear and picked up the box.

"Hey, it's heavy. Wonder what he's got to eat." He fiddled with the clasps.

Dustin's voice combined brotherly sternness with anxiety. "Put that down, dummy! It's not ours!"

A muffled shout interrupted him. Both boys leaned down slightly and looked through the tent's clear plastic window.

"Uh oh!"

A figure in the distance, dressed in a white hooded parka, was walking resolutely toward them, then running.

The boys were well acquainted with irate authority. "He's not happy. C'mon, let's get out of here." Dustin sprinted for the car.

For the first time that afternoon, J.T. took his brother's advice. Alternately running and crawling across the ice, he threw himself aboard the VW and slammed the door at the same moment it careened in a turn and headed back to the New York shore.

"Where're you goin'?" J.T. panted.

Dustin stared straight ahead. His hands gripped the steering wheel tightly.

"Back where we came from. This whole idea was dumb, dumb, dumb!"

With the hip-hop music still rattling the countryside in their wake, they traveled the short way back to the New York shore at a surprising speed, gunned up the hill to the road and sped on. In the course of their hurried travels, they narrowly avoided collision with a snowplow and a taxicab before finally pulling into the driveway of their father's house in town.

With a deep sigh, Dustin turned the ignition off, and in the resulting silence turned to his brother. "What's that?"

"Oh, no!" J.T. looked at the object on the floor of the car. "The lunchbox," he said in a puzzled voice. "I guess I just put it under my arm like a football when I ran."

He unfastened the latches and pulled open the top to reveal a neat row of CDs in their plastic cases. He whistled.

"No wonder it was so heavy!"

"You dummy! That's somebody's music collection. Now what're we gonna do?" Dustin pulled off his watch cap and twisted it. He looked at his brother. "We gotta give it back, J.T."

"We can't. We don't know who to give it back to. Unless you wanna go back out to the lake."

"Okay, okay, you're right. Um . . . I need time to think about this. If Dad finds out, we can kiss this car goodbye. He's already hot about the insurance goin' up after that last ticket.

Put it in the trunk, inside your gym bag until I figure something out."

The two boys emerged from the car slowly. J.T. obediently opened the VW's front trunk while Dustin circled the car to eyeball the tire pressure.

"How do you suppose they were gonna listen to those CDs anyway?" J.T. mused. "There wasn't any player."

"Shut up," Dustin ordered in a desperate whisper.

He was standing behind the car, running his hand over the small back window. With the other hand, he sketched the sign of the cross on his head and shoulders. Curious, J.T. stepped around the car and followed his brother's gaze, then blessed himself too.

Both boys watched television. They both knew what a bullet hole looked like.

Chapter | One

Once again, I dreamed of drowning, struggling in the dark and chilly waters of Lake Champlain, which abruptly changed to the swimming pool at the YMCA.

Then, all at once, I was in the classroom, clad only in a swimsuit. My first class of the day was due to arrive any moment. I needed to get home to get dressed, but Principal Berghauser, strangely oblivious to my dress-code infraction, was shaking his head.

The late bell rang reproachfully in my ear. I opened my eyes, blinked, and made a reflexive grab for the bedside telephone.

"Aren't you two finished honeymooning *yet?*" someone demanded.

It took several foggy seconds for my brain to sort out that the voice on the other end belonged to my friend and former neighbor, Lily Burns.

"No," I told her, switching ears as I struggled to disentangle my delicate peignoir sleeve from the telephone cord, "we have one whole week left. Surely you didn't call at—" I squinted at the bedside clock "—one-seventeen in the morning to ask me that. How did you get this number, anyway?"

"Marie, who else? I had to tell a really huge whopper to pry it out of her."

Marie LeBow, manager of Chez Prentice, our bed and breakfast back home in the Adirondacks, and the only living soul entrusted with our whereabouts, had been sworn to secrecy except in the case of dire emergency.

"Who is it?" mumbled my new husband from his side of the bed.

I covered the receiver and murmured, "The Widow Burns." It was Gil's humorous pet name for the glamorous Lily.

Gil groaned and rolled over, making a head sandwich with his pillows.

"Aren't you getting tired of all that tropical sunshine by now?" Lily asked heartily. "It's nice and brisk here. Wind chill, two below. As Gil says in the newspaper, 'January: the way nature intended.'"

Memories of my nightmare were fading and being replaced by irritation. "Lily, if this isn't an emergency on the scale of an earthquake, so help me, I'll turn you in for burning those leaves in the street as I should have in October; I'll tell—"

"No, you won't. You never do. Amelia, I was your matron of honor. Doesn't that count for anything?"

"Don't whine. Just what is it you want?"

"It's Alec." Lily's relationship with her hirsute, hymn-humming swain, Dr. Alec Alexander, was on-again, off-again. "I've been thinking about it, and I decided you're the one to talk to him. He likes you."

"I thought he was pretty fond of you too," I said.

The last time I had seen them was at our wedding. Alec was kissing her under the mistletoe.

"Not anymore."

"Oh, Lily, you didn't dump him again!"

"If you must know, it was the other way around. We were at dinner at the Lion's Roar tonight—"

"He took you there again? That's three times since you started dating." Alec's courtship of Lily must really be setting him back.

"Four, but who's counting? Anyway, all I said was that I might have another date to the ice festival and—"

"And do you?"

"What?"

"Have another date?"

"Of course not. But I have been kind of hoping that somebody else might ask me."

"Lily, how could you?"

"I'm not married to that man." Lily's voice was taking on a familiar petulant tone.

We'd known each other forever. I could picture her sitting at the kitchen table where she always chatted on the telephone. She'd slipped off her earrings and three-inch high heels she considered de rigueur for dressy occasions and was probably massaging her toes, the nails of which had been professionally painted Lily's favorite shade, Passionate Plum.

"Lily, this is ridiculous, it's the middle of the night."

Gil rolled out of bed and staggered to the bathroom. If he'd been a student of mine, the expression he muttered would have earned him several years in detention hall.

"But you will call Alec for me, won't you?"

I kneaded my forehead with my fingertips. "Why? What for?"

"To bring him to his senses, of course! He said, 'I'm cuttin' ye loose, Miss Lily.' Used those very words. But he was miserable about it, I could tell. I need you to change his mind."

Poor Alec. He'd been crazy about Lily. It must have taken a lot of courage to say that.

"Why?"

"Why what?"

"Why do you want him back? I thought you said—"

"Amelia, I'm not made of stone. I'm not positive this thing with Alec can't work. I know he likes me a lot. He just gave up on us too soon. So are you going to help me or not?"

"I'm not sure I should," I said carefully.

"What are you talking about? Were you at the same wedding I was? Did you or did you not aim your bouquet at me? I thought you wanted us to get together."

She had me there. Alec had been infatuated with Lily for months, and I'd found his devotion so touching that I'd taken every opportunity to promote the match. But there was a limit to everything, and this was it.

"Lily, you're just about the oldest friend I have and I do care about you," I said. "I know I should've said all this a long time ago, but I kept thinking things would get better. Your treatment of Alec's been shocking. You've led him on and used him and made fun of him behind his back. That lie you told about seeing the Lake Champlain Monster was beneath contempt. It could've set his work back several years or seriously undermined his scientific credibility."

"Now listen—" Lily protested, but I was fired up.

"And all this time, the man's been a perfect gentleman, hoping against hope you'd come around. It seems to me, Lily, if Alec's dumped you, well, he's finally come to his senses." I took a quick breath and plunged in again. "I know from experience you probably won't take my advice, so all I can say is, do whatever you want. And . . . and . . . .don't call us, we'll call you!" I slammed down the phone, my chest heaving.

"Amen, sister!" called Gil from the bathroom.

I smiled halfheartedly. The lingering shadows of my nightmare gave this new spat with Lily a momentous feeling, as if I were cutting some kind of lifeline. After all, months ago, when I really was drowning, she'd been there for me.

As I settled back into bed, I was already feeling guilty. Lily Burns was vain, opinionated, exasperating, and a terrible gossip, but she was my oldest friend. And if not for her, Alec, and the grace of God, I would surely have become a large, overeducated portion of fish food in the inky waters of Lake Champlain.

"What did Mother Teresa want this time?" Gil asked as he returned to bed, smelling pleasantly of expensive hotel soap. "And how did she track us down?"

"Tell me, Mr. Editor." I cupped his face in my hands and kissed him. "Do you really want to talk about Lily Burns?"

"Nope," said Gil, and grinned.

Chapter | Two

"**S**tudent?" I was totally mystified. We were standing in the foyer of Chez Prentice, my old family house recently converted into a bed and breakfast, staring at the manager Marie LeBow. "What student?"

"The one Mrs. Burns called me about. The one who was gonna commit suicide. Did you call him? Is he okay?" Marie's voice held a tone of desperation.

Gil and I exchanged glances. So that was the whopper Lily had used to get our phone number last week.

"Is he okay? Did you get to him in time?" Her face was pinched in anguish. Her own twenty-year-old daughter had died last year, but it was typical of self-centered Lily not to give a thought to how such a tall tale would affect Marie. "I've been worried about it all week. Is he gonna be all right?"

I took a deep breath. "Everything's just fine now." I hugged her. "I'm afraid I can't say anything more about it, though."

Marie's right hand had been pressed to her heart. She dropped it. I noticed the skin of her once chronically chapped hands were now a creamy olive, and she had an elegant white-tipped French manicure.

"Oh, thank goodness!" She sighed, then immediately resumed her manager persona and became all business, leading us into her office—formerly Papa's study—to show us her schedule book.

"We're doing pretty good these days. The laundry's quite a job, but I've got a couple of high school girls coming in part-time to help Hester out. You know, just fill in here and there. Still, we need to put more people in these rooms if we want to pay the bills. The ice festival will help bring them in, but there's plenty of spots still open."

She tut-tutted and shook her head at the blank spaces on the calendar. "It's getting better, though. Mrs. Daye—that lady reading the paper in the parlor—she's from Ohio. Paid cash in advance 'n everything. She tells me she's got family here in town, so she'll probably be back, off and on. And there's always the drop-ins, and we'll be full up for another whole week in June with the education conference. Plus, of course, the Kiwanis have their weekly breakfast meetings in the dining room." She pointed to large K's in each Friday square. "And the mayor's daughter wants to have her wedding reception here in August. I guess a little bird told her how good yours turned out," she said, twinkling.

"A little bird named Etienne, perhaps?" I twinkled back. Marie's husband Etienne was my partner in the business.

"Oh, Amelia, he's so proud of this place!" Even after two weeks, her face still glowed as she spoke of her once-prodigal husband. "He's got another wonderful idea for putting us on the map—but I'll let him tell you that later."

Their reconciliation must be going well, I thought. *Another prayer answered.*

Marie squared her shoulders and buttoned her well-tailored navy wool blazer. "And I'm gonna make you real glad you give me this job."

"I already am, Marie."

For the past two decades, after being abandoned by her husband, Etienne, Marie had eked out an adequate living for herself and her daughter doing whatever honorable work she could find, from waiting tables to pumping gas. When the opportunity finally arose, Marie eagerly accepted the position of manager at Chez Prentice as a chance to prove what she could do.

It was an inspired choice. Marie was shrewd and intelligent, with a gift for administration that had gone unnoticed in her other jobs. Her long-term goal was a college degree in hotel management, which she was working toward in small steps during her free afternoons and evenings.

"The flowers in the foyer are lovely," I said.

Marie seemed to shrink slightly. "D'you think it's all right? Chuck Nathan says he can let me have a bunch a week for half price. I didn't tell Etienne yet."

"All right? Of course it is! It's a beautiful, gracious touch."

"And to get such a good deal from that tightwad is quite an accomplishment," Gil added wryly.

"Before I forget, I got something else you need to sign," Marie told me. "While I find it, you go on back to the kitchen and get some coffee. It's just made. Val's boy brought some fresh baked stuff this morning: apple strudel and croissants. I want you to try one of them with Hester's McIntosh apple butter."

I turned to consult Gil, but he was already on his way to the back of the house.

Marie's sister Valerie, an amazing cook, lived on a family farm in Vermont. Her wonderful baked goods were delivered across Lake Champlain thrice weekly by her teenaged son.

I heard conversation as I entered.

"Part of the fun's not knowing what Val's gonna send us, y'see," explained Hester Swanson, who came in daily to help with breakfast preparation and cleaning. "Tuesday it was prune Danish and raisin walnut bread." Hester, no slouch at cooking herself, rolled her eyes in enthusiastic memory, nearly missing Gil's cup as she poured his coffee.

"Things are really shaping up around this place," Gil commented, gesturing with his cup at the fresh wallpaper and newly painted glass-front cabinets.

Hester parked fists on her generous hips and gazed around the high-ceilinged old kitchen. She was built like one of the heftier carved figureheads on the bow of an old sailing ship, feminine but substantial.

"We got things buttoned up in here," she agreed, "but Etienne and me's got a bit more to do in a couple other rooms, for sure."

She turned back to the kitchen counter and cut the two sandwiches she had made into diagonal quarters. "Bert's lunch," Hester informed us, and after tenderly sliding them into plastic bags, she laid them in a silver-sided dome lunchbox. "He'll be here to pick it up later today."

She opened a jar of apple butter and laid a spoon next to it. "There. Try that on some of the rolls. I made a great big batch last week. Etienne wants to get some labels printed up."

She ran a hand around another, unopened jar. "It'll say 'Chez Prentice' right on top here, then, 'Hester's Authentic McIntosh Apple Butter' right there."

Our section of New York State is famous for its apple orchards, specializing in McIntosh apples, and Hester was McIntosh's biggest fan.

"This is delectable, Hester," I said.

Gil, his mouth full, nodded enthusiastic agreement. "Mmm."

"Yeah, delectable, that's what it is. You're always coming up with the big word. Guess it comes from being an English teacher. Delectable. I like that. 'Course I do all that stuff the health department says I have to, but my apple butter's not what you call health food or nothing," Hester warned. "It's got sugar in it, of course. Marie keeps saying our guests are gonna want health food. I told her alls I know is Bert Swanson's been eating my cooking for twenty-five years and if he ain't healthy, I'm that Audrey Hepburn woman."

She patted her short gray hair and smiled crookedly. She had made her point; her burly husband positively radiated good health.

"Here's that paper to sign, Amelia," Marie said, coming into the kitchen. "It's an entry form for the snow sculpture contest. It's all filled out. I'll run it over to the mayor's office as soon as you sign it. Etienne and me—and I?—thought it would be good publicity, out there in the front yard. We'll line some-body up to make it, so you don't have to do a thing."

I watched Marie as she spoke, exuding enthusiasm. It was a nice change from the depressed person she had been before.

"I think it's a great idea," I said.

She was wearing smart, low-heeled leather boots and pulling on a red wool coat with black velvet tabs at the collar. It was a radical departure from her ubiquitous old green and yellow parka. She grinned at Gil's surprised expression while pulling on sleek black leather gloves.

"Been shopping. Etienne says I need to look kind of exec-utive."

Gil toasted her with his cup. "You're CEO material, Marie."

She dimpled and blushed.

While sipping Hester's excellent coffee, I skimmed the document and proudly signed: *Amelia Prentice Dickensen*. My new name.

"Thanks." Marie snatched up the paper and headed out the back door. "I'll be right back."

Hester poured more coffee all around and joined us at the kitchen table. "This job's been the saving of her," she told us, nodding toward the door Marie had used. "You saw her, Amelia, after Marguerite died, all kind of fading away. She'd been living for that girl, and when the kid died, well, she was going down for the third time, you might say."

Hester had been Marie's next-door-neighbor before Marie and Etienne moved into the new downstairs suite at Chez

Prentice. "But you come along and needed her help, you see. And you'd been sweet to her girl. She told me."

"But what about Etienne?" Gil asked as he smeared more apple butter on a remaining morsel of croissant, "Didn't he help Marie too?" He popped it in his mouth and chewed happily.

"That was Father Frontenac's doing. He told Etienne not to show himself till later, you see? It was good he waited, you ask me. She wouldn't've ever been able to kiss and make up, all weak like she was at first."

Hester knocked on the table to drive her point home, then sat back to let her words sink in. She took a big swig of coffee.

"Hester, you're a natural psychologist," said Gil, and turned his high wattage smile on her.

It was his secret weapon. Until recently, it had had the power to render my own respiratory system temporarily unreliable. A concentrated honeymoon dose had given me a certain tolerance.

Hester simpered. "Well, I dunno about that." She popped up from the table and looked around vaguely. "Excuse me. Laundry. Gotta go fold some towels." She scurried away, so flustered she left her half-finished coffee behind.

During most of the lifetime I'd known Gil, I'd refused to let myself admit how attractive he was. The evidence had been there all the time: thick, wavy hair (now steel gray), warm hazel-brown eyes, expressive black eyebrows and blitzkrieg smile. There was also the solid-but-not-fat physique and a tiny dimple near his chin, but it was the smile that could do the most widespread damage. Best of all, I didn't think Gil was completely aware of the power he possessed.

"Any coffee left?"

A white-haired, plump woman peeked in through the kitchen door. She introduced herself: Mrs. Felicity Daye from Toledo, Ohio. Her husband would have come, she said, but he was busy working.

She had relatives in the area, she said, and added, "But I don't want to be a bother, so I decided to stay here."

"That's what Chez Prentice is here for! Come on in. Have a seat." Gil rose to place his empty plate in the sink, "There's plenty of coffee left. And it's fresh. Be sure to have a roll with some of that great homemade apple butter."

"Want to run around the block and see the Widow Burns?" he asked as we left through the old familiar front door.

Lily's house stood back-to-back with Chez Prentice.

"I don't think so, Gil. She's probably furious with me."

He frowned. "She's got no reason to be. You told her the truth."

"Maybe, but the truth wasn't what she wanted to hear. And I was pretty rough on her."

"Give it time, Amelia." Gil put his arm around my waist. "You two have been friends forever. She'll come around. I did, didn't I?" He kissed my cheek quickly. "Woof! It's cold out here! Come on; let's go home. I want to carry you over that threshold before I lose my nerve."

Chapter | Three

I t was seven miles from town to our lakeside cottage.

"Okay, sweetheart," Gil said when we reached the front porch, bending over to hook an arm under my knees. "Up you go!"

I backed away. "Gil, we can't do this. There's ice on the porch. Look."

"Hmmm." He stroked an ear thoughtfully. "Maybe you're right; it might be risky." He pulled me close and looked down into my eyes. "Think you could give me a rain check?"

"I'll remind you when the weather gets better," I said, smiling sweetly and vowing inwardly to do no such thing, ever. We were both in our forties, and I intended to keep this man in working order as long as humanly possible.

Gil unlocked the door and we carried in our luggage. The interior was surprisingly well ordered, considering that Gil's nephew, Vern Thomas, graduate student and known slob, had taken up residence in our spare room.

I dropped my bags and looked around. It was truly neat, with not so much as a sock hanging over a doorknob. I sighed happily. It was good to be home, in my House.

Chez Prentice, where I had been raised, was a twelve-room Victorian as luxuriously appointed as my old and moderately well-to-do family could make it. Every room was furnished in the tastes of my forebears, from the hand-painted framed prints out of Godey's Ladies' Book in the entrance hall to the delicate china shepherd and shepherdess on the mantelpiece in the parlor.

While I'd loved my family and still cherished the things that had once been theirs, they had never been truly mine. It was more in the spirit of loving duty than genuine enthusiasm that for most of my adult life I'd played curator of what had virtually become a family museum. I had assumed I'd live and eventually die at Chez Prentice.

Until the day I saw this House.

From the moment I stepped into the roughly paneled hall and beheld the deer head with the quizzical expression, the lumpy fieldstone fireplace with the carved wooden plaque reading "1890," and the screened porch that overlooked Lake Champlain, I knew I had finally come home.

Papa, who'd owned a lumberyard and knew good building techniques when he saw them, would have been surprised, maybe even aghast, at my choice of a house. The place was drafty and jerrybuilt, with odd rooms added to the original cabin as necessity had dictated. The kindest term one could use to describe the plumbing would be eccentric. The fact that the kitchen had been remodeled only served to point out the shortcomings of the other rooms.

Things weren't much better outside. The cedar shakes that covered the exterior made the little three-bedroom house a potential firetrap, and it took ages to get to town by means of a twisty two-lane road.

Still, this place spoke to me of peace and welcome in a way Chez Prentice never had. While it had taken Gil and me twenty-plus years to finally realize we were meant for each other, it had taken House and me only five minutes.

"Hello, House," I purred, "I'm home."

"Oh, no, not that House thing again," said Gil, dragging my largest suitcase down the single step into our icy master bedroom. "You're getting weird on me, you know that?"

"Be afraid, be verrry afraid," I intoned, quoting one of my students quoting movie dialogue. I waggled my fingers menacingly at him.

Gil grinned. "Come over here and say that again."

I did.

There was a knock on the door. We sprang apart guiltily, then laughed.

"Caught—like a couple of randy teenagers," Gil said.

"You're never going to let me forget that, are you?" I had once used that expression to describe him.

"You got that right," he said, bounding to the front door and opening it. "Vern! Did you forget your key again?"

Ignoring his uncle entirely, Vern took three huge paces into the house and swept me off my feet in an engulfing hug. His khaki parka was still cold from the outside.

"Auntie Amelia! You're back at last!" Grinning, he snatched off his watch cap, set me down, and planted a wet and noisy kiss on my cheek.

Turning to Gil, he stroked him repeatedly on the top of his head and said, in a tone one uses to address a dog, "Good uncle, good uncle! I wanted an aunt for Christmas and you got me one!"

Gil rolled his eyes tolerantly. Vern really was a dear.

"You've cut your hair," I observed.

His blond mop was now a severe crew cut with closely shaved sides. He turned his head both ways for my inspection. His cheeks and the edges of his ears were cherry red from the cold.

"What d'you think?"

"A drastic change, but it suits you; very masculine."

His eyes swept the room. "I cleaned up. Did ya notice?"

"I did, indeed."

"I even vacuumed that deer head." He pointed backwards, over his shoulder in the direction of the entry way. "Got a new job too. That is, another one." Vern drove a taxi part time. "I'm tutoring kids at the high school. That makes me kind of a teacher now. We'll be colleagues."

"I'd like that."

We stood smiling at one another for some seconds before the ringing of the telephone broke our concentration.

Vern sprang into action. "I'll get it." A dramatic vault over the back of the sofa and two long strides later, he had the receiver in hand. He handed it to Gil.

"It's Wendy at the paper. She says it's important."

Gil retired with the phone to a corner of the room while Vern took me on a proud tour of the cleaning job he had done. At his insistence, I was beholding the relatively immaculate kitchen sink when Gil joined us.

He replaced the phone on its cradle. "Sorry, I've got to run. They found somebody dead on the lake."

"Golly! Was it some kind of accident? Who is it?" Vern asked.

"Don't know yet." Gil pulled his coat on. "You know all I do at this point. When I get more, you can read about it in the paper." He grinned. "'Bye." He planted a quick kiss on my cheek and headed out the door.

"Well, so much for the honeymoon," Vern said and grinned.

"Right." I closed the refrigerator door. "You've done a great job here—"

The telephone rang again. Vern's long arm grabbed the receiver effortlessly. "Yah? Oh, hi! Okay. Yeah, she's here. It's Alec."

"Miss Amelia, 'tis good to hear your lovely voice again," Professor Alexander Alexander began in that elusive Scots accent.

"It's good to hear yours too, Alec. How are you doing?"

He detected the tone of sympathy in my voice and tried immediately to dispel it. "Never better! Busy as ever!"

"And the monster?" Alec's scientific *raison d'être* involved a hunt for a Loch Ness-style creature, believed to inhabit the depths of Lake Champlain.

"Capital. I'm getting closer all the time. I'm organizing a new network of observers. But that's not my reason for calling. I have a wee favor to ask of you."

"Anything."

"Would you keep an eye on Miss Lily for me?"

His voice, so hearty a second before, was now low and hoarse. I could picture him sinking his chin into his spade-shaped, salt-and-pepper beard.

"I expect you've heard we're no longer an item—"

"So it's definitely over? No chance of reconciliation?"

"None, but I do still wish her well. She's such an impulsive little creature. Could you talk to her, Amelia? Keep her from making some kind of silly mistake on the rebound, as it were. She listens to you."

"I don't know about that."

"Oh, aye, she does. Would you speak with her?"

"I'll try, but you know I can't make any promises."

The picture he painted of Lily was idealistic in the extreme. The last time she'd actually taken my advice was back in high school, when I suggested she use wide-ruled notebook paper.

His voice immediately became stronger. "That's all I can ask. Now, put me back on with the boy. We've the ice festival to discuss."

I gave the phone over to Vern and retired to my bedroom to begin unpacking, then remembered something.

"Where's Sam?" Samuel de Champlain, my late mother's moody, obese old cat was just about the only thing I'd taken away from Chez Prentice when we married. "Not outside, I hope."

I checked the screen porch. Sam watched birds the way Vern watched college football games on television: supine, but vocal. No luck on the porch, just fuzzy patches on the indoor-outdoor carpeting where Sam liked to sharpen his claws. I scanned the snow-covered yard for cat footprints; there was nothing but smooth, pristine whiteness.

I knocked on the door of Vern's room and secured his yelled permission to enter.

"My goodness!" I gasped. Vern had cleaned the house, all right, but his own room was quite another matter.

Seated at his glowing computer screen and talking to Alec on an earphone telephone, he answered my question with a shrug and a sweep of the hand that took in a sea of wrinkled clothes, dirty coffee cups, crumpled papers, and textbooks. "He might be here somewhere. He hangs out here sometimes. I'll let you know if he turns up," he assured me, then returned to his telephone conversation.

As I navigated gingerly around a pair of gargantuan sneakers and out the door, he added, "He's around. Don't worry."

Vern was probably right, of course, but guilt is a powerful motivator. I'd never liked this cat very much, and because of that, I'd taken my inherited role as his caretaker very seriously.

"Sam?" I called into the pantry, and then the warm spot behind the clothes dryer. No answer.

Gil returned home around eight o'clock and ducked all our questions about the death on the lake. "Got to confirm our facts first," was all he'd tell us.

"Maybe Sam's hiding. You said he used to hide back at Chez Prentice," he speculated when I fretted about my missing cat at dinner. "Just put some leftovers in his bowl, and he'll turn up."

"Good idea," I agreed, remembering the way Sam could disappear at will, only to rematerialize at the first rattle of food hitting his bowl.

But even canned tuna failed to work its fragrant magic, and when Vern came in from emptying the trash after dinner that evening, the expression on his face was grave.

"Sorry, Amelia. Looks like Sam escaped." He led me to the screen porch and behind the large rolling trash bin. "See?" He fingered a curling edge of screening that had come loose from the corner frame. "He must have squeezed out through here. Look." He pulled out a tuft of gray fur.

A sick, sinking feeling filled my middle. "I didn't see that earlier."

Vern nodded. "It's hard to spot." He looked out at the field of snow. "No tracks. He must have left before the snowfall this afternoon." A long arm wrapped around my shoulders. "I'm so sorry, Amelia. I really liked the old boy."

Despite the cold of the porch, my eyes filled with hot tears. "Don't use the past tense, please," I whispered.

"What's going on?" Gil asked from the back door. The warm air from the house drew us inside.

Vern told him.

Gil led me gently inside. "Are you all right?"

I gave him a watery smile. "I don't know why this is upsetting me so. It's not like I even liked that awful old bag of fur. Sometimes, it actually seemed that Mother loved him more than she did me."

Gil pulled me to his chest and hugged. "He's your link to her. To her and your dad, that's why."

"How did you get so smart?" I murmured into his shirt.

He kissed my forehead.

Vern gave a polite cough. "I'm too young to see this, I think," he announced. "Besides, I've got a paper due. Don't worry, Amelia. He'll come back." He disappeared into the abyss that was his room, leaving Gil and me to our cuddling.

Chapter | Four

"Miss Prentice? Are we going to have to do a Shakespeare paper this term?" was the poignant plaint from sophomore Hardy Patschke as I made my way through the hallway teeming with teenagers.

" 'It must follow as the night the day,' Hardy," I quoted over my shoulder, not bothering to correct his use of my old name. There would be time enough for that later.

Despite Sam's disappearance, there was a smile on my face today that I couldn't control by muscle power alone. It was nice to be married, I thought, and the mornings with Gil—even in a drafty pre-dawn bedroom—were the nicest.

The first day back at school after Christmas vacation had never been my favorite, and I wasn't alone in that sentiment. In September, students are at least temporarily happy to be back, resuming friendships and plunging once again into the familiar routine, but things are different in January.

The two-week taste of freedom during the holidays serves merely as a cruel reminder of the imprisonment to which they must soon return. Of course, my students never asked me whether I was happy to be back. They probably pictured me rubbing my hands and cackling with glee at the prospect of renewed opportunities to torture them.

I hung up my coat in the classroom closet and headed for the teachers' workroom. In the now-packed hall, there was a steadily intensifying din from slamming lockers and assorted mating calls of the Human Adolescent. My ears caught random vignettes as I shouldered through the crowd.

"So what'd ya get for Christmas?"

"Yeah, we broke up. I can't believe he's taking her to the ice festival."

"—skiing at Whiteface. He's in a hip-to-ankle cast."

"Amelia! How are you?" said someone, inches from my right ear. It was Judith Dee, the school nurse, shouting above the racket. Her helmet-style hairdo was unscathed in the churning throng. I doubted if even a hurricane could dislodge a single strand.

Funny, I thought, *it has never occurred to me before, but her hair is the same color as Sam the cat's: a flat blue-gray.*

Saving my lung power for the classroom, I smiled and bobbed my head back and forth in response, then beckoned for her to follow.

We entered the workroom together. The place was empty, I observed gratefully. I had lots of copies to make before the class bell rang. Because of painful memories, I no longer made copies at the public library.

Judith shut the door with a sharp rattle. "Whew! It's wild out there! Say, did you hear about the Eisler boy? Broke his kneecap skiing. And Mrs. Brannon's psoriasis is back."

I frowned. I'd already seen Jimmy Eisler's well-decorated cast and didn't want to know about the Latin teacher's skin problems. Judith had a bad—and, I was sure, unprofessional—

habit of discussing the medical condition of members of the populace at large.

I opened the top of the copier. "Would you like to copy anything?"

She smiled archly. "No thanks. I'm just waiting out the traffic jam." She waved her hand toward the hallway. "But don't mind me. You go right ahead."

While I busied myself at the copy machine, Judith pulled a compact from her purse and began dabbing at an already well-powdered nose.

"Did you have a nice Christmas?" I asked, making conversation.

Judith squinted into her compact. "Just lovely, thank you. I went skiing in the Laurentians," she said, referring to a popular Canadian vacation spot. "I always promised myself I'd learn to ski someday, and I did. Of course, I'm no expert, but I know how it's done now."

"That's marvelous, Judith."

I was surprised. Such a trip was expensive. How on earth could she have afforded it? As a part-timer, she earned even less than I did.

Her eyes slid over toward me. "How's married life treating you?" she asked, returning her compact to her purse.

"Just fine, thanks." I left it at that, but I could see by her expression that she wasn't satisfied.

I was fishing about in my mind for another evasive answer when the door rattled open, and science teacher Blakely Knight strode in. The din from the hallway was abruptly cut short when he slammed the door unceremoniously behind him, muttered something unrepeatable, and headed for the row of message boxes on the back wall.

Judith, deterred neither by the racket nor my vagueness, probed some more. "How was the honeymoon?"

"Honeymoon?" Blakely demanded as he shoved his dome-topped lunchbox into his cubbyhole and pulled a sheaf of notes from his memo box. "Who had a honeymoon?" He held his messages up like a hand of playing cards and peeked over them to leer at me. "You?"

Before I could throttle her into silence, Judith blurted, "That's right. She married Gil Dickensen over the Christmas break. You know, the newspaper editor."

"Really?" He tossed most of his notes into the wastebasket and one dark, sardonic eyebrow lifted as he looked me up and down. "I'm disappointed, Amelia. I thought you might wait for me to finish sowing my wild oats."

I gave him the cold stare such a comment deserved. "Your oats and anything else of yours, for that matter, is—I mean, are—no business of mine."

I flounced out the door, followed closely by Judith and the sound of Blakely's mocking laughter. *So much for trying to make a snappy rejoinder.*

The hallway was quieter now, and Judith's voice carried, though she spoke sotto voce. "Blakely can be a bit of a rascal at times."

Boor is more like it.

"It's almost understandable when you know his family background. His father grew up here, and he was quite a dog in his day, if you know what I mean." She tittered in a flustered manner. "I knew his mother too. She named Blakely after a hero in a romance novel, and I must say, he is intelligent and attractive."

As we parted company at the foot of the stairs next to the nurse's office, she rolled her eyes provocatively. "You two might have gotten together if you hadn't gotten married." Her tone implied that I'd missed a golden opportunity. She sighed. "We'll never know now, will we?" Smiling regretfully, she closed the door of her office.

"No, we won't, thank goodness," I muttered and headed down the hall.

"Miss Prentice," said Hardy Patschke accusingly as I entered my classroom, "the late bell just rang."

I smiled at him and pointed to the blackboard where I had written, "Mrs. Dickensen." "That's my new name. Five extra points on Friday's quiz for everyone who remembers to use it."

There was a chorus of greetings. "Good morning, Mrs. Dickensen."

"Are you gonna give us homework, Mrs. Dickensen?"

"What does Mr. Dickensen look like? Is he cute?"

"He's adorable," I said dryly, "Now get out your lit books and turn to the poem, 'Stopping by Woods on a Snowy Evening.'"

At lunchtime, I used the pay phone in the dining hall to do what I had been putting off for days: keep my promise to Alec, regarding Lily.

Lily answered on the first ring. "Oh, you're back, then," she said coolly.

"We're back. We've been back since last week. Question: what on earth were you thinking, telling Marie that a student of mine was suicidal?"

"What? Oh, that. I just wanted her to tell me where you were, that's all."

"I know that, but it was wrong."

"What if it wasn't?"

"Huh?"

Lily went on, "I mean, what if it was true; wouldn't you want me to get in touch with you?"

"Well, yes, but—"

"And it could have been true, you know, so what's the difference?"

I sighed. What was the use? I changed the subject. "Listen, Lily, about Alec—"

"How's Sam doing?" she interrupted. She'd always been inordinately fond of my cat, and spoiled him at every opportunity.

"I don't know."

"What do you mean?"

"I told you, I don't know. He disappeared while we were out of town. I feel terrible about it, but right now, what I called for was—"

"You should feel terrible. I could have told you that that idiot nephew of Gil's wouldn't take proper care of him."

"It wasn't Vern's fault. He just—ran away. Lily, Alec called last night and I think perhaps—"

"Don't change the subject. What are you doing about Sam?"

"We called the Humane Society and Gil put an ad in the paper. It's been in there for days. Look, I understand your concern, but it's not really your business to—"

She interrupted me yet a third time. "What? Sam, not my business? How dare you, Amelia. I love th—that dear creature. And that makes it my business!"

"Lily, of course you're right, but right now I wanted to talk to you about Alec."

There was a pause. I could hear her drawing a long breath. "That, Amelia," she said at last, "is none of *your* business." She hung up.

"Put away your books," I ordered, rising from my desk at the beginning of the next class, "and pass these back." I handed a stack of test papers to the front person in each row.

There was a collective groan.

"You'll have until the end of the period. Don't finish too quickly. This is a tough one, but there's an extra-credit question."

Quiet descended on the room, and I returned to my reverie.

"Why are you smiling?" an accusing voice murmured.

I looked over at Serendipity Shea, slumped in the front row seat I'd assigned to her. Her high-gloss lipstick gave her mouth a curious pouting prominence. Now it was firmly turned downward.

"I love my job," I said pleasantly and held up a copy of the exam.

I could tell by her expression she thought my answer revealed me to be the vilest sort of sadist.

"Everyone should love her job as much as I do," I added sweetly.

Serendipity scowled and hunched once more over her paper. A wing of her white-blonde hair flopped down, concealing her face, but from her body language I could guess that she was having trouble with this test.

I fervently hoped not. In fact, I longed for the girl to get all A's, especially if it meant I didn't have to meet with her mother again. Mrs. Brigid Shea was a strident, assertive woman who refused to concede that homework was actually a good thing, not a torture devised by yours truly to ruin her daughter's social life.

Think positively, I told myself, scanned the room for paper-peekers, then returned to pleasant thoughts of Gil.

"There's the bell," I declared unnecessarily thirty minutes later. "Put your papers on my desk as you leave, please."

Hardy Patchke was the first to leave. "Piece o' cake," he said as he handed his test over, and swaggered out the door. I was happy to see most of my students had relieved expressions on their faces as they filed out.

Serendipity, however, was in a foul mood. She slammed her paper on my desk, hitched her designer purse over her shoulder and stalked out in as dignified a manner as her low-slung designer jeans would permit.

Every day after school, it was my habit to walk to Chez Prentice. As a partner in the business enterprise, it was my duty to check on things. Besides, I needed the exercise.

On this particular afternoon, as I stepped carefully over the icy patches, I thought about the students' reaction to my new name and married status. It had obviously never occurred to them that a teacher would have a personal life, especially someone as ancient as I. Many times recently, I'd found myself blushing at the speculative stares.

"Well, hello there, married lady," a male voice said behind me, and Blakely Knight fell into step at my right. "How are the happy honeymooners?" he asked in that insinuating tone I found so annoying.

None of your business, I wanted to say, but I had been raised to be polite. "We're doing well, thank you, quite well."

"If you don't mind my saying so, you don't look well." Blakely commented. "Let me help you carry that." He reached for my black leather book satchel.

I stopped walking and backed away. "No, thanks."

Blakely shrugged. "Okay, whatever."

We resumed walking.

"Actually, Amelia, I caught up with you because I wanted to ask a question."

"Yes?" I said as politely as I could.

I was feeling a trifle guilty over my curt rejection of what was, after all, a relatively kind offer. What was it about Blakely that made my skin crawl so?

"Do you know if Lily Burns is seeing anyone?"

"Lily Burns!" I said, fairly shouting the name in my surprise. Of all the possible questions I might expect from Blakely Knight, this hadn't been one of them.

"What's the matter?" Blakely seemed surprised at my reaction. "She is your friend, isn't she?"

"Certainly," I said, more calmly. "You want to know if she's, um, available?"

This would be quite a couple: diminutive Lily and tall, muscular Blakely. My father always called odd pairs such as this Mutt and Jeff, whoever they were.

"Well, I know she was dating that old windbag Alexander for a while there, but I heard that was *kaput,* so I thought, well, I just wanted to know if I'd be wasting my time if . . . " He trailed off, waving his hand.

"I'm not exactly on Lily's list of favorite people right now. I think your best bet would be to call and ask her yourself. Better yet, you're heading in the direction of her house. Why not just drop by for a visit?" Oh, to be a fly on that wall!

He appeared to consider the suggestion. "Hmm. I don't know. Dropping by so hale fellow well met and all . . . it's not quite my style."

He was describing the professor. His leering grin was back, and the sympathy I had felt for him dissolved.

"No, I guess it isn't," I agreed crisply.

"But you never know, do you? I might just do it."

We walked for another half block and were standing at an intersection waiting for the light to change when pink-cheeked, white-haired Mrs. Daye seemed to step out from behind a tree.

"Hi, folks," she said pleasantly in a deep alto voice.

She had on a long white hooded parka and dark, stretch ski pants. Even though the lapel bore the logo of an expensive couturier, with her comfortably rounded figure, wide shoe-button eyes and pale hair, she looked exactly like a snow-man.

"Mrs. Dickensen, isn't it?" she asked me.

"That's right. Mrs. Daye, this is Blakely Kn—" I turned to introduce him, but stopped mid-word when I caught sight of the man's expression.

Blakely's brown eyes had widened significantly, but only for a split second. Immediately, he rearranged his features and reached out a hand for her to shake.

"Knight, Blakely," he said in a smooth tone, "fellow toiler with Amelia in the academic salt mines. I'm sorry, what is your name, again?"

"Daye, Felicity. Nice to meet you."

The woman's plump face was pleasant as she gazed up at Blakely. She shook his hand and fell into step on my other side.

"May I join you? I'm trying to get in a little exercise; gotta stay well."

"Indeed," said Blakely dryly.

We walked some more.

"So where is it you live, Mrs. Daye?" Blakely asked.

"Toledo, Ohio. For twenty-eight happily married years," she answered with special emphasis.

"How lucky you are," Blakely said, making the Dayes' accomplishment sound unbearably dreary.

Honestly, Blakely, I thought, *is no one safe from your acid tongue?*

It seemed especially boorish to aim his cynicism at such a nice woman, even if she probably didn't realize she was being mocked.

We reached Chez Prentice in another minute, and Mrs. Daye and I turned to go up the sidewalk. "You go on ahead, dear," she said to me. "I want to have a word with Mr. Knight about something."

She turned back toward him, but he hadn't paused and his long legs had already carried him almost out of sight.

Chapter Five

A week later, when all the excitement happened, I had slipped into class just ahead of the last bell, opened the roll book and begun hurriedly marking homeroom attendance when Serendipity Shea appeared at my elbow.

"Miss P—Mrs. Dickensen," she corrected herself with a glance at the blackboard, "here's that book report I was supposed to turn in before Christmas."

I gave her a sharp look. "Serendipity, I already told you—"

She interrupted me quickly. "Remember you said you wouldn't, like, take off points if I turned it in right after, but I left it at my grandma's house and she brought it with her when she came to visit yesterday and since we're not having class today, I thought . . . " She shrugged as she trailed off.

That got my attention. "Not having class?"

She made a questioning moue. "You know, the assembly thing we have every month. Starts right after the first bell." Her tone was one of disgust at my appalling ignorance. "It's some scientist guy this time."

I pulled a tissue from the box on my desk and offered it to her. "Here. For the gum."

She hadn't been obviously chewing and had probably parked the wad in the back of her cheek, but I had an unerring instinct for such things. If Serendipity had been required to pay for the removal the disgusting stuff from the bottoms of chairs and desks, she might have better understood my mild obsession.

She rolled her eyes, but complied.

The rest of the class ignored our exchange, except for Hardy Patchke. "It's the monster guy," he informed me.

I was completing the roll taking. "Who's what, Hardy?" I asked distractedly.

"The guy in assembly today. He's the one who looks for the monster." His pale green eyes sparkled eagerly under butterscotch-colored lashes that exactly matched the color of his curly hair and tawny skin. "You know, Champ."

"You mean Dr. Alexander?"

"That's him."

I cringed inwardly, but let it pass. I had given up requiring my students to say the clumsy but more correct, "That is he." *Sic transit* grammar.

The class bell rang, and as the room emptied, I debated the issue of my attendance at the assembly. I hadn't been tapped as a monitor this time and therefore was not required to go. Should I?

I was of two minds on the subject. These elaborate time-wasters were the brainchildren of our fearless leader, Principal Berghauser, who, when but a lad in the wilds of Minnesota (where their winters made our Northern New York cool snaps feel like Florida, he liked to remind us) he found his young intellect stimulated by itinerant musicians and lecturers in the finest nineteenth-century Chautauqua tradition.

I had to applaud his good intentions. I, too, had enjoyed such assemblies during our long, balmy Adirondack winters. In particular, there had been a handsome male dancer from the New York City Ballet Company who inspired me to nurse dreams of a career *en pointe* until I realized that my hips, while not massive, tended to interrupt the smooth line favored by ballet masters.

And, incidentally, I had no talent.

I had decided instead to become a teacher. Fortunately, body proportion is seldom an issue in my profession, as is clearly evident from a glance at the yearbook's faculty pages.

The main problem with these assemblies was that Mr. Berghauser hadn't taken into account the sophistication of the modern teenager. After having experienced deafening wrap-around sound and dazzling special effects at the Cineplex and garish violence and sensuality in video games, not to mention the appalling images of death and destruction in the news, these quaint little talks—delivered explosion free, by ordinary, fully-dressed human beings—must have seemed tedious at best and at worst, an excuse to misbehave. Consequently, at any given assembly, at least fifty percent of the faculty was pressed into service to sit among the restless natives and maintain order.

Mr. Berghauser preferred teachers to attend, suggesting the value of making use of the assembly subject in our subsequent classes.

A further argument in favor of going was that I had never heard my professor friend speak publicly on his favorite subject. I decided to be there for Alec.

The hallway was now almost empty. I joined a handful of stragglers as we hastily made our way down the staircase and across the hallway to the auditorium.

"You're not going to that sideshow, are you?" Blakely Knight caught up with me with his easy stride.

I paused at the door and straightened my shoulders. "I most certainly am."

"Oh, that's right, I forgot. You're big buddies with that old fraud, aren't you?" He made it sound sordid.

"Yes, we are," I said, including Gil in the conversation. "But Alec's no fraud. He's a fellow scientist. You should respect his research, not scoff at it."

Was it intellectual contempt or jealousy motivating this man? I wondered. After all, both he and Alec were interested in Lily.

"Yeah, right. And once he catches the big scary dinosaur, can Sasquatch be far behind? What the hey, might be good for a laugh. Come on."

He laid a hand on my shoulder. I ducked away, darting into the auditorium, and collided with the principal.

"Oh, I'm sorry, Mr. Berghauser."

"Mrs. Dickensen, really!" He shook himself slightly and then said in a low murmur, "We need you to help in the front row. And please stop by my office this afternoon during your free period. Bring your grade book." He turned and strode down the aisle to the stage.

"Oh, dear." That could only mean that some parent had a bone to pick with me.

The auditorium was packed and groaning at the seams—a new one was at the top of the school board's wish list—and the only seats available were half a dozen in the front row, an area made vulnerable by its visibility from the stage and Mr. Berghauser's stern eye. The incorrigibles were required to sit here, and from the body language of the roughly ten students who stumbled their way sullenly to their assigned seats, the only things needed to crown the misery of their incarceration in the front row were leg irons.

"What's it this time?" snickered one slumping student to another, "Some old fa—" he broke off as the expression on his companion's face warned him of my approach.

Turning, both boys fixed me with a blank stare. It was the Rousseau brothers, J.T. and Dustin, famed for their unique acts of reckless derring-do.

"This seat taken?" I asked brightly.

J.T. shrugged, but gestured for me to sit. I sat carefully and occupied myself watching two boys on stage setting up a large portable movie screen.

Without fanfare, Alec ambled onstage and took a seat between the president and vice president of the student council. Lily's contention that he belonged on a box of frozen fish sticks seemed less apt today, perhaps because he wasn't wearing his favorite slicker and rubber boots. Also, he had lost some bulk around the middle, and the dapper suit he'd worn at our wedding now seemed a little too large. His spade-shaped, salt-and-pepper beard, though neatly trimmed, seemed a bit more on the salty side today.

I frowned. Was our irrepressible Alec beginning to get old?

His eyes darted around the auditorium until they met mine, and my heart lightened immediately. Alec's beaming smile, at least, was still vigorous as ever.

I winked broadly at him.

He responded by laying his hand over the top button of his no-longer-tight suit vest and wiggling his fingers in a surreptitious wave.

I heard a snort. "Look at him," J.T. said, jabbing his brother with an elbow, "wavin' at somebody!"

There were ill-concealed guffaws, and the telltale fragrance on someone's breath reminded me that we would have to redouble our efforts to patrol for smoking in the restrooms. But all that would have to wait. I sat back, crossed my arms and lifted my gaze to the podium above, where Berghauser was gently waving his hands in a palms-down gesture, as though deflecting tumultuous applause.

"All right, people, all right. Let's settle down now."

The microphone rumbled and squealed, and he gestured to the wings, where adjustments were made. A series of shhh's echoed across the room, and relative quiet at last descended.

"Well, now, today I have good news and bad news," Berghauser began archly.

There was a collective groan in reaction to the spectacle of an adult in authority attempting to be funny.

The principal continued, undeterred, "The bad news is that Dr. Hawley Felder's fascinating slide show entitled The

Life of a Tooth; Oral Health and You has been postponed until next time."

The incorrigibles exchanged several unrepeatable asides and snorted derisively.

"But the good news is," Berghauser's moustache, which up until now had drooped sadly over his upper lip, leapt to life, "that we have with us Dr. Alexander Alexander!"

"What kinda name is that?" whispered J.T., whose own appellation happened to be John Travolta Rousseau.

" . . . . has earned three doctoral degrees: oceanography, philosophy, and history. Now he has turned his attention to the relatively young branch of science known as cryptozoology. Having distinguished himself in so many fields, cryptozoology remains Dr. Alexander's favorite. So now—"

I winced at the dangling participle. Cryptozoology didn't distinguish itself, Alec did. This particular error in grammar was becoming alarmingly common.

"Let's all give him our best red and black welcome!" Beckoning like a latter-day Ed Sullivan, Berghauser invited applause, joined it, and then took his seat.

Alec stepped forward and adjusted the height of the microphone. In his pleasant lilting tenor voice, he declared himself thankful for the introduction and requested that the lights be lowered. Directing our attention to the movie screen, he pressed a clicker at the end of a thick electrical cord.

There was a collective gasp. I, too, started uncontrollably in my seat at the hideous picture on the screen.

Chapter | Six

"*Megachasma pelagios*," announced Alec dramatically, "better known as Megamouth because of its four-foot-wide mouth."

There were scattered nervous giggles. J.T. leaned forward in his seat.

We were staring at an amateur black-and-white photo of a large, gaping dead fish. I was reminded of the whale in Disney's *Pinocchio*.

"Before '76," Alec continued, gently rolling his r's in the Scottish manner, "we didn't even know this creature existed. He's a kind of shark, found off the coast of Hawaii, just about a year too late to appear in the movie *Jaws*."

Some students laughed.

He's good at this, I thought. *He's already got them on his side.*

He clicked the changer again. "More recently, in Papua, New Guinea, scientists found an undiscovered mammal, the golden mantled tree kangaroo." The next slide showed a smiling young man cradling a creature the size of my cat Sam with a long banded tail and a sweet-looking, narrow face. The girls in the auditorium responded, "Awww."

"You see, cryptozoology means the science of hidden animals, the ones we haven't discovered yet."

Another slide appeared.

"Someday, many of us hope to add another one to this list. His Latin name is *Champtanystropheus*, but we call him Champ, the Lake Champlain Monster."

"Cool," whispered J.T. under his breath.

I'd seen this photo before: an expanse of choppy lake, a row of thick forest on the shore beyond, and a fuzzy something in lower foreground. It appeared to be a long neck and head of a dinosaur-like creature. It had been taken in 1977 by a couple as they frantically scrambled to pull their wading children to shore.

"Five minutes!" Lily Burns had said when she showed me the *New York Post* article about the incident. "Those people supposedly watched that thing for *five full minutes* and the only picture they got of it was that? Hah!" Lily contended that it was nothing more than a man with a dark tan, skinny arms and a pot belly doing the Australian crawl.

There was a time when I'd have agreed with her, but no longer. I had experienced something Champ-like up close and personal the night I almost drowned.

Had it been Champ? Alec seemed to think so, and had added my account to his eyewitness file. "Almost the very same thing happened to a woman in British Columbia in '74," he'd assured me.

Alec was continuing his talk. There was another slide, with a larger shadow superimposed over a map of the lake. "Eight to ten thousand years ago, we would've called it the Champlain Sea, because it was part of the Atlantic Ocean. As the glaciers . . . "

While Alec continued explaining the geological history of the lake, my thoughts wandered. I mentally rearranged my lesson plans. Members of the first period class had, unbeknownst to them, dodged a bullet and escaped a pop quiz. I'd have to postpone second period's vocabulary assignment, but the rest of the day would be relatively unchanged.

Well then, that was all right. I looked up again.

"Ye've all heard of the Loch Ness Monster in Scotland," Alec was saying, "Compared to that creature, our study is in its infancy, but evidence is mounting. There are Native American legends and the explorer Samuel de Champlain described seeing a large creature . . . "

I thought about my Samuel de Champlain. How would Mother's poor old cat hold up in this frigid weather? My stomach lurched, whether from hunger or anxiety, I couldn't tell.

Abruptly, J.T. jarred my elbow as he raised his hand and waved it vigorously in the air.

"Yes? In the front row," Alec said, pointing.

J.T. jumped to his feet. "Didja ever go fishing for Champ?"

Alec tilted his head, "Well, no. Conventional wisdom would dictate—"

J.T. cut in impatiently, "You know, cut a hole in the ice, fish for him, like? I mean, like ice fishing or something?"

"The creature wouldn't likely respond to that," said Alec, shaking his head slowly. "For that matter, I've never heard of any winter sightings, I'm afraid."

One Gervais sister whispered something to the other, and a shrill giggle rang out.

J.T. ignored it. "Do people ever hunt it? I mean, shoot at it with guns and stuff?"

Alec frowned. "No, not at all. I certainly hope no one here is contemplating such a—"

"No, that's not what I mean," J.T. said, shaking his head vigorously. "What I mean is—"

Gerard Berghauser shouldered Alec aside, stepped to the microphone and stood on tiptoe. "That's enough questions, John Rousseau. Sit back down—now!" He gestured vigorously to me.

I put a gentle hand on the boy's shoulder. "Come on, J.T. That's enough. The girls heard you." It was no secret that he and his brother had a crush on a pair of pretty twins.

The boy slumped heavily back into his seat. His brother Dustin whispered at him fiercely, then fell silent.

Alec resumed his place at the microphone and took two more questions, dealing with UFOs and the Abominable Snowman, respectively. "I'm afraid these subjects are beyond my area of expertise," he demurred.

He looked at the rest of the crowd bristling with waving arms and glanced at Berghauser, who shook his head and frowned. "We seem to be out of time, but remember, keep your eyes open, and if ye spot the fella, call me. I'm in the book." He smiled, sketched a wave in the air and strode off the stage to enthusiastic applause.

The benevolent spell Alec cast over the student body lasted exactly one class period before the habitual ennui returned. Half of my fourth period class claimed to have misheard the deadline date for an essay. Members of my fifth period carried a rapidly spreading case of somnambulism, lapsing into narcolepsy, which I managed to fend off with superhuman effort.

"Coffee. Oceans of strong coffee," I mumbled as I trudged into the lunchroom at noon. "That's what I need."

One look and I skipped the *spécialité du jour*, mystery meat in thick, beige gravy with khaki-toned, watery broccoli and a square of rapidly melting red gelatin. My stomach lurched at the sight.

The only thing one could predict about the food at school was its unpredictability. One day, it would rival that of the elegant Lion's Roar Restaurant, the next, Dannemora Prison. It was why I kept several cans of chocolate diet drink hidden in the depths of the refrigerator.

"Back on that diet again, eh?" Mrs. Breen remarked as I skirted the lunch counter and headed for the back of the kitchen. "Don't you want a nice veal cutlet?" Her teasing was usually harmless, but today it really grated on me.

I pulled open the refrigerator door. "Thanks, but I had trouble getting my skirt buttoned this morning and . . . "

I stopped myself. Why had I said that? I didn't owe her any explanations.

"Oh, that's right," she said archly, "you've got the mister to keep happy these days." She waved a serving spoon at my midsection. "You sure there's not a little one on the way?"

"Oh, I'm sure," I said, grateful that the clinking of plates and buzz of conversation had drowned out most of our exchange. In the Gossip Olympics, our cafeteria ladies held the gold medal for Free-Style Supposition.

"Really sure," I added grimly under my breath. There are some things only one's gynecologist is entitled to know.

I shook the can vigorously and pressed it to my cheek as I dispensed two cups of coffee and generously creamed them. "Wake up," I ordered myself.

At a long, empty table near the exit, I spotted Vern seated with J.T. Rousseau. I hesitated. The two seemed to be having some kind of whispered disagreement.

As I approached, I heard Vern say, "You shouldn't have been out there, you know."

"Hey, I know that, okay? But you're gonna help, aren't you?"

"Maybe. Okay. Eat up, J.T. We need to get started," Vern interrupted, spotting me. "Amelia! Join us."

I knew Vern's welcome was genuine, but J.T.'s disapproving frown threatened to curdle my liquid lunch.

Tough toenails, J.T., I thought, mentally plucking an idiom from my vast storehouse of sundry adolescent expressions. I took a seat, set down my tray, opened the can of Fudge Fantasy with a satisfying plock and slid a straw through the aperture.

Vern had scarcely disturbed the swiftly ossifying surface of the concoction before him. "Is the food here always so bad?" He turned to the gelatin, stirred the red liquid sadly and put down his spoon. "Lame."

"Yah. Real lame." J.T. reached into a paper bag, pulled out a thick sandwich, and took a large bite.

"What brings you here today, Vern?" I took another sip of my lunch.

"Remember? I told you: tutoring." He leaned in and waved a hand at his companion. "Giving J.T. a hand with his French." He rapped his large knuckles on a textbook lying next to his tray. "He has a study hall after lunch on Mondays, so we get a little work done right here." He flipped the book open to a marked page.

"Has Vern been any help?" I asked J.T. pleasantly.

I had expected a sullen shrug, but J.T.'s answer was surprisingly civil. "I guess. Dustin's good at it, but I su—I mean, I stink at it. I wouldn't even take French, only our grandmother, y'know, my mom's mom, wants to talk it to us when we go to see her in Montreal." He pronounced it the locals' way: Mun-tree-ul. "French is all they want to talk up there."

"It's a valuable thing to know another language," I pontificated, and added what I hoped was a more tempting inducement. "You and your brother could carry on a conversation with each other without some people understanding what you're saying. My sister and I used to say *au secors* when we needed help for something. *Au secours*," I repeated, giving more expression to the phrase.

"That might work here, I guess, but not at Grammar's," J.T. pointed out, giving the French word *grandmère* an English-sounding twist. "She talks it all the time."

Vern slid the open textbook toward the boy. "C'mon, pal, let's get busy."

My can of Fudge Fantasy half consumed, I turned to the coffee. I picked up a mug, held it to my lips and immediately put it down again. It smelled like dishwater. Forget that. I pushed away the coffee cup and resumed sipping the chocolate drink.

Vern slid his lunch tray to one side and turned to his pupil. "Let's look over your exam paper and find out what your weak points are."

"I'm supposed to memorize these?" J.T. indicated a short list of idiomatic phrases.

Vern ran his finger down the list and smiled. "They're kind of fun, J.T. Look at that. It means over there. Go on, say it."

J.T. frowned. "Lah-*boss*."

"No, you have to say it the French way: Lah-bah. Y'see? That 's' is silent. And remember, there's not really any particular syllable accented in French."

My Fudge Fantasy was gone. I stood and peered over their shoulders at the lesson. La-bas, I read.

Vern was valiantly trying to put enthusiasm into the lesson. "Come on, J.T., try another one: *On y va*, let's go. It means the same as *allons-y*, only more casual."

J.T. rolled his eyes. "Great. Whoopee."

This was getting painful to watch. "I'll leave you fellows to it, then. Hang in there, J.T., you'll be fluent in no time. Meanwhile, I'm going to put my empty can *la-bas*," I added, indicating the trash can in the corner. J.T.'s exasperated expression told me I was trying too hard.

"Catch you later," Vern said pleasantly, waving a pencil.

With a growing sense of dread, I made my way down the hall to the main office. "Mr. Berghauser wanted to see me," I told Olive Chapel, the principal's secretary.

"Um hmm," she agreed, never looking up from her computer terminal. She jerked her head in the direction of the office door. "They're in there."

"They?"

She grimaced, but kept on typing. "They, the Sheas, your favorite parents."

"Parents, plural? Mother and father, both? No way."

"Way." Olive nodded firmly as she made an adjustment with her mouse. Her eyes remained fixed on the screen. "Definitely way. Way-way-way-way," she rattled rapidly, tapping rhythm on her keyboard. "You must have really stepped in it this time, girlfriend. They're not happy campers."

I sighed and put my hand on the doorknob. "Will you see that I'm given a decent burial?"

Her gaze had never wavered from the screen. "Only if I get your parking space."

It was hard to out-quip Olive.

Chapter | Seven

"Ah, yes. Miss Pr—Mrs. Dickensen, come in. We've been waiting for you." The principal was seated behind his big polished desk and seemed relieved at my arrival. The tips of his moustache lifted in a half smile.

A trio of unsmiling faces swiveled my way. The three members of the Shea clan had been given the place of honor on the brown leather couch to the left of the desk, as befitted relatives of a mayoral candidate. Kevin Shea had thrown his hat into the ring a few months ago.

Mr. Berghauser waved his right hand. "You know the Shea family, don't you? Mister and Mrs., um, Shea, and their daughter, Sa-Sa—um." He stumbled over the name.

"Serendipity," Mrs. Shea and I said together.

I glanced at her sympathetically, but only got a sharp glare for my trouble. Mrs. Shea looked even more baleful than she had at the last parent-teacher conference. Despite her well-styled ash-blonde hair and expensive Tyrolean sweater, she didn't look all that good. There were dark circles under her eyes and her face was pale. She looked like a washed-out carbon copy of her daughter.

The young lady in question crossed her arms and snapped her gum defiantly. Her father just sat and stared at me, inscrutable, like a freckle-faced Irish Buddha.

Berghauser gave a little nervous chuckle. "Yes, well, I stand corrected. Please, Miss—Mrs., um, take a seat." He gestured to the straight-backed chair directly in front of his desk.

The witness box.

Or more appropriately, the defendant's chair.

I sat, clasping my grade book protectively to my chest.

"The Sheas have a few questions about Sa—that is, their daughter's English grade for the last six weeks."

"Yes?" I said sweetly, surveying the assemblage with an air of benign, but artificial, calm. "What questions are those?"

With an effort, I lowered the grade book to my lap and opened it to the relevant class page. If I moved them slowly and deliberately, my hands hardly trembled at all.

"They wanna know why you're flunking me, that's what," Serendipity blurted.

"Oh. Well, let's see . . . " I traced my finger down the page to her name. "Here we are. It seems Serendipity made forty-five percent on the midterm exam in October and turned in her term paper long past the deadline." I glanced up at the principal, who frowned at me. "That will lower it two grade levels right there. I haven't had time to grade it, but considering—"

Mrs. Shea struggled to sit forward in the deep leatherette seat. "She told you what the problem was! She left it at her grandmother's in Syracuse!"

I was ready for that. "But it was already late before the Christmas break. When she explained the problem, I told her it would be due the day we got back. I'm afraid I can't keep making allowances for just one student. Remember what it said on the paper I sent home in September."

"Paper?" Kevin Shea, owner and proprietor of Shea's Quality Sporting Goods, glared accusingly at his daughter, who responded with an expression of innocent confusion. "I didn't get a paper. Did we get a paper?" he asked his wife, who shrugged. "We didn't get any paper. Anyways, that's not what we're here for. Are you gonna change the grade for my little girl or not?"

The telephone rang.

Principal Berghauser stared at it for a split second, then answered. "Olive, I'm in a meeting here—what? Who?" One side of his animated moustache started to twitch, and he blinked several times and sighed. "This is a shock. Let me think." He tapped his index finger on the desk. "Well, have them sent down here and tell . . . " He looked up at us, frowning. "That is, all the, um, business can be conducted, um, privately, in here. Good." He hung up.

The Shea family and I watched this intriguing exchange with rapt interest.

Berghauser chose to ignore the implicit questions in our stares. He briskly slapped both hands on his desktop, swiveled a smile around the room and said, "Now. Where were we?"

By the time I left the principal's office, I was sick at both heart and stomach. Mr. Berghauser, apparently in a hurry, had once more superseded my authority and changed the girl's grade to passing, calling it amnesty and giving her a lecture about future consequences.

For all the good it would do. Serendipity was well aware of the hefty discount Shea's Quality Sporting Goods gave our phys ed department and knew that as long as the high school received a steady supply of low-priced pigskin and bargain kneepads, she could jolly well do as she pleased. I watched the principal's stern words ricochet off her multiply-pierced ears and into the nearby wastepaper basket.

By the time they left, all three Sheas wore sly, triumphant expressions and were pointedly ignoring me.

The queasy feeling followed me into the restroom. The face that looked back from the mirror had an injured, defeated expression. "I used to like my job," I told the face and splashed it with cool water.

The class bell rang, and the thunder of three hundred sneakers shook the hallway.

Two girls pushed through the restroom door. "But how did you know? I mean, the—"

Their animated conversation broke off abruptly when they saw me. Meekly, each one sought the sanctuary of a stall.

I blotted my face with a damp paper towel; there was no use leaving just yet. On occasion, the high school hallways markedly resembled the streets of Pamplona at bull-running time. Wisdom dictated waiting until the crowds thinned a little.

The door slammed open. "Brenda!" It was diminutive Micki Davenport, panting. "You won't believe it! It's just so cool!"

"What?" Brenda and her companion responded in unison from behind their respective doors.

Micki spared me only a cursory glance. "There's police out there! In the hall!" She pointed, as though her friends could see through the thick stall doors. "They're taking away some guys in handcuffs!"

I didn't wait to hear more, but snatched up my things and left. The hall was emptying fast into the large study hall. I followed the stream of curious traffic to where people were lined up three deep at the second floor windows that overlooked the school parking lot. Somebody had managed to wrest several of them wide open, and frigid winter air was filling the large room.

Just this once, I pulled rank, squirming my way to a windowsill in time to see J.T. and Dustin Rousseau being led to a police car, their hands cuffed behind them.

"What'd ya climb this time?" someone yelled.

Hearty laughter followed, but the brothers weren't responding with their usual swaggering bravado. J.T. looked up, and though he was some distance away, I was sure I saw an expression of pure fear in his eyes.

He said something to his brother, who nudged him crossly before the officers separated them. A police officer laid a hand on the top of his head and guided it inside the squad car.

The police cars sped away, leaving me trembling with anger. Whatever the Rousseau boys' transgression was, they hadn't deserved this public humiliation!

"Has anyone called their father?" I asked of the crowd of snickering adolescents. They just snickered some more.

"That's enough," I said firmly. "Kenny, you and Damien lower these windows. The rest of you get to your classes. I believe there's a study hall scheduled in here this period." I received a grateful look from the presiding teacher, who had just entered and was clearly bewildered by the fuss.

I swept out of the room and stalked down the hallway to the principal's office. The windowed door clattered as I closed it hard. I was about to walk past the secretary's desk and into Berghauser's office when Olive stopped me with one word.

"Don't!" She spoke, as she always did, with her eyes on the computer screen and her hands flying across the keyboard.

I pointed in the vague direction of the parking lot. "But the Rousseau brothers—"

"I'm telling you, you're taking your life in your hands if you go in there right now. He's in one of his swivets." She stopped typing and turned toward me, allowing her chained reading glasses to slide from her nose. "It's bad, Amelia. I don't know details, but it's bad." She frowned, and her long, narrow face seemed to lengthen.

I felt shaken. Olive never paused in her work like this for anything. "Has someone called their father?"

She replaced the glasses and turned back to her keyboard. "All taken care of. He's meeting them at the police station. There's nothing else anybody can do."

"We'll see about that," I muttered as I left.

I was late to my next class.

"Don't worry, Miss Pr—Mrs. D," Hardy Patchke piped as I stepped through the door. "We're doing tomorrow's assignment." He pointed to the page numbers I had posted on the board earlier in the day.

Sure enough, aside from the three who abruptly left their lounging posts at the window and resumed their seats upon my arrival, most of the students were leaning over their books, pencils in hand. Would wonders never cease?

I was much calmer by the time my afternoon free period rolled around as I slipped down to the cafeteria and the pay telephone on the wall. Gil answered on the first ring.

I spoke without preamble. "You're the newsman in the family. What do you know about the Rousseau brothers?"

"It's bad, honey. Really bad."

"So I keep being told, but what kind of bad? Did they climb the Macdonough Monument this time? Put detergent in the college fountain again? What kind of stupid prank rated those poor boys being dragged out of school in hand-cuffs?"

I was warming to my subject, becoming more outraged by the word.

"Calm down. I was—"

"Are you aware of how infuriating it is to be told to calm down?"

Gil spoke slowly. "No, but I'll file it away for future reference." I could hear the amusement in his voice. His good nature, as usual, began to drain away my irritation.

"I'm sorry. You have no idea the spectacle that took place today." I glanced at my watch. "What's more, I'll be late to my seventh period class if I don't hang up right now. Quick—tell me something, anything—"

Gil broke into my harangue. "It's murder."

"*What?*"

"Remember that body found on the lake?"

"Yes, of course." The coverage of that event by Gil's news-paper had been a bit too sensational for my taste.

"It's about that. I'll tell you all about it at home tonight. Now go on, get to your class. I love you!"

I was really, really late to my next class, because I threw up in the ladies restroom. Upset though I was about the Rousseau brothers, I had no idea it would affect me like this. Fortunately, I recognized the warning signs just in time. It was a brief bout, easily handled, and it was surprising how much better I felt when it was over. Furthermore, I made it to fresh-man English just before total chaos broke out.

"You hear about the Routheaus, Mrs. Dickenthen? They whacked a guy fithing out on the lake," one of my students said in greeting. The clarity of his sibilant s's was hampered somewhat by a set of braces in the school colors.

The high school grapevine seemed far more efficient than any of Gil's journalistic sources. I tried to divert attention to matters academic.

"Get your syntax straight, Frank. Who was fishing, the victim or the perpetrator?"

"The guy. Dead guy," Frank amended. "They thot 'im, then drownded him, then thtuck hith head through a hole in the eythe."

I almost corrected him—*drowned*, not *drownded*—but the subject was simply beyond the bounds of civil discussion.

"He froze right into the ice," another student put in, eyes glittering. "At least, his head did."

"That's enough. There's work to do." I was talking as much to myself as to the students. "Let's open our books to page one hundred fifty-three."

Even Edgar Allen Poe was preferable to this real-life horror.

Chapter | Eight

Vern had spent a lot of time with the Rousseau brothers lately and I wanted to talk to him about the situation, so immediately after school, I stopped by LaBombard Taxi. It shared a small strip mall with a pizza restaurant and an auto parts store, about twenty minutes' walking distance from the high school.

Vern's battered red Honda was sitting in the side parking lot. I checked my watch. If memory served, he had another half-hour to work.

It had been a cold and windy walk. I perched hesitantly on a bench in front of the large storefront window and shivered. I hadn't bundled up enough this morning. My cheeks stung. A brisk breeze, courtesy of the nearby Saranac River, went right through my coat. I was not enjoying myself.

There was a knock on the big window from the inside. Mrs. Fleur LaBombard grinned at me through it. She opened the office door.

"Come in," she said, gesturing, "no use freezin' to death."

"Thanks so much, Mrs. LaBombard."

"Call me Fleur." Inside, the office was blessedly warm, almost stifling. "You're here for the boy, I bet." She indicated a plastic-covered settee. "Sit," she ordered, "help yourself to coffee. He'll be finish' pretty soon."

I declined the offer of refreshment, but expressed my gratitude for the shelter and asked after her husband, Marcel.

"He don't feel too good these days," Fleur said.

"Oh, dear. Has he caught the flu?" There was a certain irony in my question, since Mr. LaBombard favored spraying his taxi with antiseptic spray after each fare.

She shrugged. "Nope, just don't feel good. Kind of blue, can't make himself to get out of the bed, except go to the john. I tell him, get back to work, keep busy, that'll snap you out of it, but he don't listen."

It sounded serious. "Has he seen a doctor?"

"For what? He's got no temperature, no sore throat, nothing."

"Well, tell him I hope he feels better soon."

"He better. Right now, we only got one driver, besides Vern there. If business picks up any, we'll be in a pickle."

She resumed her seat at her desk and shook a long, filtered cigarette from its pack. "You mind?" she asked, pointing the cigarette at a two-foot-high plastic tower with a well-filled ashtray at the bottom. "I got this thing, works real good. Bought it over to Chuck Nathan's." The florist carried a wide variety of gift items and gadgets on the side. "It's kind of cool. Sucks up the smoke, sort of." She held her cigarette poised, waiting for my response.

I nodded my permission. I'd never developed the smoking habit, but before she quit last year, Lily Burns had never been without a cigarette in her well-manicured hand. If I hadn't developed a tolerance by now, I never would.

Smiling graciously at me, Fleur bent her head over a lighter shaped like the Champlain monument. I watched with interest. She bent the diminutive Samuel de Champlain back from his pedestal, flicked the base with her thumb and a flame shot up. Soon the tip of the cigarette glowed almost as brightly as her fluorescent hair. She inhaled with apparent enjoyment.

I tried to settle into the stiff sofa. It made a rubbery creaking noise every time I moved. Reluctantly, I turned my attention to the smells in the room: a mix of long-forgotten cigarettes, over-brewed coffee, and Lysol.

Lysol was by way of being a theme with the LaBombards. Taxi #1, driven by Fleur's husband, always smelled of it. The car Vern drove, #2, reminded one only slightly less of a chem lab.

I swallowed uncomfortably. Just thinking of this subject was setting my stomach on edge.

I moved my gaze around the room. One side of the room was occupied by two vending machines, one for soft drinks and one for snacks, on either side of a large trash container. Behind Fleur's desk were four metal lockers, standing side by side, prominently hand-lettered: "Fleur," "Marcel," "Vern" and "Sub." The last, I assumed, was short for substitute. Two of the lockers had dome-topped metal lunchboxes perched on top.

A coffeemaker on a folding commercial table faced the vending machines, and above it on the wall were several framed and faded school pictures of the LaBombard children, now mostly grown. There were six in all, if I remembered rightly, most of them good students and most of them married by now. I had taught all but one of them myself.

I took a deep breath of the smoky, chemical-laden air and decided to watch Fleur work. Her job, I came to realize, involved long periods of boredom, which she passed by reading well-worn magazines, punctuated by telephone calls and static-filled discussions with the two-man taxi fleet over the walkie-talkie system. The messages came in brief spurts and, among the cryptic professional terms, were pretty easy to decipher.

She finished a conversation abruptly and turned in her chair. "You know about the Rousseau boys?"

I nodded.

"Heard about it on the police scanner." She waved in the direction of a radio-like gadget and shook her head sadly. "I always thought they was good kids. My Yvonne babysat for them after the mother died."

I remembered Yvonne, the youngest LaBombard child; a sweet, rather pretty girl, but a bit too impressionable. I saw a lot of that among my female students.

"Yeah, those Rousseau boys were cute little ones, all right."

"What's Yvonne doing now?" I asked idly.

Fleur frowned, tapped her cigarette in the ashtray, and took another drag. She squinted and shook her head. Smoke curled from her mouth as she spoke.

"Don't hear from her much. She's waitressing, living up in Champlain, almost to the border. Her picture's over there." She pointed to a photo posted on the bulletin board behind me.

I turned and saw a windblown but smiling Yvonne, huddled next to a barrel-chested, curly-haired young man with huge dark eyes and thundercloud eyebrows. He looked very serious and earnest.

"Engaged to this foreign guy, Matt something; has an accent—English. At least, I think it's English. He's a case, that one. Don't like her coming to see us." She rolled her eyes and her sigh ended in a sharp cough. "She's livin' with him, which just isn't—well, you know. And he's not even Catholic. I'm not prejudiced at all, y'understand, but the mister and me just wish . . . " She trailed off.

She leaned forward confidentially. "Not too long ago, that boy and him had a fight like you wouldn't believe, right here in this office." She tapped her desk. "I was afraid somebody'd get hurt—Marcel's not getting any younger—but it was just yelling. You ask me, it's why he's feeling so poorly. But he won't listen; isn't that the way with men? They just don't listen!" She shook her head sadly.

Static from the radio interrupted her and she swiveled in her chair.

"Number Two here." I recognized Vern's voice. "Dropped off the fare at the hospital. My shift ends in two minutes. I'm headed for the Gamma house. Out."

Fleur tapped her cigarette in the ashtray and replaced it in her mouth, where it bobbed with each syllable. "Negative,

Number Two. Your aunt's here, needing a lift. Come on in."

"Amelia? There? Okay." He sounded surprised, but not altogether pleased.

"Him and that girl," Fleur said to me, jerking her head in the direction of the radio. "Takes up all his spare time these days." She took another long drag and laid the cigarette in the ashtray before answering the telephone, "LaBombard Taxi."

Girl? This was interesting. It would explain the new haircut and the renewed interest in clothes.

In the six months I'd known him, Vern had sporadically dated a variety of girls, but nobody in particular. I was new to the in loco parentis business. Should I ask him about this, or leave it alone? Would he need a woman's advice or would I be interfering? I shifted uncomfortably in my seat.

It certainly seemed hot. A wave of nausea had begun at the pit of my stomach and was gurgling upward. I drew shakily to my feet and headed for the door, waving vaguely at the busy Fleur.

"Getting a breath of fresh . . . fresh . . . " I pulled opened the door and drew deeply of the ice-cold oxygen.

It had started to snow. Tiny dancing flakes, few and far between.

I closed the door behind me and sat heavily on the outdoor bench. The air was the kind that frosted the insides of your nostrils, but it felt like bracing medicine at this moment. I bent forward, because it seemed the thing to do.

Whew, that was a near thing, I thought.

The noxious exhaust of a car floated my way and I had another bad moment; then there was the slam of a car door followed by quick, heavy footsteps.

"Amelia? You okay?" It was Vern; I could tell by the giant sneakers that came into my line of vision.

"Just a little woozy. Something I ate, probably." I sat up, looked into his dear, concerned face and felt better.

The office door opened. "Gee whiz, Miss Prentice, I'm sorry. I was busy on the phone just now. You feel faint? You want a coke or something? I'll get you one from the machine. Mrs. Dickensen, I mean."

Summoning up every ounce of my spare strength, I requested she call me Amelia and assured them both that all I needed was to get home.

"You go see the doctor, okay?" Fleur requested as I hastily gathered my black leather satchel from the plastic-coated sofa, holding my breath the whole time. "It's flu season. He'll give you a shot or something."

I nodded.

"She's right," Vern added his two cents once we were in the car. "You need to get that checked out. It could be serious."

"I feel better already." I tilted my head back, closed my eyes and decided to change the subject. "Who's the new girl?"

There was a moment of silence, then, "What?"

I kept my eyes shut. "Fleur mentioned you were seeing a lot of one particular girl."

Vern shifted gears. "Well, I guess you could say Melody Branch and I are kind of dating."

I opened my eyes. "Melody? What a pretty name. Where did you meet her?"

"In one of my classes at school."

"Is she nice?"

"Amelia, that's about the stupidest thing I've ever heard you say. Of course she's nice."

"And pretty?"

"No, she's hideous. Look, don't get any ideas. She's just a girl, okay? No big deal." Vern navigated a tricky left turn. "I heard about J.T. and Dustin getting busted. Did you see it happen? What's going on?"

"I saw them being arrested, if that's what you mean. Vern, Gil says they're accused of murder."

"Golly!" Vern's eyes widened. "Oh, gee!"

He ran his hand over his severely shorn head. He did look more mature this way.

"I mean, gee whiz, they're no angels, everybody knows that, but murder? How did they say it happened?"

"I don't have details. Gil said he'd tell us when we get h—"

The short whoop of a police siren and flashing lights interrupted my sentence.

Vern glanced over his shoulder. "What the—"

A squad car was directly behind us.

"Vern, how fast were you going?"

"Slower 'n Christmas," he mumbled, pulling over to the curb. "I always do when Mrs. Magoo's in the car." It was a slightly derogatory pet name he'd given me, a comment on my studied, myopic driving style.

Vern slumped in his seat and pulled his wallet from a hip pocket. By the time he was ready with his ID, the officer had arrived at Vern's window.

"Vern Thomas?"

Vern went dead pale and held up his license. "Yes, sir."

"Don't need to see that. We just want to ask you a few questions. Would you mind following me to the station house?"

Vern pointed at me. "Well, I was taking her home, but it's all the way out on the lake shore—"

"I'm sorry, sir, but it's important. Maybe the lady can take the car and drive herself home."

"I—I, uh, I can't a drive stick shift, officer," I piped up shakily.

"Look—can I take her to Chez Prentice over on Jury Street, then meet you? Won't take a second."

The officer nodded. "That should be fine, sir. Just don't take too long, please." He turned and ambled back to his car.

I could tell Vern was unnerved by the way he drove. The gearshift made an appalling grinding noise as we pulled back into traffic. He swore under his breath.

I didn't know what to say. We traveled the few blocks to Chez Prentice in an uncomfortable silence.

"Sorry about this," Vern said as he braked at the curb. "I'll come back and get you after—um, the, whatever, or maybe you can call Gil—"

"I'll be fine. Are you all right? What do you think it's all about?"

"Hey, I don't know. Maybe my taxi license is expired or something." He took a deep breath and turned a half-grin on me. "I'm kidding, okay? Hey, Amelia, don't look so worried. You'll be the person I contact with my one phone call."

"Vern, don't—"

He looked at me. "Come on, cut it out. I'll be fine. *Les gendarmes* are our friends." He reached across the stick shift and gave me a clumsy, one-armed hug. "Now cheer up and get out of here."

I opened the car door, scowling fiercely to prevent a burgeoning flow of anxious tears, and stood on the curb watching until the little car turned the corner in the direction of the police station. One tear, then another, escaped and trickled down my cheek.

I retrieved a tissue from my pocket and hastily wiped them away. When had I become such a crybaby? More to the point, should I call a lawyer or someone? The only one I knew at all well was, ironically, our distinguished district attorney, Elm DeWitt.

What could I do?

The realization came suddenly.

Gil.

I would call Gil and tell him all about it. He'd know what to do.

Oh, it was good to be married and have somebody else to worry with you! I turned and trudged up the walk toward the familiar front porch.

Chapter | Nine

Gil wasn't at the newspaper office when I called. "He's running down this lake murder story. Try him on his cell phone," suggested Wendy, the secretary/receptionist. I did, and a deep electronic voice suggested I leave a message, which meant he either had turned the thing off or the line was busy.

"You okay?" Marie LeBow asked as she entered the B&B office, bearing a small tray with two steaming mugs.

"I'm sorry. I'm in your chair."

She waved a hand. "Sit back down. I'll ask you to move when I need to do some work." She set down the tray. "I brought you some coffee, real cream like you like it."

She set the cup before me on the desk pad. The strong fragrance filled my nostrils. It was strange, and slightly offensive, dishwater-like.

"Is this some kind of flavored coffee?" I asked. "Hazelnut or something?" I wasn't fond of hazelnut.

"Nope, it's premium brand regular beans, fresh ground, fresh made."

I picked up the mug, then set it down. "You know, Marie, I don't think I want coffee right now." I got up. "If you don't mind, I think I'll go fix myself a piece of toast."

Suddenly, the simplicity of it sounded heavenly. My mouth watered.

Marie smiled indulgently. "Well, I do need to get back to work. I'll drink the other cup myself."

Back in the kitchen, Hester wouldn't let me lift a finger. She insisted on toasting some new bread, freshly delivered from her sister in Vermont.

"Got whole wheat in it, and nuts and stuff. Etienne says it's what people want these days." She dropped two slices in the toaster slots. "Two pieces all you want? Where's that nephew of yours, Vern? He'll eat half a loaf if I'm a judge of big boys like him."

I couldn't think of what to say. I stared at the table.

"Golly, Miss Prentice, what is it?" Hester pulled a chair up and laid a warm, damp hand on mine.

In fits and starts, I told her about Vern's appointment with the police.

"Is that all?" Hester laughed heartily. She stood and hastened to retrieve the toast as it popped up. "Don't you worry yourself about that. Why, if I got that shook up every time one of Bert's people got invited to visit the police, I'd be old before my time, that's for sure."

She laid the plate of toast before me, accompanied by the jar of apple butter and the butter dish. "There, get some sugar into you. You'll be right as rain." She poured me a tall glass of milk. "And you need this to go with it."

She was right. The homely snack was apparently exactly what I was craving. I dug in hungrily and thought about asking for more once I'd finished this portion.

Hester shook a generous amount of scouring powder into the sink and continued her commentary. "No, you don't want to borrow no trouble yet. Why, years ago Bert's father was over to that place all the time." With a large sponge, she began scrubbing enthusiastically. "Didn't do him no harm." She held up the dripping sponge. "Maybe you heard that he did a little bootlegging out of Canada."

I nodded, because my mouth was full. I had heard. She had told me on the occasion of our first meeting.

Hester chuckled. "That dad of Burt's was a case, all right." She put down the sponge, rinsed her hands, and came over to the table. "There wasn't a place on a car that he couldn't fiddle with and hide stuff in."

"Bootlegging never made sense to me," I said. "Those bottles of liquor must have been bulky and noisy, clanking together. A lot of trouble, and there's always a chance you'll go to jail."

"It wasn't only bottles, y'know. It was money, too, to pay for the booze. The old man would drive up with cash stuffed in all these little cubbyholes—in the seat padding, behind the glove compartment, even in those convertible tops they had back then, y'know, with pleats in 'em. One time he was on the border near Champlain and it started to rain, and the border guy says, 'Aren't you going to put the top up?' and Bert's dad had a heck of a time trying to explain why not. When they finally made him open it up, the money fell out!"

She laughed. "That story's my favorite. I can't swear any of 'em is true, but I get a kick out of 'em."

She returned to her sink cleaning, tossing her comments over her shoulder at me. "What I mean to tell you is, don't worry. All's they're going to do is ask questions, and all's he has to do is say he don't know."

"Don't—doesn't know what?"

Hester shrugged. "Does he know the Rousseau boys?"

"Yes, he's been tutoring one of them in French. But what could he tell the police?"

"Who knows?" She squeezed out the sponge and rinsed her hands. "It's just a fishing expedition," she said with a sage squint. "That's what they call 'em on the TV, fishing expeditions. Trying to find out stuff anywheres they can."

She took a clean kitchen towel and dried out the sink. It seemed like a self-defeating task to me, but Hester was an expert housekeeper and knew her job far better than I.

"Mind you, I knew Martin Rousseau in high school. That's the father, y'know. Could've been sweet on him, too, but he never really fell for a girl till he met that Aimee." She folded the towel and made a face. "You said it A-*may*, not A-*mee* like regular people. She was way younger than him, and kind of full of herself, y'know, and spoiled. That was a one for the movie stars, that girl. Named her babies after two of 'em: John Travolta and that guy, what's his name, in *The Graduate*. Martin took over where her dad left off, everybody said. It's too bad she died on him," she concluded, rather heartlessly, I thought.

She observed me retrieving stray crumbs with my pinkie. "Here, you need another piece of toast, at least."

I didn't protest, which wasn't like me. To tell the truth, for many years, food had been only a peripheral component of my existence, at least the preparation thereof. From the time before my parents died, I had subsisted on light suppers of Campbell's soup and saltines, and since our marriage I had expanded my repertoire only to include the better brand of microwave dinners and large cans of hearty stew. The second serving of toast smelled even more wonderful than the first, and I fell to consuming it with enthusiasm.

"I'm glad your worries didn't spoil your appetite today; does me good to see you enjoy your food. Most days, you're not much of an eater, that's for sure."

I finished chewing and swallowed. "It's your cooking, Hester."

Hester laughed. "That's right. I really know how to use a toaster. I get to laughing every time I remember when we first met and I give you my special recipe for apple pie. Shows I didn't know you too good. I bet a buck you lost it."

I finished the last toast crust and restrained myself from licking stray apple butter off the plate. "No, as a matter of fact, I put it in my mother's old all-purpose cookbook and etiquette guide." I pointed to a bookshelf tightly-crammed with cookbooks among the cabinets. "But I haven't found time to try it yet."

Hester chuckled. "Probably used it for a bookmark."

I drank the last of the milk in guilty silence. The truth was, several months ago I had used it to mark the chapter on weddings.

The doorknob on the big front door made its familiar clink-jangle, and a chill breeze quickly made its way through the dining room and into the kitchen, dancing around my ankles for what seemed an intolerable length of time.

"Whoever it is, shut the door!" Hester shouted. "You're freezin' us back here!"

"Sorry," said a familiar voice and we heard the door close with a thud.

I took a deep breath and closed my eyes with relief.

"I've often wondered," Vern remarked as he strolled to the kitchen table, snow clinging to his shoulders and his short haircut, "why don't you have a storm door like most people?" He brushed off his jacket. "You have a deep enough frame on that door to support one. I looked."

"Yeah, while we was turning into blocks of ice," Hester said with a chuckle. "Y'want something to eat?"

"No, thanks. But I mean it. You need to tell Etienne."

I couldn't stand it. "Oh, for heaven's sake, Vern, tell us what happened!"

"What happened? Oh, you mean at the cop shop?" Vern shrugged and worried the tip of his nose with a knuckle. "Nothing, nothing to speak of. Just asked me a few questions."

Hester said, "What did I tell ya? It was a fishing expedition, just like I said. Isn't that right?"

Vern gave her a blank glance. "I guess so. Look, Amelia, can we get going? It's starting to snow. I've got a paper due next week, and I've got to get home to my computer."

He stood, arms akimbo, bouncing impatiently on the tips of his size 12 sneakers. I was reminded of a sprinter waiting for the sound of the gun.

Disappointment was written all over Hester's face. "Sure you don't want a little snack, there? You could take it with you, even. I could put a couple cookies in a napkin."

"No, thanks," Vern said, a little too sharply. "Come on, Amelia, shake a leg." He took my coat off the back of the kitchen chair and draped it clumsily around my shoulders. "Let's go. Put on your coat."

I complied, puzzled and a little concerned. Something was obviously bothering him. I hurried to gather my things, confident that he would enlighten me in the privacy of his car.

I was to be disappointed. Not only did he not confide his experiences at the police station, he was close-mouthed the entire trip home, answering my forays into conversation with terse, single-syllable words: "Yes." "Nope." "Maybe."

Once inside the house, without a word, he hung up his coat and ambled into the cluttered den that was his headquarters, closing the door firmly.

I knocked. "You okay in there?"

A pause. "Fine."

For the next hour, I occupied myself correcting papers and tried to ignore the strangeness that had settled over the house.

It wasn't fair, I fretted. He must know that I was dying to find out what happened to him at the police station. Maybe he thought I was being nosy.

I immediately rejected the thought out of hand.

Nonsense! I just care about the boy, I thought, circling a stray misplaced comma with unnecessary vehemence. The point of my red pencil snapped, leaving a jagged line.

If the circumstances had been reversed, I told myself as I dug in a desk drawer for a pencil sharpener, he would have long since wormed the information out of me. There was no way he would have tolerated such a petulant silence. I rose abruptly from my chair and walked to his door.

"Vern—" I began.

The front door opened and Gil ushered in a cold breeze. "What's this I hear about the kid at the police station?" he asked without so much as a perfunctory peck in my direction. "Where is he?"

I pointed.

Abruptly, Gil handed me his coat and leather computer case and knocked on Vern's door. "Hey, pal," he said, turning the knob and barging right on in, "what gives with you and the cops?"

I heard a low-pitched mumble from the depths of the room.

"Talk," Gil said before closing the door, virtually in my face.

With a frown, I returned to my students' papers, hardly seeing the words before me.

Is this how it's going to be around here from now on, I asked myself and circled a superfluous comma, the Boys against the Girl? Every time a crisis arose, would the family members of the male persuasion circle the wagons and leave me outside—literally?

I scrawled a C- at the top of the page and moved on to the next essay.

I thus immersed myself in adolescent interpretations of *Great Expectations* until a rattling gurgle in my middle interrupted. "Maybe Butch and Sundance are ready for dinner too," I murmured petulantly as I unearthed and nuked three Hungry Man frozen dinners.

A vigorous tattoo on Vern's door yielded no response. "Dinner!" I called with what I hoped was a cheerful, unresentful lilt in my voice. "Yoo hoo! Soup's on!"

No answer.

I had consumed the little plastic triangle of turkey and dressing, along with the mashed potatoes and was starting on the much-touted Apple Crumble Dessert when Gil and Vern ambled up to the kitchen bar and took a seat in front of tepid plates of Home-style Meat Loaf and Old Fashioned Pot Roast, respectively.

If I had expected an explanation, I was again disappointed. Gil was stolid and silent as he ate, while Vern had a furtive, guilty air. He wolfed his food and retired to the apparent safety of his room in record time, while Gil continued to scowl into his segment of succotash.

Miraculously, I was able to keep my own counsel during this interlude and was rewarded at last by a confidential murmur.

"Say again?"

"He's hiding something." Gil glanced over his shoulder, though we both knew that the walls of Vern's room were as thick as his head. "He didn't tell me everything, I know it."

"Are you sure? You two were in there long enough to recite *The Iliad* in its entirety."

Gil picked up his now-empty plate and carried it to the trash pail. "I know. I tried everything short of horsewhipping that idiot to get him to tell me what it was, or to at least tell the police. But no go. Stupid kid!" he said with a snort as he deposited his burden forcefully. He looked at me straight for the first time since he arrived home. "You want coffee? I want coffee. I'll make some."

"What did Vern tell you?"

"Says he's just been tutoring J.T. in French and helping Dustin with his English, and that's as far as it goes."

"Tell me what it is you know."

"The two boys are definitely the favored suspects in this lake murder and are currently in the county jail."

"Oh, no!"

Gil worked his jaw ruefully and spooned coffee into the coffeemaker. "Couldn't be helped. With their wild reputations, the DA—they've got Elm DeWitt himself working on this one—was disposed to ask for remand, but Judge Ryan is a kindly sort and he's letting them go home and stay under house arrest."

"They'll hate that."

"They'll just have to suck it up. And the public defender they're getting is a new guy, a real go-getter I hear, so they'll get a fair shake."

"Tell me exactly what they're supposed to have done. From what I've heard, it happened on the lake." I reached for two coffee cups.

"Yeah. They were driving in their car and—"

"Car? On the ice?"

Gil nodded.

"What were they thinking?"

He poured coffee into each cup. "Who knows? The way the police tell it, the boys encountered a man out there. His identity is undetermined so far." He pushed a cup across the counter toward me.

"What, just walking across the lake?"

"No, he was ice fishing. The police say the boys robbed the man, fought with him, and drowned him. His head was hanging down through the hole in the ice, frozen."

I shuddered. So the rumor young Frank had told the class was true.

"Oh, Gil!"

Gil grimaced. "Yeah. Not nice. Not nice at all." He stirred his coffee. "I have a source in the police department who says they found a gun in the tent, but the man was drowned, not shot."

"Maybe there were fingerprints."

Gil smiled and shrugged. "My source didn't tell me."

I leaned over my coffee cup to take a sip and paused. "Is this our usual brand? It smells odd."

"Nope. Same old, same old."

I sniffed at the cup. My stomach churned and I swayed a little.

"What's the matter?" He resumed his seat next to me, rubbing my back. For once, the caress didn't soothe me. It only made me feel queasier.

I rested my face in my hands. "Nothing. I guess it's just so horrible. A man killed that way. It makes me feel a bit sick." I had once narrowly escaped death by drowning.

"We all feel like that, honey," Gil said.

"And there's something wrong with this coffee, that's for sure."

"What are you talking about?" He took a large gulp. "Mmm, pure caffeine! Just what the doctor ordered! Come on, drink up!"

I jumped from my seat and ran from the room.

"Amelia, come back! I was just kidding! I'm sorry."

I made it to the bathroom just in time.

Chapter | Ten

Maybe the honeymoon wasn't exactly over, but the following day, Saturday, I learned just how stubborn my new husband could be. I was fully recovered from my upset stomach by morning, but he insisted on serving me a breakfast of dry toast and tea as a precaution.

"And you've got to promise me to see Dr. Ben on Monday," he said, placing the plate before me at the breakfast table.

"That's silly. I'm fine. It was just all the stress yesterday. First, I had that parent-teacher conference with the Sheas, and then seeing the Rousseau boys led out of school in chains."

Gil's dimples made an appearance, though his eyes still frowned. "Not chains, honey, just handcuffs. And don't change the subject; you're going to the doctor."

I ignored the latter half of the statement. "Well, the dramatic effect was the same: those poor boys, arrested for such a horrible crime." I turned to Vern. "What do you think about all this? Could they really do such a dreadful thing?"

"I'm sorry, Amelia," he said as he drained a tumbler of orange juice. "All I know is that J.T. is starting to get a little French under his belt and that he and Dustin wanted to take the Gervais girls to the ice dance. Guess that's off."

Vern turned his exclusive attention to the rapid consumption of the plate of scrambled eggs he'd prepared. Seconds later, he heaved a deep sigh and stood.

"Better go get a shower. By the way, I want to get in some extra hours driving the cab today. And I got a few, um, other things to do. Probably be real late tonight. Expect me when you see me."

"Spending time at the Gamma house?" I asked mischievously.

Vern reddened, but maintained his easy-going tone. "Maybe," he said, and headed for the door.

"Gamma House?" Gil asked, watching Vern's departing back.

I answered him in his native language, journalese. "The story is developing. I don't know much, just a name and a sorority: Melody Branch and Gamma. Don't ask me Gamma what."

"Hmm, a sorority. Interesting, and about time. When I think of how he nagged me to chase after you."

"Pretty good advice, wouldn't you say?"

Gil picked up his cue deftly. "Oh, excellent advice. I'm a lucky, lucky man, so they tell me." He blew me a kiss, headed for the bedroom, then turned. "By the way, this special ice festival edition is giving me a pain. Looks like I'll be working all day on it myself."

I'd had an idea this morning and decided to put it in motion. "I'll ride into town with you," I said firmly. "On our honeymoon, you may recall, you promised me a dinner at the Lion's Roar, and tonight I'm taking you up on it. While you're working, I can make a reservation, consult on B&B business with Marie, and do a little shopping. Then you can take me to dinner."

"Sure, if you make it for after seven o'clock and you're sure you're up to it, but you're still not getting out of going to the doctor Monday." Gil disappeared into the bedroom and peeked around the door again. "And let the police handle the Rousseau brothers. Just stay out of it. Dennis O'Brien will make sure the right thing is done."

"I'll make note of your suggestion," I said dryly.

His eyes bored into me. "I mean it."

"Have you ever known me to interfere with police business?"

Gil came back into the room. "What about the Marguerite LeBow thing?" he asked, referring to last year's tragic situation involving the death of Marie and Etienne's daughter.

"You know as well as I do that I didn't start that—it was thrust upon me!"

"I guess you're right."

"You bet I am. Go get dressed."

Gil once more disappeared into the bedroom.

There was a thumping from behind the sofa in the den. I leaned over the kitchen bar. "What's going on?"

"My tie!" muttered Vern, scrambling on all fours around the coffee table. He only owned one, a wide one in shades of tan, orange, and green with a portrait of Wile E. Coyote in the middle.

"Why would you want a tie? You never wear one."

He lifted his head, but avoided meeting my gaze. "I, um, kind wanted to get dressed up a little."

He crawled away from me. Obviously, he didn't want to go into detail.

"Well, you won't find your tie in there," I pointed out as I loaded the last breakfast coffee cup in the dishwasher, "Why don't you check in your room?"

Still on his knees, he pulled a seat cushion off the sofa and plunged his hand in the crevice. "It's too messy. I'd never find it. Hey, there's money down here." He pulled some coins from the treasure site and counted them in his palm. "Seventy-eight cents, good deal." He pocketed them. "But no tie." He shrugged and looked over at me pitifully, still on his knees.

I dried my hands with a paper towel thoughtfully. "When did you wear it last?"

"Quite a while ago. At your wedding, in fact. Then I took it off and—oh, I know!" He jumped to his feet and ran for the front door. "It's gotta be in my car!" He slammed out.

"Put on your coat!" I called after him, but in vain.

"Do you have any cufflinks?" Gil called from our bedroom door. "If we're going to go to the Lion's Roar tonight, I need to wear this dress shirt and it needs cufflinks." He waved his arms to prove that his cuffs did indeed flop without the proper restraint.

"I have several pairs of Papa's, but they're packed in the attic at Chez Prentice." I turned the knob on the dishwasher. "Why don't you wear a shirt that doesn't need them?"

"Because this is my only clean dress shirt. I bought it by accident two years ago. It's never been worn. The hamper's full, you know, Amelia."

He tilted his head in the direction of our bathroom. There was the slightest hint of gentle accusation in his tone.

"Tell me," I said casually as I followed him into the bedroom, "what did you do with dirty shirts before we got married?" I slipped out of my bathrobe and pulled a pantsuit from the closet.

"Dropped 'em off at the cleaners on the way to work."

Gil draped a tie around his neck—a tasteful silk one with navy and maroon stripes—and proceeded to perform that most mysterious of male rituals, tying a knot backwards in a mirror: wrap, loop, slip, and pull. He looked at my reflection from under brows lowered in concentration.

"But I had kind of hoped to guilt you into doing it. Isn't the Little Woman supposed to be in charge of the laundry?" He adjusted the tie's ends and positioned the knot to his satisfaction. "How about it?"

I was busy struggling to fasten a button at the back of my silk blouse. "Not a chance. I iron worse than I cook. Didn't I tell you?" I fumbled and missed the buttonhole. "Didn't you see the ones I washed and ironed for you last week?" I pulled evidence of my ineptitude from the closet and held it up.

Gil snickered.

I replaced the shirt in the closet. "Look, I have to be at work a full half-hour before you do, so tomorrow, why don't you just take your shirts to the cleaner's as of old?" I arched my back and reached over my shoulder. "However, if you ask her very politely, the Little Woman might pick them up for you after school Tuesday—ehhh!" I groaned in frustration and turned my back toward Gil. "Would you?"

Smiling, he completed the task. "Tell me, how did you manage to button blouses like this before we were married?" He patted my derriere gently, just to show there was no rancor at my wild-eyed feminist stance on the subject of laundry.

"With difficulty," I conceded, fastening the button of my wool slacks.

"How do you like that?" I heard Vern moaning from the den. "I searched the car. It wasn't even in the trunk!"

"Come on in," Gil called to him, "we're decent."

"Just barely," I muttered and went to brush my teeth in the bathroom.

"What's the problem, buddy?" I heard Gil ask. "Come on, use one of my ties," he offered after hearing the details of Vern's predicament. "This one would match your jacket, or this one."

"No offense," said Vern, "but those are Geek City. Thanks anyway. I'll just wear a turtleneck under my sport coat. I think there's one on the floor in my room."

Gil joined me in the bathroom, closing the door behind him. "Now what am I going to do with this awful thing?" He reached in the clothes hamper and pulled out the missing tie.

"Gil, you hid it? That's terrible!"

"Shhh! No more terrible than this," he whispered, holding it over his own tie and looking at himself in the mirror. Wile E. Coyote sneered. Gil shuddered. "Can you believe he paid actual money for this atrocity? Sometimes I forget how young he is. A little over a year ago, he was still a teenager."

I was brushing my hair. "That doesn't matter. He likes the tie, and you had no business hiding it—ouch!" The comb had grazed my ear, which was still delicate from an injury sustained last autumn.

Gil looked into Wile E Coyote's eyes. "I'm telling you, Amelia, no relative of mine is going to be seen in this tie in public. When he no longer wants it, I'll just return it."

"Well, you've outsmarted yourself. He's looked everywhere, so you can't just put it back where you found it."

"Sure I can," Gil said, returning the tie to the laundry hamper. "I'll just toss it behind his computer in a few days and he'll never know the difference." He held his wrists up in pitiful supplication. "Are you sure you don't have any cufflinks?"

I finally persuaded Gil that a pair of conservative gold-colored clip earrings from Mother's old jewelry box would serve the purpose nicely. He showed these to Vern, who shrugged blankly.

"What? No joke? No wisecrack? What's wrong with you, kid?" Gil locked the front door and we, cozily decked out in our bulky parkas, navigated the treacherous icy walk to our respective cars.

"I don't know. Not in a funny mood, I guess." Vern ducked into his car, slammed the door, started his engine and rolled down the driveway, much slower than usual.

"Kid's a piece of work," Gil noted with a cloudy sigh as he pulled a snowbrush from the trunk.

"Interesting," I said, wiping off the back windshield with my gloved hand. "He once used the same phrase to describe you."

Gil worked on a stubborn frozen section with the scraper end of the brush. It wouldn't budge. "Guess I'll have to melt it off. Hop in."

We took our seats in the car and Gil turned the key. I breathed a thankful prayer when it started up right away. Back in town, too many balky ignitions on too many cold mornings had put me in the healthy habit of walking everywhere. Now that we lived miles from town, that was out of the question, and I was going to have to make up the exercise somehow. My clothes were getting tight.

Patiently, we sat watching the defroster slowly warm its way through the thin layer of ice on the windshield.

"So you don't regret that we waited so long?" I asked Gil.

"Hmmm? Regret?"

"Getting married so late," I prompted. I wasn't sure how I got on this subject, but all at once there were questions that needed answers.

"Of course I regret it, Amelia," Gil said, suddenly comprehending my question. His right glove grabbed my left one, and he held it against his cheek. "I regret that I was too thickheaded and full of myself to see what was right in front of me all those years. I regret that it took that crazy Vern to open my eyes."

"But children. Didn't you want to have them?" Before our marriage, in the interest of total honesty, I'd confided to Gil about my inability to conceive, a fact of life that I'd had to accept years ago.

He frowned at me and turned on the windshield wipers, which made short work of the remaining melting ice. "I used to, once, I think," he said, "but now, nosiree, not any more. I couldn't handle the crying and diapers and mess. That's why Vern is so ideal. No fuss, no muss."

"No muss?" I said, laughing, "Vern?"

"Well, you've got a point there. But what I'm saying, Amelia, is that I'm content with things just the way they are and very, very happy." He leaned over and kissed me. "I wouldn't change a single thing."

I could feel myself glowing, even though the poor Rousseau brothers were in jail, Lily was still being distant, Principal Berghauser was his difficult self, poor old Sam was missing and a stranger lay dead in the morgue. No doubt about it, lots of things were going wrong, but at least Gil and I had it right this time.

After Gil got out at the newspaper office, I got into the driver's seat and headed in the direction of Chez Prentice. Weekends were the busiest times for Marie and Etienne, and I usually tried to stay out of their way, but as a partner in the enterprise, it was my responsibility to stay informed and available to help, if necessary.

At the traffic light just before the turn to Jury Street, I pulled up behind a battered pickup truck full of precariously stacked lumber with a red rag tied to the longest piece that jutted from the back. "Go straight, go straight," I directed the driver when the light turned green, then as the pickup's flasher gave a delayed signal and made the cumbersome right turn, muttered, "Oh, great."

The poorly loaded wood rearranged itself and the longest board slid backward, threatening to carry its cheery red bandana straight through my windshield. I gasped and slammed on the brake. Thank goodness, the street had been recently plowed and sanded. You never knew who was going to take to the road. I gripped the steering wheel harder. This was why I preferred to let Gil do the driving.

One had to look on the bright side, however. Chez Prentice was located six houses up the street on the right. Once I reached the B&B, this pestilential nuisance could drive itself off into somebody else's nightmare. Gritting my teeth, I slowed to a snail's pace behind the truck, being careful to keep several car lengths behind the red rag at the end of the sagging, bouncing board.

But it didn't drive off. It slowed to a near stop to the right of my old family house and began a heart-stopping ascent up the low incline of Chez Prentice's newly graveled driveway. Gravity had its way at last, and the longest board slid completely out of the truck bed, accompanied by a few of its shorter fellows and, after a clattering roll, came to a stop directly in front of my car.

No sooner had I pulled to the curb and emerged from my vehicle than a burly figure came ambling over, his work-gloved hands raised in apology. "Sorry 'bout that, Miss Prentice!"

"It's all right, Bert," I said politely. "I didn't recognize your truck."

Hester Swanson's handyman husband grinned and bent to lift the errant plank. "That's because you never seen this one. It's my fishing truck. I keep it out at camp." He grunted at the effort, but managed to drag the board back to the truck.

Bert's allusion to camp meant neither a military base nor a place where children spend the summer, but simply a dwelling where locals vacationed. One's camp could range from a sagging shack to a fully equipped modern home, but it must, by definition, occupy land on the lakeshore. Come to think of it, our own house might qualify as a camp.

I followed him as he retrieved the other fallen pieces of wood. "What's this all about? Are you making more repairs?"

"Nope, me'n Etienne's got another business going." He heaved the boards back on the truck. His eyebrows shot up his forehead. "Say, you don't mind, do ya? I mean, he said it'd be okay if we worked here." He pointed toward the rear of the house with a gloved hand.

"Of course not. I'm sure whatever you two are doing is fine."

"That's good, then." Bert mounted the cab of the truck. "Well, I better be getting back there before the Frenchman gets in trouble."

"I'm glad to hear that."

I couldn't help but smile. It was to Etienne's credit that the two men had developed *camaraderie, esprit de corps,* and *vive la compagnie!*

At the turn of the driveway, I abruptly stopped mining my memory for French expressions. There at the back of the yard, beyond Chez Prentice's new gravel parking lot, was the old detached garage. During my tenure as sole resident of the place—and indeed, most of my life—this outbuilding, containing cast-aside furniture, broken tools, cartons of old magazines, and a little-used car, had been kept padlocked. Now it stood with its wooden doors flung wide. Bert's truck was moving so slowly that I passed it easily on foot, stopping at the garage door, head swiveling to take in the spectacle.

"My goodness, you two have been busy."

"You're right there," Bert huffed as he dragged wood from the back of the truck and laid it in a pile to the right of the building.

"But it's empty. What happened to the things that were inside?"

"Don't worry. I didn't throw out nothing. It took me all day yesterday to drag your folks' old stuff up to the attic. The Frenchman—" He grinned as he used the word. "Etienne, I mean—cleaned up the rest this morning." Bert pulled off his watch cap and wiped his forehead on a sleeve. "The stuff weighed a ton. No kidding, Miss Prentice, why would anybody want to keep all them old *National Geographics* anyway?"

I answered him absently as I moved forward into the dark cavern. "My mother thought they'd help with our school work. What's this?" A large machine occupied the center of the place.

He replaced his cap and resumed loading. "Band saw. We rented it."

"What exactly is this project?" I called after Bert as he rounded the truck for another load of wood.

"Swanson and LeBow, Angler 'ousing."

Etienne LeBow, his arms full of packages, walked up to me. His handsome face was flushed with cold and, I suspected, enthusiasm. In the years prior to his reconciliation with Marie, he had begun and built seven successful businesses, all due to his canny good sense and energy.

"You're building fishing shanties?"

"Custom fishing shelters." He deposited his burdens on the floor of the garage and looked around. "Prefabricated, convertible, and tailored to the individual fisherman. That is the difference. It will set us apart, right, Bert?"

"Whatever you say, Fr—boss," Bert concurred as he dragged an unwieldy sheet of plywood inside. "You want this here?"

I left Etienne and Bert to their worthy endeavors and headed indoors. Deftly evading Hester's ubiquitous offer of snacks and ignoring the kitchen wall telephone, I made my way into the dining room, across the entry hall, and through the open door in to Marie's office.

She was using her own phone and cocked a questioning eyebrow at my entrance. I held up thumb and pinkie to indicate that I, too, wished to make a call.

"Would you hold, please?" Marie clapped a hand over the receiver and stage-whispered, "Room B; it's empty. Use the phone in there."

I nodded. Guest rooms at Chez Prentice lacked televisions, but each was now equipped with its own telephone.

Marie adjusted her facial expression and resumed her telephone conversation. "What kind of discount can you give me if—"

I mounted the stairs in a philosophical mood. Chez Prentice had clearly become a going concern, but it was still the house where I grew up. How did it look to a stranger's eyes?

I'm a guest, heading for my room. Hmm, the carpet runner on the stairs is a bit worn, but elegant nonetheless. I like the smooth feel of the banister under my hand. No dust, that's good. Room B, she said. Here's A.

Room A, formerly my parents' room, now boasted a queen-size bed tucked in the nook under a gable window. Current occupant, Mrs. Felicity Daye of Toledo, Ohio. In his improvement of my family's old house, Etienne had covered the hardwood floors of the hallway with a new oriental-style runner carpet, so I was silent as I moved past Room A.

Room B, the smallest of the bedrooms, was logically between A and C. In another incarnation, it was probably sleeping quarters for the maid who served the occupant of room A. We had surmised this when renovations revealed that Room B's tiny, shallow closet had once been the door-frame for the communicating door between the two rooms.

I sat down on the charmingly dressed twin bed and looked around, trying to imagine myself a servant here a century ago. What an overwhelming job it was, taking care of this place. I knew from experience.

I reached for the telephone on the bedside table and paused. There was a voice coming from beyond the door-frame, someone in room A, engaged in intense conversation.

"No, I won't stop!" a woman's voice rang clearly. "It's got to be done! Don't give me any more nonsense about it."

I heard no reply.

"How much liquid have you had today?"

Strange question.

Her next comment was muffled, and it was then that I realized I was eavesdropping. Mrs. Daye was talking on the telephone with someone, and it was certainly none of my business.

Shaking off my curiosity, I turned to my own telephone call, picked up the receiver with one hand and with the other, undid the button of my slacks. The waistband was biting into my middle a bit, the result, no doubt, of too much driving and too little walking.

"Martin?" I asked when he answered the phone, "It's Amelia Dickensen." Years ago, Martin Rousseau, J.T. and Dustin's father, had worked at my father's lumberyard. "About the boys," I began, "I was in school yesterday when they were arrested. I called to see if I could help in any way."

"Gee, thanks, Miss Pren—I mean Mrs. Dickensen. I don't know. They're in hot water, all right, but the judge let me take 'em home."

"I'm glad, Martin. This must be terrible for you."

"It's hard, I gotta admit. All this craziness makes it tough to get to work." Martin worked at the local paper manufacturing plant. "And all the stuff people are saying! I mean, they're good kids, Miss. You know that. I mean, the stuff they done before didn't hurt nobody. They just got high spirits."

"Of course, Martin. And call me Amelia."

"But it's eating at me. They're not telling me everything. I know my boys."

"It's important they tell what they know, at least to their lawyer," I said. "Are they aware that he has to keep anything they say confidential?"

"I dunno, maybe. They watch lots of TV, so I guess they do. I'll tell 'em, though, just in case."

"That's a good idea."

Martin Rousseau sighed heavily. "I wish their mom was here, but then I'm glad she's not, y'know?"

"It's certainly understandable. Listen, Martin, I've got to go, but if there's anything at all I can do—"

"I know something!" he said suddenly.

"Anything," I replied, and wondered somewhat ungrammatically what I was letting myself in for.

"Their homework. They're not allowed back at school right now, but I don't want 'em to miss their homework. Dustin might not graduate on time if he gets behind. Could you see they get some lessons to work on?"

"There are workbooks that we use when students are out for extended periods due to illness," I mused aloud. "I imagine they'd serve the purpose. I'll check on that."

"Great." Martin's voice held a more positive tone for the first time. "That's the ticket, workbooks. And I'll see they do 'em, don't worry!"

Well, I thought as I hung up, *the boys probably won't thank me for it, but it will be helping.*

Next I called the local animal shelter. Yes, they still had Sam's description in their lost cat files. No, there hadn't been any feline fitting that description found since we first called. Yes, they'd let us know as soon as he turned up. I wasn't to worry. These cats had amazing survival instincts. Had I seen the movie *Incredible Journey?* I hadn't and rather doubted that my elderly cat was Hollywood material, but thanked them anyway.

Finally I called the Lion's Roar and got a reservation for eight o'clock. I was lucky, they told me. This was their busiest night, but there had been a cancellation.

After hanging up, I gathered my purse and coat and cocked an ear again in the direction of Room A.

Silence. Mrs. Daye had apparently finished her telephone call.

I stood and re-buttoned my waistband. We were going to dinner in the county's most elegant restaurant. In my wallet resided a venerable and virtually unused charge card for downtown's last remaining department store. There was much to be done before eight o'clock tonight.

Chapter | Eleven

At 7:55, riding in Gil's four-wheel drive green Cherokee, we were dressed in our best, though under our thick, sexless parkas, it was hard to tell. The North Country's winter conditions made glamour difficult, at least outdoors.

"And no more fretting about Sam or the Rousseaus. I want you to forget all about anything negative for the next few hours," Gil ordered as I leaned my head back against the headrest.

"Okay," I said, but with a minimum of enthusiasm.

The prospect of our romantic evening out had begun to pale. I felt tired, sleepy, and a little queasy. I lowered the passenger's window to let a thin stream of cold air blow on my face.

Concentrate on the present, Amelia, I scolded inwardly. *Think about your glamorous new velvet cocktail dress—albeit fifty percent more expensive and one size larger than the old one—and enjoy yourself.* I took several deep breaths and rolled the window back up again.

"I haven't been to this place in years," I told Gil. "I hear the food is still great. I wonder if they have the same menu."

"They do," Gil assured me. "I've eaten here lots of times."

I filed that bit of information in my mental database.

The Lion's Roar, located on the lakeshore road about four miles from our house, was the premiere dining spot in the county. Built in the early 1800s and named for a British warship, it began life as an inn. Tradition held that in the 1920s bootleg liquor was purveyed there.

I'd been told that unless one subsisted solely on the famous basketsful of tiny, handmade yeast rolls and limited one's liquid refreshment to ice water, a meal was likely to run up a hefty tab, not including dessert. And one didn't want to miss dessert at the Lion's Roar.

"I've only been once in my life, when Papa took us to celebrate Barbara's high school graduation," I said.

"It has been a while. You must have been about sixteen. Remember what you ordered?"

"Distinctly. It was prime rib. I ordered it because I'd seen the name in a book. I'd thought it was just a fancy name for spare ribs, and when they brought that great big bloody slab of meat, oh, my!"

Mute with horror, I'd nibbled at the wild rice and green beans that accompanied the entree—being careful to avoid the pink liquid that trickled all over the plate—and consumed at least a dozen of the feather-light, golf-ball-size rolls. So many, in fact, that I was almost too full for dessert.

But Papa had ordered the specialty of the house for everyone, Bavarian cream with butterscotch. The warm, rich sauce and the delicate fluff made me forget my horror.

My offending entree was wrapped up in waxed paper and taken home to our nonexistent family dog. It was much more appetizing after being stewed for several hours in Mother's homemade vegetable soup.

"And ever since that meal, I've compared every dessert I ever had to the Lion's Roar," I told Gil.

"Here we are," he said.

The car crunched across the gravel driveway, the snow already bearing the tracks of dozens of vehicles. I pressed my face to the chilly window and squinted at the old inn, illuminated by floodlights. The Lion's Roar was a barn-like building, made of dark, aged wood. The front steps and the broad, welcoming front porch had been swept clean of snow and decorated with small evergreen bushes in weathered half-barrels.

"They put great big rocking chairs out here in the summertime," Gil said.

"I remember," I said, smiling.

There was music floating on the frigid air as we navigated the slushy ruts in our good shoes. Our breaths came out in individual clouds.

Other cars were already pulling into the parking lot. A pair of hooded parkas entered the building ahead of us; a man and a woman, judging by the legs.

Assisted by Gil, I shed my wrap in the entryway and turned to smile greetings at the other couple.

"Amelia!" said Lily Burns.

She had just slid out of her coat and was wearing an elegant pink angora sweater dappled with tiny spangles and matching wool slacks, a new outfit, I was sure, because I'd never seen it. Until recently, we'd had intimate knowledge of each other's closet.

She was sporting a new hairdo, too, blonder, shorter and feathery around her face. No doubt about it, Lily Burns was an attractive woman.

She stepped back in surprise, and rearranged her features to reflect a controlled coolness. "And Gil," she added in a silky voice, "back from your honeymoon at last." She gave me a direct look that left no doubt that she remembered our rancorous telephone conversations.

She turned to her companion, who was hanging his coat on a peg on the wall. "I think you both know Blakely Knight."

"Of course," I said in an overly polite tone. "How are you, Blakely?" Apparently his pursuit of Lily was moving apace.

"Doing very well." Blakely aimed a repellant smile down at me, lowered one eye in a slow wink, and turned to extend his hand to Gil.

The two shook hands firmly in the distant but civil manner men have.

Clutching a tiny, silver evening purse, a Christmas gift from me, Lily linked her arm through her escort's. "Come on, Blakely." she said, airily adding, "See you later," with a waggle of her Passionate Plum fingernails.

The two proceeded through the entrance. I could hear music playing inside.

"Well," said Gil, "is she still mad? Could you tell?"

"As a wet hen," I said, "a wet hen dating a . . . wolf."

"Animal metaphors?" Gil's face registered surprise.

"It fits doesn't it? We all know what wolves can do to chickens. I don't know how Lily can stand him." I sighed. "Wonder what Alec is doing tonight, poor guy."

"Honey, Alec's not one of your school kids. He doesn't need your pity. He can handle this."

"You're right!" I blinked and shook my head. "What am I doing? I'm wearing a brand-new dress, I've just landed the most eligible bachelor in town, and we're out at the ritziest restaurant." I kissed Gil's cheek and took his arm, waving at the door where Lily and Blakely had entered. "Let's go have that romantic dinner for two we promised ourselves."

It was remarkable how unchanged the place seemed. The same huge fireplace—this evening housing a bonfire-sized blaze—the same dark-paneled walls and heavy tables topped with chintz tablecloths, fresh flowers, and small oil lamps. A massive antique church podium just to the left of the entrance served as a reservations desk. Behind it, a staircase rose to the second-level gallery leading to former guest rooms. A small sign indicated that they were now available for meetings and banquet rooms.

"Something smells delicious," I murmured to Gil as we approached the podium. Suddenly I was starving.

"Oh, yes, Mr. Dickensen, right this way," said the maitre d' in response to Gil's inquiry. We followed him through the busy dining room. The live music was coming from somewhere in the rear, in what I remembered as an enclosed porch overlooking a small brook. By the sound of it, there was a three-piece combo, skillfully playing old standards. I recognized the last few bars of "As Time Goes By" as we entered and "New York, New York" as we arrived at our table.

As Gil pulled back my chair, I slid into the seat with a feeling of happy unreality. I'd lived so long as a single that the

two-ness of us was still wonderfully novel. I watched ador-
ingly as my husband moved around the table and sat.

He caught me staring. "What?"

I gave him my dreamiest smile. "Just appreciating you." I
took his hand, strong, square, and larger than mine. "I like
the way those few hairs on your arm peek out from your shirt
cuff."

Gil blushed. "Cut that out." He pulled his hand back and
fingered his cuff, pulling it over his wrist, but the corners of
his mouth twitched upward. With his lips barely moving, he
whispered, "Listen, woman, don't go starting anything we
can't finish here and now."

It was my turn to blush, but any response was squelched
by the arrival of our waiter, bearing menus the size and heft of
the Sunday *New York Times*.

I selected the evening's special, filet mignon, twice-baked
potatoes, *petit pois*, and house salad.

Gil, with a puzzled look at me, chose the same.

The waiter listened attentively, then asked, "Would you
care for soup to start? A nice lobster bisque?"

Gil and I both spoke at once.

"No, thanks."

"Yes, please. Guess not," I quickly amended.

"I'll bring out some hot bread right away." With a sidelong
glance and an enigmatic smile, the waiter withdrew.

"Amelia," Gil said, "go ahead and have soup if you want."

"No, I ordered enough for an army already. They say marriage puts a few pounds on you, and I'm living proof."

I could tell he was trying not to smile. "That usually refers to the husband, because of the wife's good home cooking. However, in our case—"

"That's enough about my cooking, mister, or lack thereof. Here come the salads."

Gil bowed his head with me as I gave my silent thanks. When I opened my eyes, I caught him gazing at me thoughtfully.

Dinner was wonderful. I attacked my underdone cube of beef with enthusiasm and declined dessert only for appearance's sake.

"I feel like I'm in a scene from *Tom Jones,*" Gil murmured as I buttered the last roll in the second basket. "I had no idea marriage would bring out such . . . bawdiness in you."

"A healthy appetite is bawdy?"

He took my hand and grinned. "I'm not criticizing. It looks good on you, with your flawless table manners. I—uh, oh—don't look now." He dropped my hand and sat back.

With a sense of dread, I turned and spotted a familiar, shimmery pink figure approaching, followed by her tall escort.

"Told you we'd see you later," Lily Burns chirped. "You know, Blakely, first these two stay away for weeks and weeks, then all of a sudden we can't get away from them!" She emitted a peal of artificial, silvery laughter and looked down. "We just finished dinner, and Blakely insisted we pay you a little visit." She spoke in her usual fluttery social voice, but I could tell she was not happy about it.

"Make yourselves at home," Gil said, with an elaborately casual gesture. He stood and pulled out a chair for Lily.

The waiter asked if we needed anything else. Lily ordered a trendy Cosmopolitan, and Blakely, a scotch on the rocks. Gil ordered a cola and I opted for ginger ale. It sounded good to my slightly queasy stomach, which had suddenly started giving me little, faintly rebellious qualms.

"You're not drinking, Gil?" Blakely asked.

"Just can't spare the brain cells, pal," Gil parried deftly as he reached for his drink.

The ice clinked against the glass. Blakely couldn't have known about the history of alcoholism in Gil's family, which was my husband's primary reason for abstaining.

Lily's voice had the same crisp, icy sound. "Have you heard anything from Sam, Amelia?"

I sighed. It was a painful subject for me and she knew it.

"No, nothing."

"Sam? Is this an old boyfriend?" Blakely put one long arm around the back of Lily's chair. "Should I be jealous?" He picked up her hand and kissed it.

Lily actually blushed. "An old cat, as in feline," she told him. She looked over at me and spoke each word firmly. "A sweet, precious old pet, lost due to appalling neglect."

"I have informed Amelia that we were only going to discuss happy subjects tonight, Lily," Gil put in. "That's not one of them."

Lily frowned. "What male chauvinist nonsense."

"Well, I think it's a good idea." Blakely shuddered. "Besides, I can't stand cats. Underhanded, sneaky creatures."

"That's not true—" Lily said.

"Sam's not—" I said.

We spoke simultaneously and stopped, exchanging surprised glances.

Lily said, "This cat is an exception to that rule, Blake. He's as affectionate as any dog."

Yes, when you feed him sour cream and butter, against veterinarian's orders, I thought, but did not say.

"A cat's a cat," Blakely said. He withdrew his arm and hunched over his drink.

I glanced at Lily and caught a faint catlike tightening around the eyes. Blakely had blundered. I wasn't a cat person, per se, but even I knew better than to say something like that in front of Lily Burns.

"What do you hear from the jailbirds, Amelia?" Blakely asked, looking over the rim of his glass. "The raging Rousseau Brothers." He took a sip.

"I, uh . . . "

"Seems to me people have finally gotten wise to those boys. They've been out of control far too long."

"Sorry, that subject's on the on the taboo list too," Gil said firmly. "So, Blakely, are you entered in the ice fishing contest?"

"I'm afraid I'm not much for the great outdoors, Gil. Hunting, fishing—none of that. I like lifting weights, working on my six pack." He patted his midsection and hefted an imaginary dumbbell with his fist. "Doing laps at the Y pool, like that. You might say I prefer indoor sports, if you get my drift." He glanced at Lily.

Gil purposefully ignored the implication of the remark and went on making pleasant conversation. "I understand you just joined the faculty this winter. Where are you from origi-nally?"

"The Midwest." Blakely waved his hands vaguely. "Say, what's this?" He plucked at the catch of Lily's clutch purse and pulled back a grayish tuft.

I smiled. Strike two against Blakely. If there was anything Lily hated, it was to be picked at.

"Just lint," Lily said briskly, snatching the speck from Blakely and dropping it on the floor. "Will we see you two at the Ice Dance?"

"Um . . . probably. Yes." Gil cast a glance over at me and I nodded.

Lily had just cleverly informed me that she'd lined up Blakely as her date to this particular event.

He took Lily's elbow. "Come on, Lily. I think these two want to be alone."

Lily gathered up her glass and her evening purse in a con-fused manner. "Well, goodbye. Good luck hunting for Sam." She clattered after her escort on her high heels.

"Alone at last." Gil held up his glass in a toast. "Here's to long honeymoons."

We clinked glasses, smiled at one another and settled into a pleasant, companionable silence, listening to the music coming from the dance band.

"I remember that song," I said, humming along. . . . *you are the wind beneath my wings* . . .

"Me too," said Gil. "By the way, I like your new dress. You look nice in that color. It makes your eyes look really green.

And I like that—" he gestured in a sheepish, masculine way that I found particularly endearing, "—front part."

My minor weight gain had enhanced my bosom somewhat, and the bodice of this new dress draped nicely over it. I smiled dreamily at him.

"Thanks."

"Come on, let's dance."

We were threading our way around the tables in the crowded dining room when a now-familiar feeling hit me once again. I pulled on Gil's arm. "I've—I'm—I've got to—"

Without another word, I rushed toward the sanctuary of the sign marked Restrooms and threw myself against the one designated Ladies. I was just in time. Suffice it to say that my lovely dinner in its entirety immediately deposited itself in the nearest porcelain toilet. And all I kept thinking was how thankful I was that it was such a clean restroom.

"The flu, maybe," I told myself afterwards as I mopped my face before the mirror with a damp paper towel.

The reflection of a pretty face appeared behind me. "Mrs. Dickensen, are you all right?"

"Yes, thanks, just a little woozy."

The girl frowned in concern. She was tall and young, perhaps nineteen or twenty, with dark brown hair that formed a halo of delicate curls around her pale face.

"Is there anything I can do?"

"No, thanks, it's all right. I feel a lot better." Probably a former student, I thought. "I'm sorry; I don't remember your name."

She smiled, and her blue eyes sparkled with amusement.

"That's because we've never really met. Vern sent me in. We're sitting in the corner across the dining room, sort of behind a post. We didn't want to disturb you, and when that other couple showed up, Vern said we really didn't want to get into that mess—I mean," She paused, realizing that her quote might not be tactful. "Then when you came in here so suddenly, Vern sent me to see if I could help. I'm a nursing student, you know."

"You're Melody Branch!"

She smiled, surprised. "Vern has mentioned me to you?" The idea seemed to please her a good deal.

"Oh, yes."

It was a half-truth, because I had actually dragged the information out of Vern, but I was a sucker for romance and encouraged it whenever I could. I was about to say more, when there was a chirping sound.

"Excuse me," Melody said apologetically, "my cell." She rummaged in her small purse and pulled out a square cell phone resembling a tiny television, tapped it and said, "Hello?"

Trying to give her some privacy, I turned away and began to soap my hands under the tap, but Melody's clear young voice rang through the peripheral sounds.

"What? Sure, I remember you. Why?" There was a pause while she listened. "Well, didn't he tell you where he was going?"

Melody paced and curled one strand of hair around her finger thoughtfully. "No, I know. Of course you can't. We'll come get you right away. No, it's okay. I've got an air mattress we can put on the floor. We'll figure all that out when we get there. Stay cool." She stowed the cell phone back in her purse.

I didn't ask, but she seemed eager to talk. She stepped up to the mirror with a comb and began to repair the damage she'd done to her hairdo. "Sorry about that. It's an old school friend of mine. She's pretty stupid sometimes. I told her she shouldn't go live with this guy. She barely knows him. Now he's run out on her, and she's frantic. Her parents won't speak to her, and she and I haven't been especially close since high school, but I guess I'm all she's got." She shrugged.

You're a nice girl, Melody, I thought, rinsing my hands.

Melody sighed and put away her comb. "If Vern doesn't mind, we'll go pick her up. She can stay with me at the sorority for a couple of days until she gets her head straightened out, poor kid." She went to the door and opened it.

I said, "I don't think Vern will mind. He's a really good fellow."

She dimpled. "Oh, I know that! It's just that it's so far. Almost to Canada, so I guess you better not expect him to get home early. See you later!"

The door closed and I was left to dry my hands and think.

Vern and Melody were heading out of the dining room by the time I made it back to our table. "The young lady with Vern assured me you were all right," Gil said as he stood and held my chair. "Are you all right?"

"I'm fine. In fact, I'd like to have some dessert, after all." I decided that he didn't need to know that I'd lost my dinner and was starving again.

"Good idea." Gil signaled the waiter. We put in our order for the house specialty, Bavarian cream with butterscotch.

While we waited, I explained about Melody and the telephone call. "Unless I miss my guess, the poor kid in question is Yvonne LaBombard. Her mother told me she was living with a man somewhere in the Champlain area, near the border. They don't like him very much."

"Whoever the girl is, she has a good friend in Melody," Gil observed.

"That's true. I'm so glad Vern has finally found a really nice girl. Ohh," I murmured with pleasure as the dessert was placed before us.

"Aren't you being a little premature?" Gil picked up a spoon and dipped it in the thick butterscotch. "I wouldn't go ordering the wedding cake just yet, if I were you." He tasted the dessert. "Mmm, it *is* good."

"It's the bride's family who provides the cake," I corrected him. "The groom's family gives the rehearsal dinner. Double mmm." I closed my eyes. "Well, if they do get serious, I only hope they're as happy as I am at this very moment, Gil."

He lifted his glass of cola. "Here's to things staying just the way they are right now." His voice grew husky. "I intend to spend the rest of my life keeping it this way."

"Cross your heart and hope to spit?" I said, quoting one of my students with a smile.

He drew a cross over his heart. "You'll have to imagine the spitting part. This is a classy joint."

I imitated his gesture. "And I promise the same thing."

Chapter | Twelve

"**B**ut that's impossible!"

It was Monday and I had just wasted the better part of two hours, first in the doctor's waiting room, then shivering in an examination room, wearing a flimsy backless smock, missing my morning classes. I never would have come if I hadn't been distinctly queasy again in the middle of church the morning before.

It had happened just as we were about to sing the offertory, and Gil said that even from his seat in the congregation, he could see my face turn a pale shade of green, right in the middle of the alto section. At his insistence, I'd reluctantly agreed to call the doctor today and had been "squeezed in." I'd also been poked and prodded and had various bodily fluids collected. It had been no fun at all and I was in no mood for jokes.

"The test is quite reliable, Amelia."

With a faintly amused expression, Dr. Benjamin Stout pulled a sheet of paper toward himself on his big desk and peered at it through his reading glasses. He fit his name almost too well: barrel-chested under his white coat and double-chinned when he lowered his head to look at me over his reading glasses. He and old Dr. Henry Lewis before him had been my lifelong GPs.

"Reliable, unlike some doctors!" I snapped. "I was told, in this very building, by your late partner, that I was unable to conceive."

Ben picked up my thick file and flipped back through the pages. "That was . . . just a second . . . here it is. That was over twenty years ago. We've learned a lot more about hormone levels since then. Turns out, you've been capable of conception ever since we corrected that thyroid imbalance."

"Then why wasn't I informed? I got married in December!"

Ben put the chart down with a wry smile. "It was in the booklet I gave you."

I sighed. "It was so long ago, and I never thought . . ." We both knew what I meant. I never thought I'd ever get married.

"Look, I'm sorry, Amelia, but you're an exceptionally healthy woman and an intelligent one. You know the facts of life." Infuriatingly, he crooked his fingers in quotation marks.

"But these symptoms, the nausea, the fatigue, aren't they a little early?"

He shook his head. "They can occur as early as a week into the pregnancy. Hmm, a honeymoon baby; rare, but not unheard of. By the way, I'm sorry we were out of town for your wedding. Alec told me it was bonnie." Ben and Alec were golfing buddies.

"But—but, I mean, this is going to change everything! I never imagined . . ." Tears sprang into my eyes.

He pushed a tissue box toward me. "Cheer up, Amelia, it's not terminal. A few months from now, all this will be behind you, and you and your husband will have a little dividend to show for it."

Little dividend? I thought as I dabbed at my eyes. Gil's words echoed in my mind: *"Nosiree. I couldn't handle the crying and diapers and mess. That's why Vern is so perfect. No fuss, no muss."*

"But isn't it dangerous at my age? For the child, I mean?"

Ben smiled. "Only a little more than for a younger woman, not nearly as much as in years past." He leaned forward and said in a lowered voice, "If you want a referral to the Women's Center downstate, you'll have to ask another doctor."

"What?" I looked up, shocked. "Absolutely not! What a suggestion, from you of all people, Ben!" The doctor was a devout Catholic. I sat straighter. "I'll just have to get used to the idea."

"That's the spirit. Okay then, you're all checked out until next month. They'll schedule your appointment out front. Here are some prenatal vitamin samples and a prescription for more." He pushed several small pill bottles across the desk. "And some information you'll need." He fished a thick pamphlet from a desk file drawer and handed it over.

I dropped them in my purse.

Ben jotted a note on a pad. "You'll want to sign up for childbirth classes at the hospital."

"Hold on, Ben. Obviously Gil doesn't know about this yet. I'll call you about all that later. I have time, don't I?"

He shrugged. "Suit yourself, but the classes fill up pretty quickly. Why not drop by the hospital and see when they have an opening. Sometime in July would be best, because you're due in early September."

I left the office in a state of numbness. I had an hour before I was due back at school, plenty of time to go across the street to the hospital and sign up for the class. I walked flatfooted, carefully watching the salted sidewalks for patches of ice. It seemed I was in a delicate condition now and needed to be careful.

Shortly before her death, my mother had prayed that I not be left alone, and I had thought Gil was the answer to that prayer. Apparently there was more answer to come.

First Thessalonians 5:18, "In everything, give thanks," had been one of Mother's favorite scripture quotes.

Help me be thankful, I prayed. *And please, please, please, help me tell Gil!*

I tried to look on the bright side. Well, at least this explained the nausea and the tightness of my clothes. I was healthy. And apparently Gil was healthy too.

I paused, feeling a pang. Years ago, when we were first dating, I'd told Gil what the doctors had told me, and he'd accepted it and still wanted to get married. Now, over twenty years later, he was going to find out he'd married me under false pretenses.

What would this do to our relationship? Hadn't we promised each other only last night to keep things just as they were?

I sighed. So much for cross my heart and hope to spit.

I cast my mind back to any pregnancies I might have observed. My sister Barbara had a vigorous brood of four, but she had done all her gestating years ago in her adopted home state of Florida.

Another image swam into my head as I paused at a crosswalk, waiting for the light to change: TV re-runs of Lucy Ricardo, a human beach ball in voluminous smock and rakish beret, squishing a huge mound of clay so her child would appreciate art, waking up at all hours with odd cravings, and generally driving her husband, Ricky, nuts.

Would that be me? Would the hormones make me impossible to live with? How would Gil react? Tears sprang into my eyes.

I stopped abruptly in my tracks and frowned. *Cut it out, Amelia. Let's see a little courage here. You're going to be a mother. You owe it to little what's-his-name.*

Names! I'd need names. One if it's a boy and another for a girl. Maybe Janet, after my mother. Or something literary: Oliver, perhaps, or maybe a name from Gil's side.

Gil. I sighed again. The fatigue that had plagued me for weeks began to descend. It was just too tiring to think about how to break this to him.

It needn't be done immediately. *After all,* I reminded myself, *tomorrow is another day.*

As walked through the automatic doors of the hospital, I had discarded Scarlett as a girl's name, but was giving serious thought to Melanie.

The maternity floor was relentlessly cheery. The walls along the passageways were bedecked with colorful nursery rhyme characters, and the waiting room had a bank of telephones and a row of recliners. There was another question:

Would Gil want to be in the delivery room, or would he wait outside in the manner preferred by our fathers?

I roused a bored receptionist and was given a place in a birthing class the week after July 4th. I sighed as I slid the appointment card in my wallet.

It's starting already, Gil, I thought. *This parent stuff: the responsibilities, the obligations. Are we up to it? Are you? Am I?*

As I boarded the elevator, I heard someone calling me.

"Mrs. Dickensen! Wait up!"

I turned to see Courtney, of the lovely Gervais twins, walking briskly to catch up to me.

"Everything okay with you?"

Curiosity shone in her long-lashed brown eyes. Under her open parka, I could see the pink uniform of a hospital volunteer. On her tall young frame, it looked particularly attractive. For some reason, I had little difficulty distinguishing the girls from one another. Crystal was the sturdy one and Courtney was the friendly one.

"Fine, thanks. In fact, I'm an exceptionally healthy woman," I quipped, quoting Dr. Ben.

"Oh, that's good. I hate going to the doctor, don't you? Don't like needles and things, which is funny, because here I am volunteering at the hospital. Now, Crystal, my sister, it doesn't bother her. She used to pick scabs off her knee, just to watch 'em bleed. Mom could tell us apart that way."

"Oh, dear." I tried to picture the willowy, ethereal Crystal, who worked part-time helping Hester at Chez Prentice, as a scabby little tomboy, and couldn't.

"Yeah, weird, don't you think? Well, I don't care, I'm weird, too, I admit it. I like helping people and making them feel better, even if I can't give them a shot or operate or anything. I just want to help."

She paused, apparently out of breath, but not yet out of words. She continued, "Let's walk together, okay? I'm finished at the hospital for today, but I have to be back at school in time for gym class in fifteen minutes. I like to have somebody to walk with, don't you?"

I agreed that it made a long walk more pleasant.

"You wanna know my favorite place? The newborn nursery. I love to rock and hold the babies. And the nicest doctor is Dr. Stout. He delivered me and my sister. He wasn't the one who was supposed to, but Mom and Dad were over at St Armand's beach and we just . . . started coming. Her water broke and stuff."

"Oh, my." This story was beginning to get a little more graphic than I cared to hear, especially under the circumstances.

"Yeah, it was weird. I mean, I don't know how they did it, because of all the sand and stuff, and I guess I just don't want to know."

Neither did I. Desperate to change the subject, I hastily grabbed at another one.

"Were you at school when the Rousseau boys were arrested?" The instant the words left my lips, I regretted them. I had no business gossiping like this.

"No, I wasn't. I mean, I was outside on the field at band practice. It was horrible. I heard they took them away in chains!" To my surprise, tears filled Courtney's eyes. "They couldn't have did what they said they did, Miss Prentice, they just couldn't! Especially not Dustin!" She sniffed and accepted the clean tissue I found in my coat pocket. "Lots of people don't think they're guilty."

"I'll be bringing them their homework tomorrow," I said.

Courtney stopped walking and grabbed my forearm. "You will? Oh, please tell Dus—I mean, tell them both what I said. Me and Crystal don't believe they did that thing, not for a minute, not for a second! Tell them, please? Okay?"

Apparently, the brothers had somebody else on their side.

Chapter | Thirteen

Marie LeBow looked happy to see me. "Amelia!" she said as I walked into the kitchen at Chez Prentice at the end of the school day. "We were just talking about you!"

She was sitting at the table with a small group of guests: Mrs. Daye and a pair of nuns in sedate navy blue, young Sister Priscilla Miller and elderly Sister Margaret DeLancey, in town for a teachers' conference.

"All good, I hope," I said automatically, managing a wan smile. I was hungry. "Could I get a glass of milk?"

"In the fridge, dear," said Hester, pulling on her coat as she nodded toward the old kitchen clock, "There's cookies on the table there. Everybody help yourself. I gotta get home. Bert's gonna want his dinner early tonight."

"I gather he and Etienne are going great guns on this project."

"Got that right! Bert's cell is ringing off the hook. He's been back there in the garage every night this week, putting together them shanties." Realizing she needed to explain to the guests, she gestured with her hands. "Building little pre-fab houses and selling or renting 'em out. There's an ice-fishing contest, y'know."

I shivered inwardly, in part at the thought of long, chilly hours spent on the frozen surface of the lake, and partly at the murder that had transpired there.

He froze right into the ice; at least, his head did.

It was a mental image difficult to shake.

"Well, this snack was nice," said the more elderly of the two sisters, pushing her chair back, "but we need some real dinner. Anybody have a suggestion?"

"There's Ernie's if you like Italian food," said Marie. "It's four blocks down, across from the old post office. The best marinara sauce in the world."

" 'Allo, everyone!" We all turned to see Etienne LeBow, having just completed the sixty-mile commute from Montreal, resplendent in a dress overcoat and carrying a leather attaché case in one hand and, incongruously, a domed lunchbox in the other.

Marie hastened to give him a wifely hug. "Everything okay today?"

"Comme toujours!" He set his burdens on a counter, eased out of his coat, hung it up on a peg, and pulled open the refrigerator door as he loosened his tie. "I am starving. What is on the menu?"

"Hester made pork chops," Marie told him, "and apple dumplings for dessert."

"That sounds really good," said Sister Priscilla, "Is there any chance?" she asked with a pleading look in her eye.

"Sorry," said Marie, "breakfast only."

This really wasn't as heartless as it sounded. Our breakfasts were sumptuous affairs, with all the trimmings, served to order any time from seven to ten a.m. Hester prepared meals for Marie and Etienne and left them in the refrigerator, but, although light homemade snacks and beverages were available all the time, paying guests were on their own for lunch and dinner. It was a firm rule.

"You know what you ladies should do? You should get a Michigan at Fritzi's," said Etienne brightly, pouring himself some coffee.

"What's a Michigan?"

"It's a kind of chili dog," I explained.

Etienne frowned as he set his coffee mug on the table and sat. "Oh, Amelia, a Michigan is not just a chili dog, it's a specialty of the region! Nowhere else do you find it, and you may trust me—I have looked!"

He leaned forward. "You take a fresh bun. Be sure it's white bread," he admonished, raising a warning forefinger, "It must be a rectangle with a slit in it. Some call it a lobster roll." He formed the rectangle with his hands. "You place the steamed hot dog in this slit." He suited the action to his words. His short-fingered hands were articulate. A solid gold signet ring gleamed on his right pinky. "Voila."

I glanced at Marie, who was suppressing a grin.

"And now," He raised his forefinger again. "Over the top you spoon the wonderful sauce, but not chili—no!" He tenderly spooned imaginary sauce over the hot dog, then, frowning, explained, "A spicy meat sauce, the texture of bolognaise. Delicious!"

My mouth began watering. I could tell by the others' expressions that theirs were too.

"And on top, sweet chopped onions." He began sprinkling the onions on the imaginary hot dog, and it was all I could do not to snatch it off the table and take a huge bite. "And just the tiniest little line of yellow mustard along the top."

He actually kissed his fingers in that corny gesture you see performed by cartoon chefs, then sat back and sighed. I caught him tossing a microscopic wink at his wife.

"Was that for real?" I whispered to Marie behind my hand.

"Nah. He worked at Fritzi's for a few months right before we got married," Marie whispered back. "He loves to do that bit. He says he's practicing his salesmanship."

"Where can we get these . . . Michigans?" asked the younger sister.

"Fritzi's," Etienne said. "The best are at Fritzi's."

"Is there lots of salt in it?" Mrs. Daye asked. "And fat?"

Etienne shrugged again. "I don't know, but I would think so."

"Where is this place?"

"I'll show you if you'll give me a lift to the newspaper office afterwards," I told the nuns. "I want to get a couple of Michigans for my husband." Surely it would soften Gil up before I dropped my little baby bomb on him.

Sister Margaret turned to Mrs. Daye. "Won't you join us?"

She accepted, but without any particular good grace.

We pulled on our coats and headed for the front door. As we were about to leave the kitchen, the elder nun turned back to Etienne.

"Mr. LeBow, why do they call them Michigans?"

Etienne's response was an elaborate Gallic shrug. He tilted back in his kitchen chair.

"No one knows," he said in bass tones, "It's a great mystery."

Marie rolled her eyes at me.

"Isn't this nice?" Sister Margaret commented as we pulled into Fritzi's parking lot. "It looks like a bunkhouse in an old cowboy movie."

"Now that you mention it," I said, "I can definitely see a resemblance." There was an upturned horseshoe over the door and bandana-patterned cafe curtains at the windows.

Sister Priscilla was driving. She pulled into a vacant slot, turned off the ignition, and we all four scrambled out, driven, no doubt, by our collective hunger.

The three other women watched as I ordered the special, a Michigan red hot, accompanied by a gigantic cup of cola, which I changed to a chocolate milkshake, and French fries.

Everyone ordered and paid for their respective meals. We surveyed the dining room for a table.

"There's a booth!" Sister Margaret said, pointing.

As we headed across the room, Mrs. Daye's pocketbook buzzed stridently.

"Excuse me," she said, digging in her purse and walking at the same time. She extracted an old-style folding cell phone and turned away to answer. As the rest of us sat at the table, she drifted over next to a rolling metal tray bearing yellow and red squeeze bottles.

Her conversation wasn't audible, I noticed with relief. I didn't want to indulge in eavesdropping again. The sisters and

I exchanged light pleasantries as we waited for our order number to be called. We spoke of hometowns and colleges attended, mutual local acquaintances and the weather outlook.

I was just about to suggest that the sisters would enjoy a trip on the Lake Champlain ferryboat when over in her corner, Mrs. Daye seemed to explode.

"What? Do you want to kill yourself?" she barked into the cell phone. She gestured with her free hand, causing the light plastic catsup and mustard bottles to keel over, domino-style.

Some landed on the floor. Suddenly aware that the entire room was watching her, she murmured sharply into the phone and snapped it shut. "Sorry," she said with a sheepish expression as she gathered up the fallen condiment bottles and replaced them on the tray. She repeated her apology as she slid into the booth.

The elder sister leaned forward, concern on her broad and wrinkled face. "Dear, is there anything we can do?"

Mrs. Daye stiffened. "Oh, no. No. Thank you so much, but no. You know how husbands are." She looked across the table at the nuns and gave a little, mirthless laugh. "Or maybe you don't. Anyway, it's okay. It's fine." She looked around. "I'm hungry. When is that food getting here? Aren't you hungry?"

A server bearing a loaded tray came to her rescue. After sorting out our orders, the elder sister blessed the food, and we fell to, punctuating the silence with humming nods of approval.

Finally I polished off my last French fry and followed it by a satisfying rattle at the bottom of my extra-thick milkshake.

I couldn't believe how ravenous pregnancy made me. Good-bye to the Lady of the Saltines, Gil's sardonic reference to my sparse kitchen skills.

I had devoured the huge mound of French fries with amazing speed. My Michigan, however, I had quickly put aside. It tasted and smelled strange to me, though Mrs. Daye and the sisters apparently enjoyed theirs.

A quiet fell over the group as we sat back, satisfied.

Mrs. Daye gazed into her soft drink. She hadn't said a word during the entire meal. Then, "You know, don't you, that we've been consuming poison?"

Sister Priscilla started. "I beg your pardon?"

"Poison; this kind of food. Do you have any idea what junk like this can do to a person's kidneys? Put a drop of this cola on an old penny, and it burns off the tarnish, not to mention what the salt they put on those French fries can do." She punctuated her comment by fretfully crumpling her paper napkin.

I exchanged quizzical glances with the nuns.

Sister Margaret smiled. "Salt is pretty hard on slugs and snails too, I hear," she said and started to giggle.

"It's not funny!" Mrs. Daye said sharply.

"I beg your pardon. You're right, of course. We should all eat more healthily."

Mrs. Daye, who had seemed to expand with outrage, suddenly deflated. "Yes, we certainly should." She lapsed into silence.

"Excuse me a minute." I went to the counter and ordered some takeout for Gil.

By the time the sisters dropped me off at the front entrance of the newspaper office, orange grease was seeping through the paper bag containing Gil's two Michigans. Inside, the receptionist Wendy was pulling on her coat.

"He's still at it," she told me, jerking a thumb toward the door. "I hate to bail, but my kids are in a concert at school tonight."

She took the bag from me, opened it and sniffed. "Michigans! Ohhh, yum! Wish I could stay!" She returned it to me and patted my shoulder. "You're a good wife, Amelia," she said, and left.

"You bet I am," I muttered, holding the bag at arm's length.

Gil didn't look away from his computer screen when I entered. "Just put the cup down on the desk, Wendy. Thanks."

His hair was rumpled and his shirtsleeves rolled up. His office was in a state, with stacks of paper on every available surface. *Don't let the turkeys get you down,* the little sign Vern had given him, occupied a precarious but prominent spot on top of his computer monitor. Moodily, he moved the mouse a fraction of an inch, then tapped briskly on the keyboard.

I tore open the paper bag and set the two paper-wrapped Michigans on the desk next to him. It took a minute for the fragrance to reach his nostrils. He blinked rapidly and looked around.

"Oh," he said, and his face softened at the sight of me, "it's not coffee, it's you."

I leaned down and kissed him. The little acrobat in my chest did a flip. It was good to know the honeymoon wasn't over yet. At least not until I told him my news.

"And Michigans! You're an angel of mercy."

"Can you take a break?"

"For you? Of course." Gil slid his reading glasses to the top of his head, and held a hand out. "Gimme."

He peeled back the paper at one end of a hot dog and took a huge bite. "Ambrosia! I was going to offer to share, but you've already had some, haven't you?" he said, his words muffled by the bread in his mouth. "Onions on your breath." He pointed to his own mouth.

"I only had one bite. I've lost my taste for them. By the way, I have something to—" I began hesitantly.

"Come, have a seat," he directed, pulling an empty desk chair forward, and I complied. He reached out with his free hand and pushed a hair off my forehead. "You look tired."

"I am. But I think I know why." I tried again to broach The Subject.

He took another bite. The first Michigan was two-thirds consumed. Gil misread me. "I know, all that business with the Rousseau boys. You can't just fix this, Amelia, try as you might."

He had successfully diverted my attention. "I'm not trying to fix anything. I just want them to get a fair shake."

He popped the remainder of the first hot dog in his mouth and reached for the second. "Don't worry, honey, we can trust Dennis O'Brien to get to the bottom of this business."

"I trust Dennis, of course," I stipulated, "but I'm not sure about the rest of the police. The Rousseau boys have been such a nuisance these past few years that it probably looks like a golden opportunity to send them away."

"Amelia, do you think you can drop that for a second and let me tell you about my day?"

I sighed and folded my hands. "Consider it dropped for the time being."

"Good enough. Question: Aren't you folks teaching English grammar any more?"

"Of course! I mean, I am. Some of the new textbooks are pretty lax about it. That's why I've insisted on using the old ones. The school board wanted to make an issue out of it, but Mr. Berghauser pointed out that it saves money. I have them use the books in the classroom and any material they take home is on worksheets."

"Well, somebody must not have been paying attention. And unfortunately, they work here." He swiveled back to the monitor. "Take a look at this." He fiddled with the mouse and clicked through several different screens before stopping at a body of text. He highlighted a sentence under the heading, "Storms of the Past."

"This is a piece I assigned for a sidebar." He read aloud, "'Decimated by the storm, the mayor of the neighboring town called out the National Guard.'"

I sighed and nodded. "The dreaded dangling participle. Even Mr. Berghauser has a problem with it. And decimated, a kind of pet peeve of mine. It originally meant reduced by ten percent, but the erroneous meaning—total destruction—was used so often, it became standard usage."

"Well, I can let that little one pass, but it takes me all day to weed out about three dozen other boo-boos, even with the help of spell check."

"You'll get no sympathy from me, my friend," I said, remembering pretty young Courtney's fractured grammar, "It's no more than I see and hear every day of the week."

He scratched his head petulantly. "Yes, but you're not getting out a newspaper, where all the mistakes become public record." He reached for the last bite of hot dog and popped it in his mouth.

I was glad he was finished and the smell was fading. I didn't know how he could eat that thing. Well, time to tell him.

I took a breath and began, "Uh, Gil? I—"

He balled up the paper and tossed it in the wastepaper basket. "Whew! That was wonderful, but I better get back to work." He took a sip from a water bottle." I'll be about another hour here. Oh, sorry, I interrupted you. What were you going to say?"

"You need to work. It'll keep," I added with relief. I'd been dreading the moment.

"Is it too late for you to catch a ride home with Vern?"

I consulted my watch. "Probably. I think I'll stick around and correct my test papers." I'd have to wait until we got home to tell him The News.

We spent the time in a companionable working silence, punctuated by an occasional snort of disgust from Gil.

As for my work, I was pleased with the results of the Robert Frost exam. Two students actually scored 100 percent, and there were four nicely-worded poems. I smiled as I read Spencer Gonyea's:

The gym is empty, dark, and fun,
But I must see my homework's done
Before I play some one-on-one.

Yeah, right, Spencer, I thought, *and that's a lovely dress you're wearing, Mrs. Cleaver.* But despite the smarmy content, it was a nice effort, and he deserved every point of the ten extra credits I'd promised.

Serendipity Shea's paper, on the other hand, was abysmal. Try as I might, I couldn't wring out more than a very generous 39 points. "Oh, child," I murmured to the absent girl, "don't you understand that you never leave a true-false question blank?"

"What is it?" Gil swiveled away from his computer screen and rolled his chair over to mine.

"The turkeys," I sighed, nodding toward Vern's sign. "They're getting me down."

"Come here." Knee to knee with me, he put his hands on the arms of my chair and leaned in to give me a kiss, and another.

"Thanks," I said with a sigh. "I needed that."

He pushed off, rolled over to his computer, and turned it off. "Finished?"

"Just about." I scribbled the score on Serendipity's paper and set it on top of the stack.

Gil picked it up and looked at it. "F? Ouch!"

"Ouch is right. To coin a phrase, it really does hurt me more than it does her."

Gil brought me my coat. "Trouble with you is, you're just too nice. Always were. It's an irritating habit."

"Well then," I said, leaning up against him, "what's a nice girl like me doing with a wicked fellow like you?"

Later that evening at home, just after we slipped into something more comfortable and Gil settled on his side of the bed with a book, I slid in alongside and said, "There's something I'd like to discuss with you."

He put down his book, leaving his finger in the place. "You sound serious."

"I am."

He put a bookmark in his place and set the book on the side table. "Shoot."

"I—"

The telephone rang.

"Hold that thought." Gil reached for the receiver. "Hello? Yes . . . no, he's not. Does it have to do with work? Is there a problem I can help with?" He listened. "All right. You're welcome." He hung up.

"Who was that?"

"Fleur LaBombard." Gil had a thoughtful look on his face. "She asked if Vern was home. When I said no, she said thanks and she didn't need any help and goodbye."

"Oh, dear, what do you think—"

The telephone rang again. I answered this time.

"Mrs. Dickensen? This is Fleur again. Is Vern coming home soon, y'think? I mean, if there's a place I could call him at . . . "

"I'm sorry. I don't know where he is. Would you like to leave a message?"

"Oh, gosh, I dunno."

"Just give me a second to get something to write with." I rummaged around in the drawer of the bedside table and unearthed a pencil stub and scrap of paper. "Fleur? Go ahead."

I saw Gil smile at me and reach for his book, so I took the telephone into the other room.

"Look, Miss—Mrs.—um . . . "

"Call me Amelia, remember?"

"Oh, yeah, Amelia, listen, if Vern's not gonna get there soon, I'll just have to think of something else."

"Can I be of help?"

"I don't know. You remember my kid, Yvonne? I was speaking of her the other day?"

"Yes?"

"Well, the mister and me, as I said, we don't hold with the living together thing, y'know, especially the mister, and we're not supposed to have anything to do with her as long as she— well, anyway, I just can't leave my girl alone up here, so every now and again, when he's out, I bring her something. Sometimes it's a casserole or something I knit or something, y'know?"

"Yes?" I pictured Fleur knitting with a cigarette hanging out of her mouth, a remarkably incongruous image.

"Well, I don't let on to him, you understand, or he'd have a fit. He don't like the guy. Matt, he calls himself, Matthew Ramsey."

From that hodgepodge, I managed to decipher that she was referring to Yvonne's Significant Other. Matthew Ramsey. The name sounded vaguely familiar.

"I see. And how can I help you, Fleur?"

"Well, I was thinking Vern could come out here and give me a hand. He's good in a crisis."

"A hand with what, Fleur?" I was again losing the thread.

"I'm here, up at her place in Champlain, but she's gone! Nobody's here, not that Matt guy and not Yvonne, and lots of her stuff is gone."

"Oh, I see." Apparently, my deduction of the other night was correct. The abandoned girl had indeed been the hapless Yvonne. But if she hadn't yet informed her parents of her whereabouts, was it my place to fill Fleur in?

"I wouldn't worry, Fleur," I began and immediately realized what a stupid statement that was. I tried again. "Look, maybe she went out of town. Maybe she's with friends somewhere. Do you know her friends?"

"Not any more! She dropped all her old ones after she got involved with that . . . guy. Where did he take her? I could kill him! Where is she? If he did something to hurt her, I'll—"

I couldn't stand it. Her anguish was getting to me.

"Listen, Fleur, I heard something the other night about a girl living up in Champlain whose boyfriend left her. It might be Yvonne. She was staying here in town with a friend named Melody Branch at a sorority house."

"Which sorority?"

"All I know is that it's called the Gamma house."

"Melody Branch, Gamma house . . . oh yeah, Vern's girl," Fleur said, all at once briskly practical. "I know the place. Thanks, Amelia."

She rang off quickly, leaving me with a vague feeling of guilt. Should I have told her that? Did I betray a confidence? Would there be unhappy repercussions?

The lesson at church Sunday had been on the Prodigal Son. If ever there was a prodigal situation, it was this one, I thought, and whispered a prayer for the LaBombard family.

Please be in this situation. Bring harmony to their hearts.

I felt a curious kinship with Fleur. Maybe there was something to the cliché, after all. Apparently, I was about to become a new member of a universal club: mothers.

It was a strangely moving thought. Now was the time to tell Gil. Now, before I lost this strange and elusive sense of joy.

I moved to our bedroom door and stepped inside, calling softly, "Gil, darling?"

His response was a gentle snore.

Chapter | Fourteen

The Rousseaus' street was lined with cars, and on the sidewalk was a knot of people, most of whom held a microphone or camera. Several large vans, stenciled with names and logos of television stations from all over the state, lined the curb in front of the house and down the street.

"Excuse me," I began, shouldering my way through the knot of reporters.

Suddenly, all eyes and cameras turned my way.

"Who are you?"

"What are you doing here?"

"Are you a relative?"

"Did they do it?"

"Give us a statement, will ya?"

As the wife of a newspaperman, I knew better than to say a single word, least of all the perennial "No comment," so I clutched my black leather book satchel to my chest, continued to stare at my objective, the front porch, and kept moving. It was slow going, but eventually I made it to the front door.

I rang the doorbell. No response.

This was not surprising.

I rang again and pressed my ear against the door, trying to ignore the snapping cameras. There seemed to be movement behind the door, so I cupped my hand against it and called into the door. "Martin, it's Amelia Dickensen."

"I got a name!" I heard a reporter announce behind me. "Take it down: Mimi Dawson."

"Mimi! Mimi!" someone in the throng called. I continued to ignore them. "How do you know Martin? Or the boys? Do you know the boys?"

"Martin? You asked me to come, remember?" I said into the door.

"Are you dating the father?" somebody asked behind me.

I tried to direct a withering glance over my shoulder, but it didn't have the same effect it did in the classroom.

A few metallic thumps and the door opened a crack. A hand reached out, grabbed my elbow and pulled me painfully through the narrow aperture before slamming the door.

"Thanks for coming, Miss Prentice," Martin Rousseau said, re-locking the door. "Sorry about all that out there. It's got so I have to keep the blinds down all the time."

I rearranged my disheveled clothes. "How long has this harassment been going on?"

Martin scratched his head. "Ever since the guys got arrested. It seems like always, now. I don't mind telling you, it's beginning to get to me."

That last was obvious. He looked terrible. There were dark smudges under his eyes and his shoulders drooped. He had on mismatched bedroom slippers and what appeared to be cracker crumbs scattered over the front of his sweatshirt. He followed my gaze, shrugged again and brushed himself half-heartedly.

"I'm trying to eat something. Keep my strength up and all. Come on in."

We progressed from the enclosed front porch into the entry hall.

I glanced at the large photo of Martin's late wife on the wall and quickly turned my eyes away. "This must be such an ordeal for you."

He waved his hand. "Aw, it's going to be all right," he said bravely. "They're innocent, and it'll all come out in the wash. He glanced at the books in my arms. "Oh yeah, you brought the boys' work, didn't you? That's great!" He turned and called up the stairs, "Guys—get down here! Miss Prentice brought your homework."

Dustin's head appeared at the top of the stairs. "That's Mrs. Dickensen, Dad. She's married now."

"Keep your voice down, son, if you don't want what you say to get in the papers." He turned to me. "Sorry, Mrs. Dickensen."

"It's Amelia, Martin, remember?" I gestured to the boys to come down. "Maybe we could settle in the kitchen?"

The boys ambled hesitantly down the stairs and greeted me in a hangdog manner, glancing uneasily at the front door. They were both as disheveled as their father, with Dustin in sweatshirt and pajama pants and J.T. in cutoff shorts and a ragged T-shirt bearing the single strange word, "Bazinga!"

Martin herded them into the kitchen. "Come on, come on, get a move on."

"We can work at the table," I began and stopped at the sight of a pile of soda cans, paper plates, a pizza box, and a varied collection of TV dinner trays.

Martin sighed. "We've been a little sloppy lately. Come on, guys, let's clean this up."

"D'you think we did it?" J.T. asked baldly as he wadded up a paper bag and shot it, basketball style, into a nearby trash can.

"Shut up, J.T!" said Dustin, tearing up the pizza box with alarming ferocity. He discarded the box, wiped his hands on his rumpled jeans and stepped up to me. "It's like this: We've done a couple of stupid things before, sure." He shrugged. "Okay, a lot of stupid things. But we didn't do anything to that guy they found."

J.T. piped up. "Yeah, we just took a look in the tent and—"

"Shut up, J.T!" It seemed to be Dustin's favorite way of addressing his brother. "You gotta believe us. We're not killers, you know?" He paused and searched my face. "You know?" he said again and bit his lip anxiously.

"I know, Dustin," I said.

That wasn't entirely true. I didn't know for sure. On more than one occasion, I had been lied to by experts and sometimes believed them. Certainly these two sturdy boys were physically capable of overpowering a man and drowning him. I was reserving judgment, but it didn't seem the appropriate time to express it.

As their father watched, looking exhausted and distracted, the brothers helped me unload my book bag. They seemed almost eager to get started on the workbooks, moving rapidly around the house and quickly locating the necessary tools: paper, pencils, pens, and erasers.

"Your math assignment begins on page 79," I told J.T. "And yours, Dustin, is here, in the blue workbook, page 99."

"I remember now," J.T. said, almost cheerfully. "We learned most of this stuff last week."

"It's not as bad as I thought," Dustin agreed, wielding a pencil with enthusiasm. He looked over at me. "Thanks for bringing this. I mean, I guess we gotta do it so we don't fall behind. And I want to graduate on time. I'm gonna graduate on time," he amended firmly.

Martin went to the door. "Well, I'll let you folks get to work," he said, and left. I heard him trudging wearily up the stairs.

"Before you get started, let me explain the other assignments," I said, and for a few minutes, had their undivided attention. At last I said, "Well, that's about all. Got it?"

"Yeah." They both nodded.

"I'll be going." I rose and pulled on my coat. "Call me if you have any questions." I paused, remembering. "Oh, by the way, a friend of yours said to say hello: Courtney. She wishes you well."

The boys exchanged glances.

"Good," Dustin said, staring down at his shoes, "that's nice of her."

I finished buttoning my coat. "I thought so too. Well, goodbye."

"I'll tell Dad you're going." Dustin went out of the kitchen. "Mrs. Dickensen?"

"Yes, J.T.?" I assumed he had another question about his assignments.

"Was it that mad guy they think we killed? 'Cause he was fine when we left."

"I don't know, but tell me about the mad guy, J.T. Did you recognize him?"

He frowned down at the kitchen floor and bit his bottom lip reflectively. "No, I mean, we didn't stick around to see who it was." He shifted in his chair. "He was far away, and he had on a white parka thing with the hood up. I didn't see him long. Dus and me just heard him hollering and figured we better get out of that place quick."

"What about the fishing tent? What do you remember about it?"

"Well, it was a nice one, not the homemade junk you see some guys got. It was one of those kind you can fold up, y'know? A blue tent kind of thing. They got a lot of them where Dus used to work."

"So you looked inside. What did you see?"

"Just the tip-up; that's what you call the thing that holds the line. It was halfway out of the hole and the hole was freezing over. I started to break up the ice to get it out when the guy started hollering."

"You didn't see anything else?"

J. T. rolled his eyes. "Nope, but it was funny, because Dus said those things usually have lots of stuff inside, like buckets for the fish and stools and coolers and radios and stuff, even TVs sometimes, but this place didn't have any of that. Just the tip-up with the line connected to it and a lunchbox.

Sometimes people just go out on the lake and poke a hole in the ice, but if you already blow that much money on expensive stuff like that tent and that tip-up, you usually want to get comfortable too."

"How expensive do you think all that equipment was?"

"I don't know. Dus is the one that notices things like that, 'cause he used to work at Shea's. Like that tip-up. It was just kind of round, like a big red plastic hockey puck with a flag stickin' out of it, but Dus recognized the name. It was top of the line equipment, he said." His voice trailed off as we heard his father and brother descending the stairs.

"So they're all set, huh?" Martin gave his boys a wan smile.

"All set," I agreed. "I'll be back in a few days with more."

"Tell Vern I said to keep the thing that we—"

His brother shoved him. "Shut up!"

"That's enough, guys," Martin barked. "Get to work."

He accompanied me to the door. "What're people saying about all this, Amelia? At school and stuff?"

"Well, there's a lot of curiosity about the case," I said, trying to be tactful.

"What does Dennis O'Brien say?"

"I'm afraid he doesn't confide in me, Martin," I said. *At least, not any more,* I added mentally, remembering a time when Dennis' friendship with me actually threatened his career.

He stared off into space and reassured himself, "But everything will be all right. It will, I know it."

He opened the door and I slid quickly back into the mob. The reporters followed me down the steps and along the sidewalk.

"Mimi! Mimi Dawson! What did you do in there?"

"How are the boys? Aren't you scared to be with them?"

"Did they tell you what happened?"

"Mimi, look this way!"

I stopped at a crosswalk. A persistent portion of the gaggle had followed me the length of the block. I waited for the light to change and fumed. Were these jackals going to tail me all the way back to Chez Prentice? Would they besiege the place as they had the Rousseau residence? What would that do to our B&B business?

The light changed and as I stepped off the curb, followed by a half dozen of the more ravenous denizens of the journalism profession, a miracle occurred. I heard a short, sharp beep from a car stopped at my right and turned to see Vern gesturing to me from the driver's seat of a LaBombard taxi. He reached his long arm and opened the passenger door.

"Get in!" he yelled, and I complied before the crowd behind me knew what had happened.

Vern locked the doors and pressed the heel of his hand, hard, on the horn. The blare caused one man to start in surprise and hurl curses at the taxi, but Vern forged slowly ahead through the throng, honking in short beeps as a warning to the imprudent few who remained in his way.

At last, the way was clear and Vern stepped on the accelerator. We were back on a main street in thirty seconds, leaving the melee far behind.

"My hero," I said, patting Vern's elbow. "I don't know what I would have done if you hadn't come along. And Vern, one of the boys told me to tell you—"

"Let's talk about it later, Amelia, okay?" He jerked his head in the direction of the back seat and at that moment I realized he had another passenger.

I shifted in my seat and found a hand thrust directly before my face. "Cobb, James Cobb," said a handsome man in his late twenties wearing a loosened tie and white shirt under his heavy, unzipped parka, "I just moved here from Syracuse. I'm in the public defender's office. Defense counsel for the Rousseau brothers."

I shook his hand, but didn't offer my own name.

He leaned his forearms on the back of my seat and continued, "Quite a mess out there. Good thing this guy came to your rescue, I'd say." He patted Vern on the shoulder and instructed, "Just continue around the block, okay, buddy? And stop at the end of the street. I'll leg it from there." He looked back at me with unblinking gray eyes. "Who are you, by the way, if you don't mind me asking?"

Before I could come up with a quip that would indicate that I did mind, Vern put in, "She's just a family friend of the Rousseaus."

"Oh." James Cobb sat back in his seat. "Well, those boys can sure use all the friends they can get right now."

"A person always needs friends," I observed rather pompously. "But surely you don't think they'll be convicted."

"Not allowed to say," he said, "but if you're a betting woman, well . . . " he trailed off significantly.

An hour ago, I'd been unsure of the boys' innocence, but this man's attitude got under my skin. "I can tell you, these are good youngsters. I've known them for years. An injustice is being perpetrated—"

"Keep on saying that, lady," Cobb interrupted, "keeps up the pressure on the local Barneys. That's the tack to take: The cops are prejudiced against them because of their record of mischief." He seemed to warm to his topic. "Just look at the way they were arrested: brutally manhandled at school, right in front of their classmates, their teachers! If that's not prejudicial, I don't know what is!"

"They weren't manhandled," I pointed out sharply. "I saw the arrest. The police did everything by the book." I was thinking of Dennis and his scrupulous decency.

"Not where I come from," said James Cobb lightly. "The way I see it, this town is like all small towns—a hotbed of corruption, from the mayor on down, especially the DA, and the boys are just convenient scapegoats."

"For what? What corruption?"

He shrugged. "Who knows? There's bound to be something if we turn over enough local rocks." He leaned forward again. "For instance, I know for a fact that last year a girl was murdered right in the public library!"

I had close, personal knowledge of that particular unfortunate event and opened my mouth to explain it in no uncertain terms, when Vern slammed on the brakes and pulled over to the curb. "There you are, sir. You can get out at this corner and walk up to the house. That'll be seven dollars and fifteen cents." He scowled at me and put his finger to his lips.

The man counted out the fare carefully before gathering up his briefcase and stepping out onto the sidewalk. "Thanks, buddy."

I watched with some malicious satisfaction as he reached the middle of the block and was pounced on by the ravenous horde of news people.

Vern muttered a derogatory word under his breath as he did a three-point turn in the middle of the street. "Stupid lawyer didn't even give me a tip. Maybe that's the way they do it in Syracuse."

I sat silently as Vern headed the taxi in the direction of Chez Prentice. "You okay, Amelia?" he asked after several blocks.

"Yes, but I was thinking that in order to get the Rousseau boys off, that man is going to try to destroy the reputations of a number of good people in this town. And if he doesn't, and the boys are convicted, well, that's also unthinkable. This is just a huge mess. What are we going to do, Vern?"

"What do you mean 'we,' *kimo sabe?*" Vern squinted at the traffic. "I'm just the cab driver."

"Don't try to pretend you're not involved in this somehow, mister," I said. "J.T. told me to tell you to keep something. Now, what is that all about?"

"Hmm." Vern frowned. "Oh, I know. I promised to get them their French homework so they won't fall behind."

"Nice try, but I already got their assignments from Miss Leary. That's what my visit just now was all about. And for that matter, why did the police really want to question you?

Tell me, Vern, or do I have to get Gil to break out the thumb screws?"

Vern shrugged. "Sorry, Amelia, can't help you."

"Can't, or won't?"

He grinned at me, and it was hard to stay angry with him. "A little bit of each. Come on, Auntie. Give me a little credit. I know what I'm doing." He pulled up to the curb in front of Chez Prentice. "There you are, dear sweet, adorable Aunt, special delivery door to door, free, gratis, on yours truly."

"No, thank you," I said, pulling out my wallet and handing over some bills. "I pay my own way." I slid down in my seat and folded my arms. "But I'm not leaving this cab until you tell me."

"Cut it out, Amelia. I'm on a time clock here. The LaBombards are depending on me."

I pointed at the short-wave radio. "I haven't heard any more fares come in. Come on, Vern, give."

"Give what? That the Rousseau boys think I'm cool? I would have thought that would be a given." He linked his hands behind his neck jauntily, but I wasn't buying it.

"Did they tell you everything that happened on the lake that day?"

Vern dropped his hands and stared at the steering wheel, stone-faced, a sure sign that I was on to something.

"They were driving across the lake on the ice. Gil told me that," I prompted. "Then what? What did they tell you?"

"If I thought for a minute that you weren't trustworthy," he began.

"Yes, but you know I am. Come on. What is it?"

He put his hands over his eyes. "Nope. Sorry. No can do. I did promise, and I'm a man of my word."

"Vern, if you know something that can help the Rousseaus, you must tell Dennis!"

He took my hands in his. "Like I said, Amelia, I know what I'm doing. Please trust me," he pleaded. "Please?"

I sighed. "For now." I slid out of the passenger seat and stood in the open door. "But eventually, I'll know."

His relief was palpable. He nodded. "Eventually; probably."

What a frustrating afternoon, I thought as I made my way up the sidewalk to the porch of Chez Prentice. *What could Vern possibly know that could help prove the Rousseaus innocent? Or—*

I stood, frozen by a terrible, more plausible thought: *Or would it prove them guilty?*

Chapter | Fifteen

"Through Vern's Room with Gun and Camera," I entitled an imaginary documentary as I circled around, gathering up coffee cups, saucers, plates, and utensils, all with the dried-on residue of snacks consumed long ago.

It had been three days since I'd last tried to tell Gil about the pregnancy, and I'd fallen into a state of vague semi-denial. Tomorrow and tomorrow and tomorrow had crept along in its petty pace, and somehow inertia had taken over. Right now it seemed easier to just let nature take its course. In early September when labor pains began, maybe then I'd tell him. Meanwhile, I had dinner to prepare, not my favorite chore by a long shot.

"Honestly," I chided the absent Vern, withdrawing a greasy fork from under a sneaker, "if I didn't need all these dishes and things to make dinner." It was definitely going to be a long time before I got food on the table because everything was going to require some energetic scrubbing.

Most of the cups were stacked in several precarious little towers on his computer desk. I sat down at the desk and tried to consolidate my load, but gravity would have its way, and as I pulled it toward me, one of the stacks wobbled and fell over, causing me to overcompensate. All the cups on the desk fell, separating themselves and heading in countless different directions.

Fortunately Vern's discarded clothing on the floor made an effective cushion and none of the cups broke. One of them did, however, roll under the desk, and it was while I was retrieving it that I encountered the silver lunchbox.

It was wedged up against the wall behind the rectangular computer entity that muttered and flashed from time to time as it breathed and ruminated.

"How long has this thing been here?" I muttered. "Any leftovers in here should be really ripe by now."

Seating myself on the floor, I pulled the box onto my lap. It was rather heavier than I'd expected, and the closure was a bit more elaborate than the usual lunchbox latch. It had a keyhole, but apparently wasn't locked, and it wasn't hard to deduce that in order to open the box, one slid the metal square to one side, rather like luggage.

"Vern, what have you been—" I began, and stopped at the sight of the contents: approximately a dozen music CDs in their plastic jewel cases. "What a novel idea," I said, and lifted out several, "and a good way to protect your music." The walls of the case were thickly lined with some kind of stiff packing foam, and fit around the CDs tightly.

Vern's collection was eclectic, to say the least. Most of the names were unfamiliar to me, but I did recognize one by George Strait and another CD featuring the original Broadway cast of *The Last Leaf,* a musical that held unique memories for me. I ran my finger down the list of songs.

"Oh, here's 'What's Your Pleasure?'" I said aloud. It was one of my favorites, a kind of rollicking patter song performed by the show's star, Jerry Orbach.

Surely Vern wouldn't mind if I played just one song. I looked around as I pulled the disc from its case. Vern probably didn't have a CD player any more. All the young people I knew used MP3 players now.

"But you play CDs, don't you?" I said, addressing the gray rectangle that had only recently stopped making noises like a coffeemaker with sinus trouble. "I've seen how Gil does it. You just find the little door." I pressed a tiny button on the front of the computer and a shallow drawer, clearly shaped for a CD, presented itself.

Carefully turning over the CD to expose the music side upward as we used to do with records, I dropped it in the slot and touched the drawer gently. It responded by sliding back into position.

"What's going on here?" It was Vern, towering over me, a scowl on his face.

"Um," I said, and suddenly realized how very odd I looked: kneeling on the floor on a pile of discarded sweatshirts, next to the wide-open lunchbox, surrounded by assorted dirty crockery with an empty CD jewel box in my hand.

"I, uh . . . " Quickly, I thrust the jewel box back in the silver lunchbox and struggled clumsily to my feet. "I was out of coffee cups and plates and I knew you had some in here. It took a while to find them all," I added and picked up a rumpled T-shirt from the back of the computer chair. "You keep your place pretty messy, you know."

Vern, ignoring my accusatory tone, swooped down and grabbed the lunchbox. "What were you doing with this?" He slammed it shut.

"Well, I thought it was a real lunchbox—it surely looks like one—and that it might have some trash in it. I mean, things like this." I fished a crushed potato chip sack from behind the computer monitor. "Anyway, when I saw it had music in it, well, I like show tunes."

Vern's stern expression softened slightly.

I felt a strong sense of shame coming over me. "Oh, dear, this is terrible, isn't it? I'm so sorry. I seriously breached your privacy. I should have waited until you got home, but I needed the plates and things. I shouldn't have opened the lunchbox—is that what you call it?—and I promise, I won't do anything like this again."

Vern continued to hold the box tightly, but he was clearly in a forgiving mood. He shrugged. "Well, no harm done, I guess. And I should have put the cups and stuff back in the kitchen, so maybe it's partly my fault." He shoved the offending item back under the computer desk and helped me to my feet. "Just ask me next time, okay?" He retrieved several cups off the floor.

"Okay," I echoed meekly, beating a hasty retreat to the kitchen with my arms full of crockery.

I had finished putting the cups in the dishwasher and was scrubbing some stubborn dried cereal off of a bowl when Vern burst out of his room and approached me with a renewed scowl. "Amelia! What did you do with the CD in here?" He held up the empty *Last Leaf* jewel case.

I dried my hands on a dishtowel. "It's in your computer. I put it in there to play a particular song. I thought you saw me do it. I guess it didn't play. I'm not very good with computers, I'm afraid."

As Vern followed, I walked rapidly into his room, sat down in his computer chair, and pressed what I thought was an appropriate button. "I just wanted to hear this song."

But instead of playing music, the computer screen suddenly, silently, filled with columns of numbers, steadily moving upwards.

"Amelia, what'd' you do?" Vern barked and edged me rather peremptorily out of the chair.

I wrung my hands. "Oh, dear, I don't know. I just pressed Enter. Isn't that right? But it's not playing show tunes, is it?"

Vern's tone was suddenly thoughtful. "No," he said, "it's not." He leaned forward and followed the ever-growing list of numbers with his index finger. "It's kind of familiar, though. These dashes, three digits, dash, two digits, dash, four digits, over and over."

"But why numbers? It's supposed to be a music album, isn't it?"

He turned toward me in his chair and blinked. "Yes, and it is. I've played every one of these CDs to make sure. But why is it acting differently now? Show me what you did."

I leaned forward and pressed the tiny button. "I just put it in to play like this." The narrow drawer opened smoothly. "See, there's the CD."

Vern leaned forward and lifted the disc out gingerly on the edges with his fingertips and grinned. "Oh, I see. You put it in upside down." He turned it over and examined the decorated top.

"But I thought you—oh, never mind." I sighed. I was never going to get the hang of computers at this rate. I was just grateful, I decided, that I hadn't done any actual damage.

Vern squinted intently at the colorful label decoration. "Here's what it is," he said quietly, almost whispering. "Right here, this shiny part on top. There's room to burn more information on it, on the wrong side. If anybody was to look at it, even play it—the right way," he added, turning a wry cocked eyebrow at me, "they'd think it was a real music CD. It's very, very clever." He replaced the CD in the slot and resumed his examination of the numbers.

"So it isn't a real CD?"

"Sure it is. They just altered it."

"Who?"

"Good question."

"And why would anyone do that?"

Vern frowned. "I don't know."

"Those look rather like Social Security numbers."

"Of course!" Vern said, leaning back in his computer chair. "The dashes should have told me. Wow." He clicked on one of the numbers. Immediately, the screen changed and a name and address appeared.

I folded my arms and leaned forward. "There must be hundreds, maybe thousands, of numbers here. What is this? Some government document?"

"Maybe." Vern brought his face close to the screen. "No, I don't think so." He fumbled in the silver lunchbox, extracted the George Strait album from its case and examined it closely. "See that silver band? It cuts off part of his cowboy hat and slices off a corner of the title, too. Somebody altered this CD, just a little."

He exchanged it for the Broadway show album in the computer, being careful to put it in silver side up, and pressed Enter again. This time, the screen was filled with pale green rectangles with printing and fingerprints and small head-and-shoulder photos.

"What are those, driver's licenses?"

"Nope," Vern said, leaning forward. "Look, it says Permanent Resident Card. They're green cards, or rather pictures of them."

"Vern, where did you get these things—the CDs and the silver case, I mean?"

The boy looked down at his hands and said nothing.

"This is clearly illegal material! We've got to get this to the police!"

"We can't."

"What?"

Vern was taking long, deep breaths. He said in a near-whisper, "You see, I promised."

"Promised what?" I could feel my blood pressure begin to rise.

"To help some . . . friends. They asked me to help them figure out how to get this . . . lunchbox thing back to whoever it belonged to."

Whomever, I thought to myself. "It's the Rousseau boys, isn't it?"

Vern sighed. "Yes, but listen, they didn't have any idea what this thing was. Neither did I, for that matter. They gave it to me last week in school, before they got busted. Dustin said they sort of accidentally walked off with this thing and wanted to figure out a way to return it."

He turned a pleading face toward me. "I thought I could help. I mean, if I could find out who owned it and get it back to them without a fuss, everything would be cool, but then this, um, murder happened, and I was in a bind, you see?"

"You can't shrug off responsibility here, Vern. This obviously has something to do with making false IDs. Do you think the boys could be involved in an illegal—"

"No way!" He glared at me.

"We need to call the police."

"No!"

"But it's stolen property!"

"Accidentally stolen."

"That may be, but Vern—"

A blast of cold air sweeping down the hall and into Vern's open door announced Gil's arrival. "Hello? Anybody? Where's my little family?"

I sighed. "Here, Gil."

Vern widened his eyes, pleading.

My husband appeared in the doorway. "Amelia, didn't I warn you that this room would swallow you up like a Venus Flytrap? What's going on?"

Vern shot me another glance containing the deepest pathos. I ignored him, but not without an inward wince. This would probably mean the death of our cordial auntie-nephew relationship.

"Come look at this," I said to Gil, indicating the computer screen. As he sat in Vern's chair and leaned forward, squinting, Vern turned his back with a ferocious snort of disgust.

"Wow," he said under his breath. "Where did this come from?"

I showed him the lunchbox and repeated what Vern had told me.

"Ooo-kay," he said when we'd finished. He bit his lip and looked up at me. "Amelia, do you have O'Brien's home number?"

Vern whirled around. His expression was heartrending. "Gil, isn't there some other way to handle this?"

"Look at this stuff." Gil pointed at the computer screen. "There's nothing else we can do. Listen, Vern," he added, not unkindly, "just be glad we have a friend on the force who might be inclined to believe your story."

Vern sat heavily on his unmade bed and stared at his hands, clasping and unclasping them. "I'm a dead man." He threw a dark frown at me.

Gil dialed the number I gave him. Dennis was home.

"He wants us to meet him at the station," Gil said after finishing the muttered conversation. "C'mon, Vern, let's pack this thing up." He pulled his handkerchief from his pocket and used it to remove the CD from the computer and replace it in the jewel case. "No need adding another set of fingerprints to the mix," he pointed out, putting the assembled lunchbox in a grocery bag I'd fetched for him.

"I'll say a prayer for you," I said as uncle and nephew suited up for the trip into town.

Vern's expression was pure resentment. "Yeah, you do that." After a dramatic zip of his parka, he slammed out the front door.

Gil kissed me. "I won't lie and tell you the kid's not in trouble, but I'll do all I can. Keep your chin up." He started down the hallway, then turned around. "Do me a favor and call Ned about this. I doubt he'll be any help, but he has a right to know." Gil scratched his forehead.

"He moved to Saratoga last spring. Use directory assistance or something." He threw me another kiss. "Don't wait up."

I stood in the doorway and watched them drive away.

Chapter | Sixteen

I actually did pray for Vern right then and there, while sitting at the kitchen bar next to the telephone. I prayed also for Gil and for the Rousseau brothers and finally, for myself and my baby.

Less than six months ago I had complained in prayer that I was alone. That prayer had been answered bountifully, overwhelmingly. Now I had new things to pray about. Of course, when opportunity came my way, I had cooperated fully with Providence and many good things had resulted.

"Lord," I murmured, quoting a T-shirt I'd seen somewhere, "please give me the strength to endure my blessings!"

It was time to hunt for Edward Thomas, Vern's father. It wasn't a chore I relished, and not only because I'd be the bearer of bad news.

Vern's late mother, Carol, had been Gil's sister and her death several years ago from a virulent form of cancer had so embittered Ned that his son had moved away and taken up residence with his uncle.

The subject of Ned was *verboten* in our household, at least in front of Vern, but Gil managed to keep tabs on his brother-in-law, probably using his many journalistic connections.

"Saratoga, huh?" I said, and called directory assistance.

There were six Edward Thomases in Saratoga, but only one Ned, so I tried the number.

"You know the drill," a recorded voice growled cryptically. At the tone, I suddenly realized that my news wasn't the sort one should deliver via voicemail.

"Uh, Ned, this is Amelia Prentice, you know, Gil's wife? Amelia Dickensen, that is." I gave a little mirthless chuckle and cleared my throat. "It's about Vern. Your son."

Good grief, Amelia, of course he knows the name of his own son!

"Well, he's all right, but there has been a, um, well, a difficulty has arisen. I mean, he has a problem, and we think you need to know about it. Call us, please." I added the numbers of both our telephone and Gil's cell.

As I hung up, it occurred to me that I wasn't even sure I had the right Ned Thomas. And what would I have told him if he had been home? I wondered.

Ned, Vern is at the police station. He's involved with a murder investigation and may be in trouble for withholding evidence. He may even be a suspect, but Gil and I know he's not guilty of anything except being young and loyal to his friends.

For that matter, I added to myself, *his friends aren't guilty of anything, either; I'm certain of it.*

I fixed myself a glass of milk and a peanut butter sandwich, moved to the couch, and turned on the television. I ate my dinner answering arcane questions posed by Alex Trebek, then watched as a sinister-looking fellow with a punk haircut extolled the virtues of some kind of chamois cloth costing $19.99, but wait, if I called in right away . . .

I dozed.

Cold air coming from the front door woke me. I sat up and caught a glimpse of the back of Vern's coat as he slipped into his room and slammed the door shut. I glanced at my watch: nine thirty-seven.

"They're not holding him right now, letting him go to classes and work, but they told him not to leave town and to keep completely mum about the lunchbox. I'm calling a lawyer in the morning," Gil whispered, joining me on the sofa.

"But what about Dennis—"

"His hands are tied, honey. When they questioned Vern the other day, he left out the bit about the lunchbox, and now claiming he wanted to return it sounds pretty thin. That, combined with the fact that he'd been meeting with the Rousseau boys regularly—"

"But he was tutoring them!"

"Shh! I know that, and you know that, but it looks, well, suspicious, under the circumstances."

Tears came into my eyes. "So that's it? They think they have their culprits?"

Gil yawned. "Could be. But don't worry, we'll find him a really good lawyer, not that idiot he has now." He stood. "Come on. I'm dead on my feet. We've got a busy day tomorrow."

I dried my eyes with a paper napkin. "Have you had anything to eat?" Food was becoming ever more important to me these days.

He grimaced and stood. "Some chips and soda from the police station machines. That'll hold me." He arched his back and groaned. "You coming?"

"I'll join you in a while. I'm wide awake right now."

Gil went to bed. On television, Andy Griffith was cross-examining a witness. I clicked the remote off just as the culprit shouted his confession in open court.

In the silence, my thoughts crowded upon me again. It occurred to me that I possessed knowledge of this situation that no one else had: I knew for certain that all three young men were innocent.

And how would you know that? The logical side of me asked.

I know them. All three of them. They wouldn't do this thing.

That'll really go over well in court! Exhibit A: Amelia knows these defendants, your Honor; the Defense rests!

All I know is that someone else committed this crime.

Who?

I don't know, but I intend to find out.

I knew this town and the people in it. I'd taught many of them, read their thoughts put to paper, observed how they behaved. I even knew their parents, heaven help me!

"I can do this."

I was going to need a compatriot, a sidekick, as it were, with whom I could share this task. In short, I needed Lily Burns, or a close facsimile thereof.

I called her. It was late, but she'd be up, I knew.

"Lily? It's me."

There was a long silence on the other end. "What do you want?"

"A favor," I said brightly, ignoring the ungracious tone. "Mind if I drop by tomorrow after school? Something rather, uh, interesting has come up, and I'd like your opinion."

"Here? Come here?" The concept seemed new to her. "Tomorrow?"

"That's right."

Another long silence, then a sigh. "Look, Amelia, that just isn't going to be convenient. But what's wrong with right now? Can't you tell me about it on the phone?"

"Well, I guess so," I said.

Lily's backyard bordered on Chez Prentice's and from time immemorial, we'd always talked in one another's kitchen over tea or coffee. Maybe this was her way of keeping our badly injured friendship in traction until the damage healed. More than ever I regretted my sharp words to her, and the least I could do was to comply.

"Just a second."

I didn't want to wake Gil, so I buttoned up my cardigan sweater and carried the portable receiver to the screened back porch.

I hesitated. I had to go carefully here. There were some things I couldn't tell her. Lily was good in a crisis, but as I've said before, she was also a world-class gossip.

"Now Lily," I began, "suppose, speaking hypothetically now, that you know someone—a woman, a friend of yours— who has a family member that has some evidence of interest to the police, and . . . "

"The woman? Or the friend?"

"The woman is the friend."

"Then who's hiding from the police?"

"No one is hiding from the police, Lily, in fact, they've already gone to the police."

"The friend."

"Right. I mean, no, the family member."

"What evidence does the woman have?"

"She doesn't have evidence, the family member does. And they've already turned it in."

"Which family member?"

I sighed. My breath was coming out in frosty clouds. "Let me start again."

"I'd rather you didn't. Just get on with it. Oh!" She was interrupted by a crash and a series of muffled thumps. "Look what you've done! Behave yourself!" I heard her say to someone, then to me, "Hold it just a second."

She was breathless when she returned to the telephone. "Sorry about that. I knocked something on the floor with my elbow."

Sure she did.

"Look, Lily, I didn't know you had company or I wouldn't have called." I shivered and stamped my feet.

"Company? Oh, right." She gave a little giggle. "Don't worry about that. No big deal. What were you saying?"

I'd had enough. "No, it's all right; never mind."

"Suit yourself," she said airily.

I pressed the button marked End as forcefully as my near-frostbitten finger would allow. It was now obvious why she didn't want company. It would interfere with her trysts with Blakely.

So there it was. I was on my own.

Chapter | Seventeen

The next afternoon as I trudged among the exhaust-stained piles of snow on my way from school to Chez Prentice, I tried to think how I could conduct my own investigation.

My answer came literally in a flash as I crossed the street and looked down Dover Avenue toward the old downtown section. In the distance was a ten-foot sign bordered by neon lights, reading:

"Shea's Quality Sporting Goods"

What better place to do research on ice fishing? Truth be told, I would have preferred to go to the REI store out at the mall, but that was a long drive and I was currently on foot. Due to my unfortunate involvement with Serendipity, I might be considered *persona non grata* around here, but Shea's was a large store and hired any number of shaggy young men who were knowledgeable about all things sports. The likelihood of my meeting anyone of the Shea clan could be limited if I kept my eyes open.

Besides, it's a free country, isn't it? I reminded myself. *And the store is open to the public, is it not?* I was part of the public.

I entered and winced as a bell fastened to the front door announced my presence. I paused and looked around.

Good. Nobody was anywhere in sight.

The store was arranged much like any variety store, with long aisles between tall shelves.

I moved carefully, trying not to let my boots make much noise on the wooden floor. I was passing a display of can-teens—who would imagine there were so many types?—when I heard a low conversation between two young male voices. I paused and listened.

Yes, as a general rule, I frown on eavesdropping, but I was conducting an investigation. Besides, we were in a public place, and they had no expectation of privacy. (Or so I had heard on television.)

" . . . been squirrelly ever since she let Dus go."

"Yeah, I wondered about that. Why'd she do that? He do anything wrong?"

"Don't think so. Maybe she knew he was a killer even back then."

"I don't think he did it, Jack. Or his brother neither."

Hear, hear! You dear, ungrammatical young man, I thought.

"Sure they did. They stuck the guy's head in—"

I stepped around the corner. "Excuse me."

Two young men in plaid flannel shirts looked up, startled. I had interrupted them as they unpacked pairs of snowshoes from a huge carton and arranged them in a display.

One of the young men stood and dusted off the knees of his jeans. "Can I help ya?"

Oh, how tempted I was to correct him: *May I help you?* But I was no longer Miss Prentice, English teacher, but Amelia Dickensen, Intrepid Detective, who also happened to speak all the local dialects. It was also time to stow any Latin idioms that might pop, non vocatus, into my head.

"Yah, maybe ya can." I swept my gaze around the store. No sign of a Shea, so far.

"I need to see your ice-fishing tents."

He looked down at me with some amusement. "You fish?"

I glanced down at my prim wool coat, medium-heeled winter boots, ladylike leather purse on one arm and leather satchel containing workbooks for the Rousseau boys in the other. "Is there any reason why I shouldn't?" I demanded, inwardly kicking myself for not getting into costume for this excursion into another world. Overalls, perhaps.

"No, I guess not," said the young man, scratching his neck uncomfortably. He beckoned. "The tents are back here. C'mon."

And it was, indeed, another world. As I scurried to keep up with the youngster's long stride, I observed row upon row of mystifying objects and cartons. On the way, I identified ropes, fishing hooks, soccer balls, small axes, Thermos bottles, weights of various sizes, elastic bands, lanterns, running shoes, and ice chests. At last we reached a back corner of the store where several ice-fishing tents were displayed.

"Where ya plannin' to fish?" he asked.

"On the lake," I said. I would have thought that was obvious. I lifted a tent's flap. This looked like what I'd heard described third-hand as the tent the Rousseau boys encountered. "May I—I mean, can I?" I asked, indicating that I'd like to enter.

The young man shrugged. "Sure. Go ahead."

Still carrying my purse and school supplies, I stepped easily inside without having to bend my head at all. This structure was about the same size as the shanties Etienne and Bert
were building.

I looked down, surprised. There was a plastic floor
equipped with three snap-shut fishing hatches for the con-
venience and comfort of the fisherman. But the boys had
described a floor of ice.

I stuck my head out of the tent, remembering just in time
to use the vernacular. "Ya got any tents with no floors?"

He gave me a quizzical look, but jerked a thumb in the
direction of some smaller tents. "Just one model, over there.
We're almost out of 'em, on account of the ice festival,
y'know," he said, trying his hand at a little salesmanship.
"They fold up real neat. They're only a couple hundred bucks,
so they move fast."

Sure enough, there in the corner was a blue, dome-shaped
shelter much smaller than the first tent.

I stuck my head inside and looked around. It was a good
deal smaller than the tent my mind had sketched, but apparently it sat directly on the ice, allowing a would-be perpetrator plenty of space to accomplish, unobserved, any number of
nefarious tasks and leave the body to cool.

" 'Tis not so deep as a well, nor so wide as a church-door;
but 'tis enough, 'twill serve,' " I murmured.

"What?" the young man said. "You gonna have church in
that?"

I laughed out loud. "No, I was just thinking of something
else."

"Jason," boomed a disembodied voice, "phone for you on line one."

"Um," said the young man, "We're kinda short-handed. I gotta go for a second." He gestured toward the back of the store.

"Please, go ahead. I'll continue to browse."

He loped away, making heavy sounds with his boots on the wood floor.

I went back inside the small tent and sat down, tailor fashion. I tried to imagine it as bare ice. Judging by the hatches in the bigger tent, holes broken in the ice for fishing were about twelve inches across. There would be room in here for one hole, perhaps two persons (sitting, one hoped, on stools) and perhaps two standard large ice chests.

I heard footsteps outside the tent, lighter ones, then the tinkling sound of a cell phone ringing. A woman answered, "Hello? Hello? What?" Abruptly, she changed to "Who is this?" a hoarse, angry whisper, "Listen, pal, if you think you're scaring me, you're wrong! Who is this?"

I made a mistake at this juncture. I should have just remained in the tent until she walked away, but curiosity impelled me to crawl forward and pull back the tent flap.

Brigid Shea must have been looking right at the tent. She pocketed the telephone and demanded loudly, "What are you doing here?"

With all the dignity I could muster, I said, "I'm looking at ice fishing tents." I raised myself up on my knees, emerging disheveled from the tent.

"What d'you think you're doing?"

"I just wanted to see your stock of tents" I repeated, clumsily retrieving my satchel from inside.

"I'll bet you're spying for that husband of yours. Trying to run us out of business with those lousy rental shanties!"

"But that's not my husband!"

"Get out!" She stood trembling with rage, pointing a finger in the general direction of the egress.

Apparently it wasn't enough that I complied. She then felt the need to come from behind, grab my shoulders and push me toward the door, talking all the way.

"I shoulda known it was you when Jason told about the nutty woman with the books. I knew right away who it was."

"Nutty? I tell you, I just wanted to look at the tents."

I tried to squirm away from her grip, but her hands were vise-like. Clearly, this woman had been using those weights I'd seen earlier.

"Yeah, to scope out the competition, you mean!" As we approached the entrance, she came around and shook a finger in my face. "You tell that Frenchman you're married to to leave us alone!" She let me loose with a shake.

A workbook fell from my arms, and I stooped to retrieve it. "But I'm not married to—"

"That's your problem. And you're not much of a teacher, either. We all know you've had it in for my Serry ever since she started high school."

"Now see here, Mrs. Shea!"

She pointed her finger again. "Out! Out! Out-out-out-out-out-out-out!"

She sounded like a barking dog. A terrier.

As I headed back town the street, slightly twisted Latin phrase popped into my head, courtesy of my student Hardy Patchke: *Veni, vidi, concouri.*

We came, we saw, we ran.

Chapter | Eighteen

"You know, Miss—Mrs. Dickensen," J.T. said as he vigorously erased a wrong answer in his workbook and blew away the debris. "You're a lot nicer here with us than you are in school."

"Shut up," Dustin whispered between his teeth. He was hunched over his math lesson.

"But it's true. In school you're sort of a tight—uh." I could see him searching his vocabulary for a word that wouldn't offend me.

"Sort of, you know . . . " He waved his pencil in the air.

I decided to help him. "Would *formal* be the word you're searching for?"

J.T. grinned. "Yeah, formal. But you're not that way when you're here. You even laughed a minute ago. Why can't you be like that in school?"

"Golly, J.T., can't you keep your mouth shut for one minute?" Dustin exploded. "How can a guy get his work done with you yapping all the time? I'm going upstairs!"

He gathered up his pencil, papers and books and headed out of the room. He stopped abruptly at the door, his face losing its stormy expression.

"Um, Mrs. Dickensen, if that's all right."

I looked at his face and was reassured. This was not a boy who could kill a man in cold blood.

"Go right ahead, Dustin. If you have a problem or need help, come back down. I'm a little shaky with numbers, but I'll be glad to do what I can."

"Don't worry. I can handle math. It's the history and English and stuff that gives me trouble." He backed out the door and took the stairs two at a time.

"Dork," J.T. murmured after his brother. "He's a real grouch lately."

"You've both been under a lot of stress."

"I guess so." He filled in the last blank on his workbook page. "There, done. You wanna check it now?"

"Sure."

I rapidly scanned the answers. There was only one wrong out of thirty.

"This is good work, J.T., only obelisk isn't a bird. It's a kind of tower, like the McDonough Monument across from city hall. I'm surprised that you, of all people, didn't know that, after all the things you've climbed."

He ducked his head and smiled shyly. "I guess I do now."

I smiled back. "That's right, just about the only thing around here you haven't climbed. Or have you?"

"*Non, c'est tout, Madame.*"

"*Tres bien.* How is the French coming?"

"It's not as hard as I thought."

"*Bon!*"

He looked at me thoughtfully. "I think I figured out why you're so mean at school."

"You have?" I said, amused.

"Sure. It's easy. You're a woman, right?"

"True," I agreed, wryly remembering how firmly that fact had been brought home to me in recent days.

"And you're not very big, either. I think you have to be kind of a bi—um, bad guy," he corrected himself, "in school so us guys won't lean on you too much." He graced me with a wide smile. "What do you think?"

"I think you need to get back to your work."

"Is, uh, Vern okay?" he asked, picking up his pencil again.

"Yes. Why?"

"I feel bad about him gettin' in trouble on account of us. I'm real sorry."

He stopped and looked over his shoulder. I knew what he was thinking. His father and brother were both upstairs and out of earshot.

"I don't know what happened with that thing. We sure didn't tell the police."

"What didn't you tell?" I was whispering along with him.

He reddened. "Oh, gosh. I thought you knew—"

"About the silver lunchbox? I do know. Is that what you didn't tell?"

"Yeah, mostly. I mean, Vern didn't know and we didn't know, either, that anybody was dead. We didn't see any dead body. We just wanted to get that stupid thing back to the mad guy without, you know, without getting in trouble."

"J.T., when—" I began, but changed my question as Martin Rousseau walked into the kitchen. "That is, when do you think you can have your essay finished?"

J.T. understood immediately. "I dunno. Pretty quick, I guess. I'll get started as soon as I think up what to write about."

"You guys doing good here?" Martin asked.

"J.T. is doing very well," I said firmly. The kind of grammar usage I had heard in this house made it clear that there was a lot of work to do.

Martin went to the refrigerator and looked in. "Gotta get some more food, I guess," he mumbled.

"The crowd outside seems to have subsided somewhat," I remarked, more to make conversation than anything.

Though the throng had dwindled to several reporters and a cameraman apparently camping by the curb in a single van, the strain was still making its mark. Martin looked worse than at my last visit. He had lost weight, and I wasn't sure he had even changed his clothes since the other day.

"Are you able to get to work more easily now?" I asked.

He looked at me over the top of the refrigerator door and shook his head. "No, I took some vacation time. I got three weeks coming. The people at the plant are being real good about it. 'Course, I'm gonna have to get back sometime."

His gaze returned to the interior of the refrigerator. He pulled out a carton and shook it.

"We're outta milk."

I moved a blank piece of paper and a pencil into position. "Tell me what you need. I'll pick up some things at the supermarket."

Martin protested, but weakly. After I assured him that I'd retain the receipt so he could reimburse me, he proceeded to enumerate some basics.

"That meatball chunky soup, milk, a couple cans of chili, the store brand's okay. A half-dozen boxes of macaroni and cheese, the blue kind, like on TV. That should do it."

Fresh fruit and vegetables hadn't been mentioned, but I mentally resolved to add some bananas, apples, and carrots, and pay for them myself.

With a can of root beer in his hand, Martin again retired upstairs, and I began to prepare to leave. J.T. stood when I did. He cleared his throat uncomfortably.

"Um. Miss—Mrs.—um, would you go one other place for me? For me and Dus? I got money I can give you." He reached in his back pocket.

"Go where, J.T.?"

He stepped close to me and whispered, almost inaudibly, "The flower shop, you know, the one next to the supermarket?"

"Blossoms by Nathan?" I said aloud.

"Shh!" he admonished me sharply, and whispered, "It's kind of a secret." He fished in his pocket and extracted some crumpled bills and an assortment of change. "Here's, um, sixteen, no, seventeen dollars and a little more. I need you to order a couple of corsages for the ice dance. But don't say it's for us, because they might not do it."

"But, J.T.," I protested, whispering, "are you saying you're actually going to the dance? It's only a few days away."

He looked at me a long minute, then shrugged. "I don't know, maybe. It's something to look forward to, y'know? I mean we didn't do it, y'know? And we got this lawyer guy who's supposed to be good. Maybe we'll get to go." He turned his gaze back to me. "You see what I mean?"

I did see. The corsages represented a normal future. I couldn't bring myself to squash any hope they might feel, no matter how tenuous.

"But to whom are you giving the corsages?" My grammar was correct, I knew, but even to myself, I sounded stuffy.

J.T. didn't seem to notice. He slid his eyes over to the back door. "Well, you don't have to have a date to go, y'know. We can go stag." He rubbed the tip of his nose with the back of his wrist, a subtle sign he was prevaricating, and looked at me. "But we need the flowers just in case, sort of."

Just in case. Right, I thought. *And the Gervais twins will just happen to show up.* He and his brother were up to something, for sure, but it probably wasn't criminal. At least, I didn't think so.

I thrust the money in my jacket pocket. "All right, J.T. I'll order them in my name and have them delivered to Chez Prentice. If things go well for you, they'll be available the night of the ice dance." That's all I needed; more secrets to keep.

As I buttoned my coat, J.T. looked at me and sighed. "I thought it would be fun, but it's not, you know?"

"What's not fun?"

"Bein' famous."

Chapter | Nineteen

"**S**eventeen bucks and change for two corsages?" Chuck Nathan of Blossoms by Nathan squinted down at me skeptically. "Including sales tax?"

I nodded, prepared to add a few dollars of my own if necessary.

His gray sweatshirt, bearing the words "Do Your Part— Recycle!" hung loosely on his gaunt form. He pushed his wire-rimmed glasses up his nose and shrugged. "Well, I suppose I could do it for twenty, plus tax. They'll be carnations, though. Most kids are ordering Gerberas this year," he said, nodding to a huge sheaf of brightly colored daisies behind the glass door of a nearby cooler and added, "Gerberas are extra." His big, pale and watery blue eyes regarded me as balefully as Alec's *Megachasma pelagios*.

"I'm sure carnations will be fine," I said, pulling the extra money out of my wallet. "In the school colors, please. And if you'll deliver them to Chez Prentice the afternoon of the ice dance."

"Okay, if that's what you want." He slapped an order pad on the counter and began writing.

I took a deep breath. I loved the smell of a flower shop, a combination of sweet-scented blooms underscored by a kind of mossy tone. Lily liked to say that Nathan's shop smelled like a funeral. I preferred to look at the other way around: Funerals always smelled like a flower shop.

"School colors, no problem," Chuck said, writing vigorously. "You ordering these for your guests over there at the hotel?"

He was clearly fishing for information. His glasses slid down his nose again, and I noticed that they were broken just over the nose and repaired with green florist's tape and that his 60's vintage ponytail was fastened by florist's wire. Chuck was our town's genuine, unreconstructed hippie and clearly followed the instructions on his shirt.

"For friends," I countered evasively as I handed over the boys' money.

He deposited the money in the vintage NCR cash register and handed me a carbon-copy receipt. My order was impaled along with a dozen others on a long desk spike. "You want to make out a card to go with the corsages?" he asked, indicating the tall desk where there were a variety of tiny decorated cards for all occasions with tiny, blue-and-white striped envelopes to go with them.

"That's not necessary."

A short, white-haired woman stood on tiptoe at the desk, writing. I wasn't sure, but from the back, she looked familiar.

"Well met, Amelia!" said someone from behind me.

I turned and beheld the amiable mass that was Professor Alexander Alexander.

"Alec, likewise!"

"My, ye look bonnie today!" He laid a large hand on my shoulder and scratched the side of his face with the other. "Let me have a look at ye. There's something there. Can't put my finger on it, but it's like there's a candle within."

I know I blushed, because I could feel the heat on my cheeks. "Oh, Alec, what a flatterer you are—"

"No, no, it's something." He shook his large and shaggy head. "Never mind, my dear. Suffice it to say you're looking especially lovely. Excuse me a moment—" He turned to Chuck Nathan. "I'll need a nosegay for a lady. Make it small pink rosebuds with baby's breath, surrounded by a kind of doily rigmarole, all in a vase, for delivery tomorrow."

He handed Chuck a credit card, glanced at me and caught my quizzical look. He looked away and mumbled into his beard, "Miss Lily's birthday."

Chuck placed the credit card on an old-fashioned card imprinter, fixed a carbon-copy form on top and ran it across with a metallic rattle.

"Oh, Alec."

I felt a variety of emotions: compassion for him and sadness at the futility of his cause, but most of all, alarm that I had totally forgotten the occasion myself. Lily and I usually exchanged birthday gifts. Would our estrangement mean an end to that pleasant custom? I decided not.

"Chuck? Do you deliver gifts too?" I asked, gesturing at the shelf of dusty china knickknacks.

He glanced up from his order pad and took a swig from a nearby can of cola. "Yeah, no problem."

I selected a pretty gilt-edged teacup and saucer painted with pink rosebuds, dusting it discreetly with a tissue from my pocket. It was outrageously overpriced, but charming, and Lily would love it.

When Alec finished giving instructions and retired to the nearby desk to make out a card, I stepped up and arranged for the cup to be gift-wrapped and sent to Lily's address too.

The woman at the desk finished her writing, quickly slid the card into a tiny envelope, and sealed it. As she licked the envelope, she turned, our eyes met, and I recognized Mrs. Daye.

"Hello!" I said, surprised.

"Uh, hi." Looking vaguely startled, she walked over to Chuck and handed him the envelope. "There."

"So you're sure you want just the one, now?" Chuck asked her, scratching the top of his head with a pencil. "It's cheaper per flower if you get half a dozen, no problem."

"No thank you," she said, glancing at me. "Just the one." Without another word, she turned and walked out.

"Get her." Chuck turned away mumbled, "I was just making sure. Gotta get the orders right. Especially odd ones like that."

I wanted to ask him which was odd, the woman or the order but decided that a person's flower order was probably confidential, a kind of florist-client privilege.

Besides, it was apparently time for Chuck's break. Without further pleasantry, he turned away from us, pulled a metallic lunchbox from beneath the counter, and retrieved a large bag of potato chips. These he began munching cheerfully, alternating chips with sips of cola, ignoring any rules of etiquette.

My stomach growled a little. It would have been nice if he had offered me some chips. I would have declined, of course, but it would have been nice nonetheless.

I filled out the card for Lily simply: "Happy Birthday from Amelia." There seemed nothing else to say under the circumstances.

"May I give you a lift somewhere?" Alec asked.

His manners were always impeccable. It was one of the many things I liked about him.

I declined with thanks. "I'm headed to the newspaper office. It's not far."

"I understand some students of yours are in a good deal of trouble," Alec commented, holding the door open for me as we exited.

I sighed. "Yes, but I just don't believe they could do such a thing, kill a man in cold blood, like that. Accidentally, perhaps, but never on purpose."

"I feel a certain responsibility for their predicament," Alec said as we reached his car and he turned the key.

"Responsibility? What do you mean?"

He ran a big hand over his face and looked down at me. "I'm a witness, Amelia, for the prosecution. I was driving along the lake shore and saw the fellows—or at least their car— nearly run another car off the road on the day in question. They were driving in a very dangerous manner. That giant grape-on-wheels of theirs is pretty easy to spot. I felt it my duty to step forward and give the information to the police. "

"Then when they go to trial, you'll be, um . . . " I paused.

He sighed. "Called to the stand? Yes, I believe I will. I feel terrible about it, but what can I do?"

We both stared at the ground for a moment, silent. It was then the inspiration hit me.

"Alec?" I said at last. "I need to solve this mystery. How would you feel about being a sidekick?"

Slowly, he lifted his eyes to mine. As he did, his back seemed to straighten. He gave his beard a stroke and burst into a beaming smile.

"I'd love it. When do we start?"

Blossoms by Nathan was the next to last shop in a row of tiny stores on Brinkerhoff Street, between the Raisin D'être Bakery and True Wines (slogan: *In Vino Veritas*) and only a few doors away from the newspaper office.

Alec and I adjourned to a corner table at the bakery where he had coffee and I had milk. We shared a Danish, and I filled Alec in on the basics of the situation. He was eager to start immediately.

"One thing, though," he said, "aware as I am of your aversion to modern technology, I still must insist you carry a cell phone." He cut short my objections. "I'll get you one, sign you up, everything, but I will brook no argument on this, Amelia."

I sighed. "Well, Gil has been wanting me to get one."

"It's agreed, then. Come along," he ordered, gathering up our foam cups and paper napkins.

"I have a number of avenues I'd like to explore," Alec said as we said goodbye on the front steps of the newspaper office.

We agreed to meet again soon and share what we had found out, and he ambled away, humming "Onward, Christian Soldiers."

"It sure doesn't look good for them," I heard Gil saying on the telephone as I entered his office.

"What doesn't look good?" I asked as he hung up.

He swiveled in his chair and grinned at me. "Hello, sweetheart! How long have you been standing there?"

"Don't try to deflect my question. Were you talking about Vern or the Rousseau boys?" I leaned down to kiss him.

"I could have been speaking of many things," he said, pulling up a chair for me. "Terrorists, the immigration problem, smuggling, politics in general. But you're right. My source in the police department tells me that the case against the Rousseau boys is—and I quote—'a sure thing.' Vern's situation is a little less grave, according to the lawyer I called. I got him an appointment for this afternoon."

I frowned and sat down. "What do they have on the Rousseaus?"

"My police source couldn't tell me much, but—" Gil leaned across his desk, retrieved a steno pad and read from his notes, "—the police know that the Dustin and J.T. had the shattered window in their VW repaired."

"That isn't necessarily incriminating," I said.

"True, but the boys claim that they were shot at."

So they had told the police that, at least. "Doesn't the repair substantiate their claim?"

Gil nodded. "It would, only a neighbor saw one of the boys smashing the back window. It looks a lot like they were trying to fake evidence. Remember, no bullet was found in the car. And no gun at the scene of the crime."

We both sighed.

I raised a shaking hand to my mouth. "Gil," I muttered through gritted teeth. "I could use a cola—no, make it a bottled water; would you, please?" The pamphlet Dr. Stout had given me said to be careful of caffeine.

He leaned in, his face filled with concern. "Are you still having trouble with your stomach? I thought you'd seen the doctor about that."

My response was muffled. "I did."

He thrust his hand in his pocket and pulled out some change. "But you seemed so much better. Didn't he give you some medicine or something? I'll be right back." He headed down the hall to the soft drink machine.

Should I take this opportunity to tell Gil about my pregnancy?

No, nothing good would come of just blurting out the news, especially considering the dire situation with Vern. I still needed to find the proper time, proper place and, most important, the proper words. All of these had so far eluded me. I closed my eyes and waited for him to return.

"What exactly did he say?" Gil asked as he put the bottle down on the desk. "The doctor."

I grabbed it eagerly, unscrewed the cap and took a gulp. It was icy cold, exactly what I needed.

"He said I'd be fine. It'll just take a little time," I answered after several more restorative sips.

"What's wrong, exactly? An ulcer?"

Gil's expression told me that he was about to conduct an interview. He unscrewed the top of his own bottle of water.

"Can we—can we talk about it later?" I said weakly, leaning a trifle on his sympathy. It was a shameless feminine trick, but not inappropriate, considering the circumstances. "It's nothing serious, I promise."

Gil nodded. "Sure, honey; just so long as you're all right."

"I'm fine, but I'm a little hungry." The cold water had been remarkably therapeutic, but it lacked something. "Gil, could you get me a pack of those peanut butter cheese crackers from the vending machine?"

He squinted at me on his return from the machine. "What's it with you and peanut butter lately?" He tossed the pack of crackers into my lap.

"It just tastes good, that's all." I tore open the package greedily, popped a whole cracker into my mouth, and consumed it in record time.

I was beginning to feel better. "Tell me more about the case against Dustin and J.T." I extracted another crisp orange square from its cellophane sleeve and took a more ladylike bite.

"There's not much more to tell. The police have finished examining the car, looking for more evidence of firearms. No luck."

"What would they be looking for?"

"Gunpowder residue, that sort of thing."

"Doesn't this prove that somebody has been shooting at them?"

Gil shrugged. "It could, but it's pretty apparent that they were up to something underhanded. Why, if they're not guilty?"

I swallowed the last morsel of cracker and frowned. "And if somebody really did shoot at them, why didn't they tell the police right away?"

"Exactly," Gil said, leaning forward and kissing me on the forehead. "Are you going to be okay? Got your blood sugar back up to normal and whatnot?" He picked a large orange crumb off my sleeve.

I looked up into his eyes. They were filled with sympathy and concern.

"Yes." I took a deep breath. Maybe this was the time to tell him, after all. "Gil, I want to—"

But he had already swiveled around toward his desk. "Good, because as stimulating as this conversation is, it's not getting my editorial written." He leaned back and hooked an elbow over the back of his seat. "Get Vern to give you a lift home after his appointment with the lawyer, okay? I'll be there about eight, bearing a pizza from Ernie's."

I stood. "That'll be all right."

There would be another time and another opportunity to tell him. And Ernie's made the best pizza in the known universe.

An hour later, I was back at the Rousseau door, bearing a sack of groceries in each arm. J.T. met me at the door. "Thanks!" he said, as he relieved me of one of the sacks. "Dad 'n Dus are still upstairs. Sleepin', I think."

I followed him into the kitchen.

"Oh, cool! Bagel Bites!" He pulled the box out and immediately began to prepare them. "I'm starvin'!" He pulled a clean paper plate from a stack on the counter and arranged the little pizzas on it. "Hey," he asked in a lowered voice, "did you see about the . . . you know?"

He meant the flowers. "Yes, I did."

"Great." He grinned and replaced the box of box of remaining Bagel Bites in the freezer. "Thanks."

"J.T.," I said softly as I placed the gallon of milk in the refrigerator, "why on earth did you smash your own windshield?"

He froze at the open door of the microwave and stared at me. "How'd you know that?"

"The cops must've figured it out, stupid," said Dustin from the kitchen door. He stretched his arms in the air and yawned. "It was pretty lame, that's for sure." He reached into one of the two grocery bags and pulled out a bunch of bananas.

"If you knew it was, then why did you do it?" I asked. "If you could show there was a bullet hole in the back window, it might have helped your case."

He shrugged, selected a banana, and began to peel. "We didn't know anybody got killed, y'see. Mostly we were scared of Dad finding out we were out on the lake. That's why we broke it. Then, when this murder stuff came up, we tried to explain, but nobody would believe us. We're stupid kids, I guess. Our lawyer thought it was pretty dumb too."

J.T. gasped. "You're not supposed to talk to anybody about what he says about our legal case! The guy *said!*" Scowling, he dialed the proper time for the Bagel Bites and punched the on button rather more emphatically than necessary.

Dustin glowered back at his brother. "Like I don't know you already been down here spilling your guts to Mrs. D." He turned quickly to me. "No offense."

"None taken."

"Besides," Dustin went on, his mouth full of banana. "The guy thinks we're guilty, and he don't even care."

Doesn't even care, I thought. But no matter how ungrammatical, what he said was true, I suspected.

"He's going to make out like we did it, but we couldn't help it," he continued bitterly, "'cause our mom's dead, and Dad's supposed to be doing a lousy job raising us, and everybody's against us 'cause we've been in trouble before and stuff like that."

He stepped closer to J.T. "Is that what you want? Huh? Even if we do get off, people'll think we did it anyways, and we'll always be those kids that killed a guy on the lake but got off! Like that football player!"

A tear ran down his cheek. He discovered it suddenly and wiped it away with an angry sweeping motion of his knuckle.

"That's not what I want! I want everybody to know we didn't do it!" He stifled a sob. "Look . . . look . . . I gotta . . . I gotta go—"

He bolted from the room, nearly knocking over his father, who was entering, wallet in hand, and disappeared up the stairs. The three of us paused uncertainly for a few seconds, looking at one another.

Martin glanced over his shoulder after his son and broke the silence. "He'll be okay. He's just a little upset. How much I owe you for the groceries?"

I showed him the receipt, and we settled up.

The microwave buzzed. J.T. moved slowly to retrieve the snack, keeping his back to me. "I'm gonna go up and give some of this to Dus," he mumbled and exited quickly.

"I don't like that lawyer guy myself," Martin Rousseau admitted, "but he's supposed to be good. And it's starting to look like we're really going to need him."

Chapter | Twenty

For the next few days, school was fairly predictable. Occasionally I'd overhear gossip about the Rousseau boys, but it remained highly speculative. It seemed there wasn't much chance for Amelia, Girl Detective, to investigate the current situation.

Maybe her new Faithful Companion, Alec, was having better luck. I resolved to call him when I could, to find out.

Right now, I needed to make some copies of a test paper during the middle of my one free period. As I expected, the room appeared to be empty, with the exception of a large florist's vase bearing one tall white calla lily.

"How lovely," I said aloud, and realized that I wasn't alone, after all.

From where he had bent to pick something from the floor, Blakely Knight straightened himself to full height. He had his grade book clutched to his chest, and his other hand was bunched into a fist.

"Amelia," he began, frowning at me thoughtfully, "Tell me about this Shea girl."

"Serendipity?"

"That's the one. How does she do in your class?"

"Suffice it to say she doesn't aspire be an English major."

"That's what I figured. She won't be a chem major, either. She's just trouble all over the place." His tone changed. "You like flowers?"

"Why, yes. I suppose everybody does." I busied myself at the copy machine, placing the first page on the glass just so.

"Well, I don't, so here. It's yours."

He placed the vase on the copy machine and looked down at his opened hand. There was a crumpled card in it. He tore it into four neat quarters and dropped it in the wastepaper basket.

"What? But—"

He headed out the door with the parting shot, "Don't ever say I never gave you anything." Out in the hall, he narrowly missed running over Serendipity Shea and her little group of sycophants.

The door slammed shut, and I was left alone to contemplate this interesting turn of events.

"What on earth?" I asked nobody in particular.

As the copy machine hummed, I regarded Blakely's spontaneous gift. It was a gorgeous flower, standing in tall, solitary splendor and framed by deep green leaves, its thick stem cleverly supported by a green wooden stake fastened with bits of green tape.

It was not unheard-of for flowers to be sent to a female teacher in school, and the logical place to leave them without disturbing classes or being trampled in the hallway was the copy room, where we had our message boxes. I had never, however, seen a man receive flowers here.

Perhaps the fact that the flower was a lily had significance. Lily, as in Lily Burns? The more I thought about it, the more likely it seemed. It wasn't typical of her, but she had been acting strangely lately. Besides, why shouldn't a man receive flowers? *It is a new era*, I reminded myself.

Flower arranging was considered quite a masculine pastime in Japan, I had once read. If a man enjoyed them . . .

But clearly Blakely didn't enjoy receiving this flower. He'd given it away. I sniffed the creamy blossom and pondered. When I'd entered the copy room, he had been bent over the wastebasket. Perhaps he'd planned to throw away the flower when my arrival had given him another idea.

I switched pages in the copy machine and punched in a request for 36 copies, then moved around the counter to where the wastebasket stood. There, on top of a stack of discarded error copies were the four card fragments. A tiny torn envelope just under them was blue and white striped.

It had to be the note that accompanied the flower.

I looked down again.

Dare I? I thought, picturing myself as Pandora, about to lift the lid of the storied box.

I hesitated.

Lily Burns' voice popped into my head. *"Pandora, Schmandora! Grab it and hide it before somebody comes!"*

Picking up the pieces of the envelope and card, I thrust them into my skirt pocket. Clumsily balancing the vase on one hip, and carrying the copies in my other arm, I managed to arrive back at my empty classroom without encountering anyone.

I looked at the clock. Just twenty minutes before the bells rang and my classroom would be filled again with students. I deposited the test papers on my desk. They hadn't been collated, nor were the pages stapled together, but my students would just have to deal, I quoted Hardy Patchke yet again.

Now, where to place the flower? Obviously, it would arouse curiosity on the part of my students. Perhaps they'd assume Gil sent it to me. But after all, what business was it of theirs? Defiantly, I placed the vase squarely on the corner of my desk, in full view.

Then I pulled the pieces of the envelope and card from my pocket and put the small crumpled pile on my desktop. It wasn't hard to reconstruct the note, nor was it difficult to make out what was written there in large, handwritten block letters:

YOU'VE KILLED HIM.

There was no signature.

Chapter | Twenty-one

The strong, sweet fragrance of Blakely's calla lily, so pleasant at first, was causing my nausea to act up. Holding my breath, I carried the vase to the rear of the room and set it on a windowsill.

Will this ridiculous sensitivity to smells end once I give birth? I wondered.

Give birth. The words, though not spoken aloud, caused me to pause in my pre-class chores. I hadn't ever thought of them in terms of myself, at least not since childhood, when I had played mama to my dolls, long before I had been introduced to the words *inability to conceive.*

Seated at my desk, I put my head in my hands, closed my eyes, and asked Heaven, *What is this all about?*

Motherhood. The word popped into my mind as the class bell rang.

I would soon be a mother. It was an immensely humbling thought. Could I possibly be as good a mother as the one I had? I knew that doing a good job wasn't necessarily automatic; as a teacher, I'd known too many parents who were, in my opinion, going about it all wrong.

As if on cue, Exhibit A of my thesis on faulty parenthood, Serendipity Shea, strutted from her place in the center of her giggling coterie and slid into her front-row chair, her eyes flashing and what can only be described as a sardonic lift to the corners of her mouth. While I watched, she pulled out a stick of gum and began to peel it.

I cleared my throat.

She looked up at me in mock surprise, smirked, and replaced the gum in its wrapper.

I don't have time to analyze her any further, I told myself, passing out the corrected test papers. "I recommend that you save these papers, people. They'll prove invaluable when you study for the final."

Serendipity looked me in the eye and methodically crumpled her test paper, sheet by sheet, into three tight balls which she lined up in a row at the front of her desk.

Uh, oh.

Mr. Berghauser's summons arrived at the end of the school day. "Mrs. Dickensen," he said in his most solemn tone as I hesitantly entered his office, "I have something important to discuss with you."

He gestured to the familiar chair opposite his desk. I sat.

"I try to be understanding when it comes to the lives of our staff outside of school, but we simply can't have our teachers harassing parents."

My jaw fell. "Harassing? Me? Whom did I harass?"

He frowned and his moustache frowned with him. "Now, don't try to pretend you didn't go to Shea's Sporting Goods and create a scene."

I yelped, "What?"

He smiled now, and his moustache wobbled. "Of course, I'm the first one to admit that Sa—Sa—that daughter of theirs is a handful, but we need to be adult about all this, don't you think?"

"Sir! I must object! I didn't—"

"Now, Miss Prentice, let's not get into a battle over semantics. A complaint has been issued against your behavior, and, despite your past excellent record, I must give it due consideration. You can see that, can't you?"

"I think so, but—"

"Do you deny that you went to the store?"

"No, I don't deny it, but it wasn't my intention to—"

"Do you deny that you were involved in an altercation with Mrs. Shea?"

"There was an argument, but I didn't start—"

"Oh, come now, are you actually going to assert the 'he started it' defense?"

It was a joke among teachers, the universal excuse, "Yes, I gave him a black eye, but he started it."

"Mrs. Shea has furthermore asserted that you have been giving her daughter failing marks because of a prejudice against her."

"Now look here! You of all people know that's not true. Serendipity's academic performance has been totally abysmal! My grade book here is proof." I held it up.

"Perhaps, but it is your grade book, isn't it, Miss Prentice? You are free to put anything you choose in it."

"There are her returned papers," I began. "I encourage the students to save them." My voice petered out. I knew the answer before I asked the question. "Has she saved them?"

Mr. Berghauser shook his head. "I'm afraid not. It isn't a requirement, you know."

"Well, it should be," I muttered.

"Perhaps, but that's an issue to be taken up with the board of education at a later date."

The mention of the almighty board brought me up short. They had the power to discipline me, fire me, arrange so I could never teach again. The utter unfairness of it all caused tears to prick behind my eyes. I frowned fiercely to squeeze them back.

I won't cry. I won't cry.

I stood. "If you'll excuse me."

The room was closing in on me. I hadn't eaten recently, and the queasiness was returning.

"Wait." Berghauser rearranged the pencils on his desk. "There's another matter."

My legs gave way and I sat back down.

I suppressed an illogical urge to laugh. What on earth could it be now? Skipping assembly? Using too much chalk?

"It has been brought to my attention that you received flowers from a male member of the faculty and openly displayed them in your classroom. As a married woman, I don't need to tell you that this is questionable at best."

I put my head in my hands and murmured, "Dangling participle."

He leaned forward. "What did you say?"

A hysterical giggle would not be stifled. "You used a dangling participle. You're—you're not a married woman, I am." I snorted.

"Miss Prentice! I mean, Mrs. Dickensen! This is a matter of ethics! You don't seem to be regarding this with the gravity it deserves."

I pulled a tissue from my pocket and dabbed at my eyes. "Believe me, sir, I am."

"Did you or did you not receive flowers from Blakely Knight?"

"I did, but it was just one flower, not flowers, plural. And I assure you, sir, that I am very happily married!"

He dismissed this with a wave. "Nonetheless, you displayed it in your classroom, giving rise to a most unfortunate conclusion on the part of your students."

"What students are those? Mr. Berghauser, that flower, one flower, singular, was given to me by Mr. Knight on a whim. If anybody else, Mrs. Dee, for instance, had been in the copy room, he might have given it to her. Ask Blakely, um, Mr. Knight, about it."

Berghauser squirmed uneasily. He cleared this throat. "I did, but he refused to be forthcoming about it. He used some most unseemly language."

I could imagine.

Berghauser added, "And he didn't give it to Mrs. Dee, he gave it to you."

"So why isn't Blakely in trouble?" I asked sharply.

Berghauser folded his hands on his desk with smug assurance. "He's not married. You are."

Of course, that explains it. Another thought occurred to me. "Who told you about the flower?"

He coughed. "That's irrelevant. You admit that you were given the flowers, uh, flower, and that settles the matter. That, combined with the matter we have already discussed, puts you in quite a precarious position career-wise."

I closed my eyes. I was sinking, drowning again in the deep, inky waters of Lake Champlain, and there was no one there to rescue me, no Lily, no professor, nothing. I'd have to swim, or try to.

"Mr. Berghauser, what do you propose to do?" I asked in a low voice.

He leaned forward. "In light of your long and commendable past record, I rather thought I'd leave it up to you. Of course, your behavior with regard to Mr. Knight is to be henceforth above reproach." He actually shook a finger at me. "If the slightest hint of more impropriety gets back to this office, there will be Steps Taken, I assure you!"

I sat, stone-like and staring, while a volcano raged in my stomach, threatening to erupt.

His tone became silky, reasonable. "As to the situation with the Shea family, well, you have a choice. You can issue a written apology to the Sheas; a copy will remain in your permanent record, of course. Or you can be stiff necked and make a fuss that will result in a good deal of difficulty for both the school and yourself."

He examined his coat sleeve for lint. "I would appreciate your answer now, please."

I stood. "I . . . I don't . . . that is, I—"

I was fighting the strongest nausea I'd yet experienced. I gagged and clapped a hand over my mouth.

"I can't just—" My words were muffled.

Berghauser looked alarmed. "Miss Prentice, are you ill?" He also rose to his feet.

The big desk stood between us, and Berghauser had reason to be grateful for that fact, because just then, I threw up all over it.

"Oh, I'm glad I'm alive to see this day," Olive Chapel declared in a fervent singsong whisper as she handed me another damp paper towel. "Here, honey." She'd responded to the principal's desperate summons and had helped me to the ladies' room. "You took that man down a notch, you did, and more power to you!"

I used the towel to wipe my hands. I was seated on a folding chair with my head down, in accordance with accepted first aid practice. I continued to maintain my compliant position as she placed the towel on the back of my neck, but I had to ask.

"What are you talking about?"

She squatted and lifted my chin gently with her index finger. As she gently bathed my face, she said, "Don't get me wrong, Amelia. Berghauser's a pretty good man deep down, but lately he's sort of turned into somebody else, like. Maybe he sees retirement at the end of the tunnel, I don't know, but it's getting harder to see the good guy and easier to see the donkey's tail, if you see what I mean."

I did. When I'd lost my lunch on his desk, he'd stared at me, wide-eyed, and said, "Really, Miss Prentice!" as he pressed the intercom.

"He did seem to act as though I'd done it on purpose," I agreed. "I didn't, you know."

"Of course you didn't." Olive eyed my face speculatively. "But are you going to be all right? You need me to call the nurse?"

"No, thanks," I said hastily. Nurse Dee's motherly ministrations would only make me feel worse. "Just a little queasiness and stress. It's nothing, nothing at all."

Olive smiled. "Oh, I get it. You haven't told Gil Dickensen."

"Told what?"

She smiled benevolently. "About the bun in the oven. Don't worry, sweetie. Nobody will hear it from me, but you better get a move on because it's gonna be common knowledge around here by the end of the week."

I was shocked. "But who would know?"

Olive shrugged. "Hard to say, but people talk. Chances are Berghauser'll hear of it before tomorrow and, whatever you do, don't let him off the hook. You got him on the run, girlfriend. Ten to one, he'll think you could sue him for something. Harassment, maybe. Keep it that way, that's my advice."

She looked at her watch. "Uh, oh, the bell's about to ring. I gotta go back and make sure the janitor's cleaning up the place."

She went to the door, looked back and pointed at me. "Remember what I said."

Chapter | Twenty-two

Olive's prediction about repercussions proved true because very little was said the next day about the incident in the principal's office. I never received the expected memo or summons in the morning, and Mr. Berghauser even smiled hesitantly at me in the lunchroom line.

"Feeling better?" he asked.

"Yes, thank you. I'm very sorry for—"

"No need." He waved away my apology and scurried off, carrying his tray.

"If I knew that was all it took, I might've tried it sooner," I murmured to myself as I accepted a bowl of vegetable soup from Mrs. Breen.

"Good choice," someone said in my ear.

I turned and beheld Alec, holding a tray. "The chicken casserole is a disgrace—I can tell ye that first hand—but I'm told the soup is nice."

He deposited his used crockery on the appropriate surface and chivalrously took over my load. "Come join us. Vern and I are having a meeting."

"Here in the school dining hall?"

Approaching the table, I smiled hesitantly at Vern, who responded with a sullen frown while chewing a mouthful of food. He'd been avoiding and ignoring me ever since the Night of the Lunchbox.

I was of two minds on the subject. On one hand, I had turned him in, so to speak, when he asked me to wait; however, if we hadn't gone to the police, he might have found himself in far deeper trouble later on. Either way, Vern's attitude, while somewhat understandable, was hurtful to me.

"The food's cheap, and I wanted to catch up with you, so I asked Vern to meet me." Alec resumed his chair and opened the top of a large spring-bound legal pad. "The thing is, Amelia, Etienne's roped us into designing and building the Chez Prentice entry in the snow sculpture contest."

"I wondered how he was going to manage that."

"The deadline for submitting our plan is this afternoon at five. We've gone through dozens of different ideas, but nothing seemed right, but just now, we had a flash of genius. By the way, we've called Etienne, and he's definitely enamored of the idea. Marie thinks we're a bit daft, but she'll cooperate." He paused and announced, "We're going to build a miniature Chez Prentice!"

"She won't like it," Vern commented, and crammed half a slice of bread into his mouth.

"Nonsense, lad. You see, Amelia," Alec explained, "Chez Prentice is built along square, straight lines. It would be relatively easy to build in snow. And the details will make it charming, unique, the clapboards, the chimney bricks, everything. It'll be one-eighth scale or thereabouts. Don't you think it's a splendid idea?"

He turned to Vern. "One thing, though, have you lined up a crew yet?"

"But—" I sputtered.

Vern ignored me. "Sure have. I called those students of yours you mentioned, and they're on board. Melody's willing to help out whenever she has time. It's a done deal. They're setting up the tarps in the front yard as we speak."

I jumped into the conversation. "You two certainly have moved fast on this."

"We had to, because of the deadline. Check out Alec's sketch." Vern slid an artist's pad across the table in an almost civil manner.

Sure enough, the sketch was of Chez Prentice, albeit cartoonish. In fact, it seemed to almost put an actual face on the house. Half-drawn shades in the upstairs windows resembled drooping eyelids; the central upstairs gable became a nose of sorts and the front door, a mouth. I smiled in spite of myself.

"Well, it is rather charming. Friendly."

"It'll be a fine image for Chez Prentice. And free advertising," Alec said.

Vern took a look at his watch. "Uh, oh, Gotta run." He gathered up his papers in one sweeping motion, stuffed them into his backpack, and was gone.

I closed my eyes, mentally blessed my food, and took a deep breath. When I opened them, Alec was gazing at me over his cup of coffee with a glint in his eye.

I picked up my spoon. "What?"

He leaned forward across the table. "Give me your hand, Amelia."

Puzzled, I extended my right hand.

Alec took it in both of his, and when I drew it back, it contained a red metallic rectangle, smaller than a powder compact.

I opened it. "My telephone? My goodness, it's tiny."

"It's one of the simpler ones to operate. I've charged it up and programmed it with my number. Ye'll know it's me by the special ring." He answered my doubting expression, "Don't worry, Amelia, you'll learn to love it."

I doubted that, but said, "Thanks, Alec."

"But that's not all," he whispered gruffly, "I have information."

Surely no agent of the CIA was more eager. He glanced over his shoulder. He was enjoying himself—Alec the Spy.

"Yes?" I sipped my soup. It was good, as he had predicted.

"Well, I had breakfast at McDonald's this morning and heard some interesting gossip from a fellow who does janitor work for Gray's Funeral Home. That woman at Chez Prentice? The guest?"

"You mean Mrs. Daye?"

"The very same. It seems she's been shopping."

"Shopping?"

"Well, browsing, actually. For coffins. And funeral plans."

I shrugged. "That's not all that suspicious, Alec. Lots of people do that."

"Yes, but she's not from here. And is it for herself or someone else?"

"That's not very juicy gossip. Nor does it implicate her in the murder. Why would the murderer plan the victim's funeral?" A thought swam into my head. "Unless, perhaps, she's somehow related to the victim. Have they determined his identity yet?"

Alec shrugged and shook his head.

"Could a little woman like that overpower a grown man, and what's more, kill him, in such close quarters?"

"You're right, of course." Alec sighed and applied a pat of butter to his roll. "I just thought it was interesting. You need to keep an eye on her, though, that's my advice." He took a hearty bite of bread.

We ate in thoughtful silence for a little while.

Alec looked over his shoulder and said in a low voice, "That's valuable information in that lunchbox. There's a lot of money to be made in false identities, green cards, and such-like."

"What kind of person might be involved in something like that?"

"Someone who moves about the area regularly, I would think," Alec said.

"And has connections across the border, perhaps?"

"Someone who might need money."

"That would describe quite a number of us, Alec," I said.

"True." He reached for his coffee cup.

"Someone involved in ice fishing?" I speculated thoughtfully.

Alec scratched his head and reverted again to a whisper. "You know whom we're describing, don't you?"

I looked around self-consciously. There were only two people left at the long teacher's table, and they were at the other end.

I whispered, "Out with it, Alec!"

"Etienne LeBow." He saw my expression and added hastily, "No, Amelia, hear me out." He began ticking off points on his fingers. "Moves about a good deal, has connections in Canada, always in need of money for those business schemes of his, and as for the ice fishing element, you can see for yourself. Besides, who knows what foreign contacts he's made over the years?"

"That's nonsense." The very idea made my stomach seem to sink within me.

"I know, I like the fellow myself, but what do we really know about his life before he returned to Marie? Think about it, that's all I'm saying."

"He's my business partner, for goodness' sake. I know all about his past."

"Yes, but consider the source. Do you really know if what he told you is true? Have you had any of it verified?" He looked at my face and smiled gently. "Ah, I thought not."

"Oh, Alec, I don't know. I can hardly bear to think of such a thing. I mean, I think I know him. I know as much about him as, well, as I do about you."

"Oh, my, y've gone quite pale." Alec reached a hairy hand across the table and patted mine. "Och, I'm sorry, m'dear. Don't give it a second thought. I've let my imagination run away with me again. I was just speculatin', ye might say." He had gotten quite Scottish all of a sudden.

I sat up straighter. "No, you're right, of course. We must try to remain dispassionate. I mean, as you listed those aspects of the guilty person, I found myself thinking—no, I must admit that it was hoping—that someone of the Shea clan fit the bill. And they do, up to a point."

"A few minutes ago, at this very table, Mrs. Dee told me she spent her Christmas vacation in the Laurentians. Where did she get the money? Bert Swanson also fits. As do I, come to that."

"Yes, darn it."

He held up an admonishing index finger. "Dispassionate, you said."

I smiled at him. "Risky as it might seem, don't you think we can at least eliminate you from our list of suspects?"

Alec glanced up sharply.

I turned around. Blakely Knight was approaching the teacher's table, carrying his lunch tray. Pointedly ignoring us, he slid into a seat at the other end of the table.

"Speaking of preferred suspects," Alec growled under his breath, "have ye given him a thought? He might be pretty good at hand-to-hand combat." Alec's own big hands formed slowly into fists as if he relished the idea.

"Do you know about him and Lily?" I whispered.

Alec's eyebrows came together in a ferocious expression. "Oh, aye." He stood and picked up his tray. "But I believe we're finished here for the time being. Must be running along, m'self. I have snow sculpting supplies to purchase. And isn't that your class bell?"

Chapter | Twenty-three

There was a strange square tent-like structure the size of a one-car garage fashioned from khaki tarpaulins and poles on Chez Prentice's front yard. A heavy electric cord leading from it snaked to the basement entrance around the side of the house. Muffled sounds emanated from within and all at once, Vern emerged from a flap in the side. He acknowledged me with a relatively polite nod and trudged away, following the cord.

"Hello?" I called as I entered the Chez Prentice foyer. "Anybody home?"

"Here, Amelia!" Marie answered, sounding anxious. "We're in the kitchen. Come here, you gotta see this!"

I hurried through the dining room.

Sure enough, Marie, Etienne, Hester, and Bert were staring at the wall-mounted television recently purchased so that our more media-addicted guests could watch the news at breakfast.

"This isn't good," Etienne said as he stared at the screen.

"Terrible," Hester agreed, shaking her head as she dried her hands on a dishtowel.

"Isn't going to help them much," Bert added. "Stupid kids."

"What is it?" I stepped forward to see the screen.

Along the bottom, a subtitle read, "Previously recorded" and a reporter was saying, "And here, once again, is footage of what happened earlier today at the suspects' home."

A shaky, hand-held camera zoomed in on a figure as it scrambled across the roof of a house. Rapidly the figure climbed into a window, pausing just before it disappeared to give a jaunty wave. The camera pulled back and moved down the house to the snowy yard and a still, dark body lying there, apparently having fallen from the roof.

My heart raced. I gasped. "Oh no! Who is it?"

Marie laid her hand gently on my arm. "Don't worry, it's okay. Just watch."

The camera zoomed in closer, moving slowly along the still form, starting with the feet and pausing significantly where the head would be. Instead, however, there was a white athletic sock, apparently stuffed to approximate a head and crudely decorated with eyes, nose, and a leering mouth.

The news anchor said, "As we said, this was shot immediately after our cameraman observed what he thought was a body falling from the roof of the Rousseau house. Fortunately, that body turned out to be a homemade dummy. Here's a comment by the boys' father."

Sure enough, there on the screen was Martin Rousseau, looking more harried and gray-faced than ever, standing in the middle of the rabid crowd of reporters. A microphone was thrust into his face. He blinked and cleared his throat.

"I want to say, I mean, the boys want me to say, that they apologize to you people for the real dumb thing they did this morning."

The crowd of reporters surged even closer. Their varied, frantically-thrown questions intertwined with one another.

"Why don't the boys come out themselves?"

"What does their lawyer have to say about this?"

"Don't they know they could have hurt someone?"

"Are they guilty?"

"Did they kill that man?"

Martin took a deep, weary breath and held up his hand. "Alls I can say is that they're sorry. We're all sorry. They're kids. They did something stupid. That's all. If you want to know anything more, talk to Mr. Cobb." He turned and began to move back through the crowd to his front door, his shoulders drooping, ignoring the roar of questions that followed him.

The news anchor said, "And here's the comment from the attorney for the young men."

In contrast to Martin Rousseau, James Cobb cut an impressive, handsome figure as he stood on a step outside his office building, slightly elevated above the crowd of reporters. "What happened today is simply an example of what stress and mistreatment can do the minds of impressionable young people, hounded beyond description by a corrupt establishment and a brutal police department. Once we are in the courtroom, we will prove the baselessness of these charges, and once they are exonerated, I will advise Dustin and John Rousseau to begin a lawsuit for false arrest and malicious prosecution against those responsible for this outrage."

One of the reporters shouted a question, "Isn't there a witness?"

"We intend to prove that that so-called witness is mentally unbal—"

"I can't listen to any more," Marie said, using the remote to turn off the television.

I sat down. "That was J.T. on the roof. I recognized him. What was he thinking?"

Bert poured coffee into his thermos. "Like Martin said, he's a kid." He shrugged. "They don't think."

"That's a copout, dear," Hester said. She hastened to add milk to his thermos.

Etienne began to pull on his coat. "No, it's not. When you're young, you do all sorts of silly things."

He had a melancholy look on his face, and I suspected that he was thinking of his daughter and the well-meant foolishness that had led to her death last year. Or was he remembering some long-ago indiscretion in his own past?

"I don't care. No matter what that lawyer says, a stunt like that just makes the boys look guilty," Marie said, hastily coming back to the subject at hand. "You can sort of see how they might kill a guy, maybe by accident or something, then panic."

She looked at me. "I know you really think they're innocent, Amelia, but maybe you have to face facts. Just 'cause you want it to be, don't make it true."

Her eyes held a hint of tears. Thoughts of her late daughter were never far from Marie's mind, either.

I nodded. There was nothing I could say. If someone like Marie could think the Rousseau boys would do such a thing, I dreaded to think what a jury might conclude.

There was a knock at the back door. Etienne opened it to Chuck Nathan, bearing a handsome floral arrangement. Once again I was struck by his resemblance to one of those '60's radicals: wild hair, scruffy clothing, and all. Yet it was ironically rumored that Chuck could, so to speak, buy and sell anyone in town, a direct result, one presumed, of his hard work and penurious ways.

Our little group welcomed the diversion. Hester relieved Chuck of his burden and invited him to join us for coffee.

He declined without any particular grace. "Nope. Can't. Got lots of deliveries to make." He looked over at Etienne. "Can I talk to you? About those ads on your fishing shanties?"

Etienne's face broke into a smile. "Of course! Come with me to the garage; I'll show them to you." He finished buttoning his overcoat and the two men left through the back door.

"Ads on the shanties? That's a new idea, isn't it?" I asked.

Bert shrugged. "That's the Frenchman for ya. He's always comin' up with stuff like that. Hey, it's a living. Take the fishing shanties, I mean, shelters—that's what Etienne calls 'em. We got a waiting list now; people really want to rent 'em for the contest."

"Bert, do you consider the sporting goods stores as your competition? I mean with regard to the fishing—um, shelters?"

Bert pulled on his gloves and watch cap. "Nah. There's people that rent and there's people that buy. Two different groups, you might say."

Marie held up a hand. "Wait. Everybody be quiet."

In the sudden silence, we could hear muffled voices, raised in anger.

We all hastened to the back door and saw Chuck and Etienne in a nose-to-nose confrontation.

"You can't just pollute the scenic environment like that!" Chuck was shouting.

The florist's height made him somewhat imposing, but the smaller man was giving as good as he got.

"Pollution, you say; what I say is the free enterprise!" Etienne roared, his index finger waggling in Chuck's face.

"Capitalist!"

"Communist!"

Muttering epithets, Nathan abruptly turned and stalked out of the yard, leaving his adversary standing there, panting.

Without donning a coat, Marie scurried out into the yard and escorted—or rather, dragged—her husband inside. Etienne was muttering something in French.

"Etienne!" Marie scolded, *"Tais-toi!"*

Etienne kissed her forehead. "Sorry, *chérie. Il est fou, ce type.* He says my advertising will pollute the lake.

"Pollute the lake?" Hester asked. "How's it gonna do that?"

"It's like billboards, he says. It ruins the scenery, he says." Etienne went to the coffeepot and began to pour himself another cup. His hand shook, and some of the coffee sloshed onto the counter. "What a dope." It was hard to tell if he was referring to Chuck or himself. *"Niaiseux."*

"Sit down," Marie ordered and hastened to take over for him. "Didn't you tell him the shelters were temporary? Only there for a few weeks?"

Etienne waved away Marie's logic. "He knows. He don't care. I am turning the lake into a junkyard, he says." He took a big swig from the mug Marie set before him and set it down decisively. "Well, come on, Bert, let's get busy. If we are making junk, we better make sure it's good junk."

Bert grinned and pulled on his gloves. "Right."

Chapter | Twenty-four

"Miss Amelia," Alec said breathlessly on my new cell phone's voicemail after school the next day, "meet me at the diner, would ye please? Right away? It's verry important!"

I'd known who was calling. Alec had assigned himself a special ringtone. My tiny telephone had played a tinny version of "Bonnie Annie Laurie," but it had rung in the middle of my two o'clock class. I'd retrieved the message at the end of the day.

"Couldn't you have told me over the telephone?" I said aloud. Even to myself, I sounded whiney, but I was bone-weary and eager to get home.

He concluded the recorded message as if he'd heard me. "It's too complex to discuss on the telephone. Please come, soon as ye can!"

I hung up, groaning. I didn't want to trudge through the snow-covered streets again.

On the bright side, the diner was only two blocks away from Chez Prentice and made a widely renowned bacon, lettuce, and tomato sandwich. A good excuse for a snack for little Cathy or Heathcliff.

I bundled up, bid Marie goodbye, and headed out.

It was just four o'clock when I pushed through the door of the shiny silver diner. The smell of frying bacon made my mouth water. Danny Dinardi called out a greeting from the grill as I made my way down the aisle with counter and stools on one side and narrow booths on the other, most of which were empty.

"You here to meet the professor?" he said, grinning. "He's waiting." Danny jerked his head toward a booth in the furthest back corner where Alec sat, trying to look casual.

Only cowering under the table would have made him look more conspicuously secretive. As it was, he had slid all the way up against the wall, clutching an attaché case to his chest. There was an empty coffee cup before him on the table.

"Stt!" He signaled me and gestured with a large, hairy hand, indicating I should sit opposite him. Alec furtively wedged the attaché between himself and the wall. "Amelia," he began in a hoarse whisper, only to be interrupted by Shirley, Danny's taciturn wife, who also happened to be his waitress.

"Get ya anything?"

Alec froze, his eyes darting back and forth.

I couldn't help myself. "BLT special and a large glass of milk, please."

Shirley noted my order on her pad and began to turn, but Alec stopped her in his melodious Scottish burr. "M'dear, would ye add to that order another one of those wonderful sandwiches," he nodded at an empty plate before him, "and a warm up on m'coffee? Give me the check?"

To my amazement, Shirley's habitually sour expression melted into a wide smile. "Sure thing, Professor. Right away."

I leaned out of the booth, watching her walk away. "How did you do that?" I whispered.

Alec dug in the attaché case. "Do what?"

"Get a pleasant reaction out of that woman. I've never seen her smile in all the years I've been eating here."

Alec shrugged and placed a handful of papers on the table. "Oh, sure, she was a bit curdlin' back when I first came in, but I dinna take the bait, so to speak. Just kept play actin' as though we were fast friends, and soon enough, we were!"

I leaned back into the aisle and spotted Shirley at another booth, her frown once again firmly fixed. "Oh, I don't know. I think maybe it's more than that."

Alec brushed aside my suggestion. "That's neither here nor there, Amelia. Getting back to the real reason for my calling you—look!" He slid the papers across to me. "You told me that the bullet wasn't found in the boys' Volkswagen, rright?" His r's rolled pleasantly as he tapped the top paper with a thick forefinger. "Look here."

I squinted at the page. It was a simple black and white sketch of a VW bug's front seat interior. "Where did you get this, Alec?"

Alec reached over and patted my hand. "I keep forgetting that you've only just joined the new century, m'dear. 'Tis simplicity itself with a search engine on the Internet. I found it on a website for Volkswagen enthusiasts and printed it out."

I rolled my eyes and sighed. Anyone who knew me at all well was aware that I did not own a computer. The first time I heard the term *search engine*, my overactive imagination conjured up the image of an eccentric, ornate Jules Verne-style contraption, a kind of snowplow derivative, equipped with a powerful headlight and perhaps a loudspeaker on the cab roof for good measure.

To my word-obsessed mind, even the term *website* had a sinister sound. Where there was a web, could a spider be far away?

Until I acquired my new cell phone, I'd managed to duck the pressure to conform to technological advances, even though Mr. Berghauser had gone so far as to give me an email address: *ameliaprentice@yahoo.com*. I'd ignored it. Frequent visits to Olive's desk allowed me to obtain all the school information I needed to function, thank you very much. But there it remained, at the principal's insistence.

Alec leaned forward and pointed at the illustration. "This is the rather elderly model the Rousseau boys have, and ye can see the glove compartment there."

"Yes, of course, but what does this—"

"Steady, lass, let me finish." He pulled another sheet from underneath the first. "You'll notice by this sketch that the back window of a Volkswagen is tiny by today's standards. So the shooter had a very narrow range in which—"

"The shooter?"

Alec looked confused. "Yes, shooter. Isn't that the correct term?"

"You mean you believe the boys' story?"

"Of course, don't you?"

"I do believe that they didn't kill anyone, but I thought perhaps the bullet-hole story was, well, a desperate attempt to validate themselves. It's just so melodramatic."

"Think, Amelia. What's more melodramatic than murder?"

"Point taken. Go on."

"Well, if that part of the story was true, I think we can give more credence to the other part, as well."

"I don't know, Alec. It just seems so fantastic. But," I mused, "that lunchbox thing does contain what I guess to be stolen IDs."

"Right! It's my contention that there was something illegal going on, and the boys stumbled onto it," Alec said, then sat back, fixed a wide smile on his face and directed his gaze into the aisle. "Ah, here she comes now!"

As Shirley Dinardi laid two heavy diner plates before us and removed the empty one, she positively simpered at Alec. *Some kind of Scottish magic*, I thought, and shrugged inwardly.

The next few minutes were occupied with consuming Danny's deservedly famous sandwiches, then Alec dabbed his lips and dusted off his gray-speckled beard with a paper napkin, signaling a resumption of our discussion.

"What we need to do," he whispered gruffly, because Shirley was taking an order in the next booth, "is somehow get into that car."

My mind was wandering. "What car?"

Alec sighed. "Amelia, pay attention! The VW, of course! You know Dennis O'Brien quite well. Surely there's a way."

I shook my head. "No, there isn't. Last time I got Dennis involved in a problem of mine, I almost got him fired. I can't impose on his friendship like that. But I suppose we could ask Mr. Cobb for help."

Alec smiled. "Of course! The defense attorney. Good thinking!" He dug in a side pocket of his attaché and produced a computer the size and thinness of a children's picture book. "A gift to m'self. It's already come in mighty handy," he said in answer to my surprised expression. "Danny doesn't have Wi-Fi, so I'll have to use me modem." He pulled a small rectangular item from his pocked and plugged it into the side of the computer.

I had no idea what any of it meant, but within three minutes Alec had obtained the telephone number of Brand's law firm and was poking it in to his cell phone, which he then unceremoniously handed over to me. "He knows you," he mouthed at me.

After some clumsy back-and-forth on my part and the admonition from the secretary that he could only spare a minute of his time, Cobb came on the line.

"Yes, Mrs. Dickensen? What can I do for you?" His voice sounded impatient.

"It's about the boys' car."

"The boys?"

"Your clients? The Rousseaus? Their Volkswagen."

"Oh, yes, of course. I can help you a little there. The father only wants a couple thousand for it. A steal, if you ask me. That thing's a classic."

"Then the police have released it?"

"Sure. They dropped it off in my parking lot. The father's going to pick it up tonight sometime."

"Haven't you looked it over? For evidence, I mean? That is, the boys said—"

"Yes. Well." Cobb allowed himself a small, derisive snort. "I'm framing the defense to go in a slightly different direction. These young men have been put through such trauma—"

"You know, Mr. Cobb, I *am* interested in possibly buying that car, or at least I know someone who might be."

Gil liked classic cars. It was possible he'd like to buy one, I rationalized. Perhaps. Maybe.

"Could I come see it this afternoon?"

"Sure. Look, I've got to get to court. I'll leave the key with my receptionist."

Alec drove, and we made it across town to the new office center in record time, as he hummed "Be Thou My Vision" under his breath.

"There it is," I said, pointing to the rather bedraggled little car, hunched in a far corner of the parking lot.

Alec pulled in a slot next to it. "I'll take a look at it while you fetch the key. Mr. Cobb might obtain a restraining order against me if I were to go up there."

"Why on earth?"

"Don't ye remember? I'm a prosecution witness, and—haven't ye heard?—I'm to be portrayed as a maniac who sees mythical creatures. Perhaps I'm even dangerous. Have a care, Amelia." He wiggled his eyebrows at me.

I sighed. "What a mess!"

"Ye're right therre. Now run along! We've noo time to waste shilly-shallying!"

"Who's supposed to be the sidekick?" I muttered as I headed into the building.

When I returned, Alec was sitting in the front passenger seat, running his hand around in the open glove compartment.

"How did you get inside?"

"I used the coat hanger that I carry in m'back seat for this very purpose. Simplicity itself."

"You? But—" I began, but stopped when Alec's face lit up.

"Amelia! I feel something! Let's see. Ungh!"

The professor seemed to be trying to cram his square, bulky body inside the compartment. All at once, he sprang back.

"I was right! See for yourself. There's a hole toward the back that you could put your fist through, and certainly a bullet! Try it yourself!" He backed out and hurried around to the front of the car, where he worried the trunk latch until it opened.

Carefully I slid into the passenger seat, reached out and ran my fingers along the interior of the small box-like compartment. "Oh yes, here it is," I said.

My hand was smaller than Alec's, and I was able to get it all the way through the hole to the trunk. I wiggled my hand and was startled to feel Alec's calloused fingers in mine.

"Oh!" I laughed and retracted my hand. "But Alec," I asked, coming around the car to join him at the front, "what does this mean?"

"It means, m'dear, that we might be able to prroove the boys are innocent."

"Oh, Alec, that's wonderful! We need to call Dennis O'Brien right away!"

"Hold your horses, Amelia, this is just part of the puzzle." He was running his hand around the trunk. "It's the bullet that'll make the difference." He grunted as he leaned over the edge and reach far into the interior, then backed out, clapping dust off his hands. "Nope, no luck." He slammed the trunk shut. "No bullet. None." He sighed, squinted and stared at the pavement. "A dead end." Then his face brightened. "But we're not defeated, are we? The good news is that the boys' story is still possibly true. That's something, at least."

The expression grasping at straws popped into my head, but I suppressed it. "So what do we do now?"

He rested a gentle paw on my shoulder. "I suggest we go home now and cogitate. Something will come to either one or the other of us, I'm sure."

Chapter | Twenty-five

"I can't be sure when I'll be back," Vern said briskly.

He was cramming a change of clothes into a bag. He'd be spending several nights at Chez Prentice so he could put the finishing touches on the snow sculpture.

"Between classes, driving the cab and this contest, I don't have time to be driving back and forth out here."

"Of course." I changed the subject. "Please, Vern, can't we talk about this . . . thing . . . between us? We used to be such good friends."

"Yah, used to be. Drop it, Amelia. It's water over the bridge now."

Under different circumstances, I might have made light of his mangled idiom, but not today. My heart hurt from the coldness.

"But—"

He zipped his duffle closed and straightened up. "Look, I suppose you did what you thought was right. And Gil took it from there. But from where I stand, it looks like a lack of respect. Respect for me and for my judgment. And that's not easy to forgive."

He heaved the bag on his shoulder and headed out the door.

I sat down on his unmade bed and once again those drat-
ted tears filled my eyes. "Forgive?" I said aloud. "Do I need
forgiving? Lord, did I do the right thing? Did Gil?"

That afternoon, after school, as I navigated the salted sidewalk, formulating ways to convince Vern that Gil and I had
done the right thing, a taxicab pulled up alongside the curb,
the passenger window rolled down, and I heard, "Miss? Miss?"

When I bent down to the window, the usually taciturn
Marcel LaBombard smiled back at me. "Get in, please, get
in," he said, beckoning.

"I'm all right walking, thanks."

"No, it's important, please, we gotta talk to you." He patted the front passenger seat. "Real important."

I climbed into the taxi, and closed the door. Immediately,
Marcel was off.

"I'm headed to Chez Prentice," I instructed him, but he
took a right turn and headed across the small bridge that
spanned the river and into a totally different neighborhood.
"Where are you going? What—" I began.

Marcel stopped at a light and looked over at me with an
anxious expression. "Sorry, am I makin' you late for something?"

"No, not really. But where are we going? What did you
want to talk about?"

"Okay, it's like this. You done us a good turn, Miss Prentice.
I mean with Yvonne and all." The light turned green and he
accelerated.

"Oh, but all I did was tell Fleur where I thought she was."

The cab slowed and turned into the small parking lot of LaBombard Taxi office. "Fleur and me's been wanting to thank you." He was out of the car in a twinkling and held the door open for me. "Please, come in. Let the wife tell you herself."

"Amelia!" Fleur was behind her desk when I entered, but she rose and came running to throw her arms around me. The scent of cigarettes was strong about her, and I had to work hard to control my gag reflex, but I managed, and returned the hug with a smile.

"Look who's here!" Fleur announced as her daughter, Yvonne, a pale, slender blonde with a tendency to bad posture, came through the door carrying a case of candy bars. "Hi, Miss Prentice," she said and went quietly about the task of refilling the candy machine.

"It's Mrs. Dickensen now, y'know," her mother corrected her daughter. "She got married. Come over here, honey, and sit down. Bring that box of candy. You want some candy, Amelia?"

I accepted a Twix bar and began happily munching.

Fleur said, "I want you to tell Amelia what happened."

With a shy smile, Yvonne complied, sitting tailor-fashion next to her mother on the worn leatherette sofa, while her father beamed at her from a straight chair across the room.

"Go on," her mother prodded. "Tell her about it."

Yvonne looked down at her tightly clasped hands and said hoarsely in a voice I had to lean forward to hear, "Well, things had got pretty bad with Matt lately. He'd get mad over the littlest bitty thing, and, well, it wasn't very nice when he was mad." Her voice became almost inaudible.

Marcel shifted in his seat, and perhaps I only imagined that he emitted a low growl.

Fleur stroked her daughter's arm lightly. "Tell what happened then."

"Not a lot, really. He left out one morning and just didn't come home that night, and I waited for him to show all the next day—it was my day off. But he never came. He didn't answer his cell phone, neither."

"The bum wouldn't let her have one," Marcel muttered.

"We couldn't afford it, Dad, that's why." Yvonne turned back to me. "Well, anyhow, I asked off the next day at the restaurant, in case he would call home, but he didn't and they wouldn't give me the next day off, and told me I was fired if I didn't come in. I didn't know what to do, because the rent was coming due, and Matt always paid that, and I didn't have anywhere near enough to pay it, and I figured he'd be mad if we lost the apartment, so I got kind of scared.

"I didn't think Dad wanted to hear from me, at least that's what Matt'd told me—they'd had kind of an argument—so I couldn't call home."

I glanced at Marcel again. His eyes were filled with tears.

"But I remembered that Melody Branch was a nice person in school, and she was in the Gamma sorority at the college, so I called over there, and they give me her number, and, well, she came."

I heard a soft sob coming from Marcel. He'd pulled out a large handkerchief and was blowing his nose vigorously.

"Mom and Dad showed up at the Gamma house the next day, Miss Prentice, and they were really nice about everything. I mean, they asked me to come home and stuff." She directed a shy smile at her mother.

Fleur reached over and patted my hand. "That was your doing, Amelia."

Marcel had recovered enough to mop his face and say, "Tell 'er what you're going to be doing from now on, Yvonne."

The girl looked shyly over at me. "I'm going to college next semester. I'm going to major in education; become a teacher." She pressed her lips together and looked away.

"She's so good with little children, Amelia," Fleur added.

The prodigal has truly come home. Thank You, I prayed. Then another thought popped dramatically into my head. "Yvonne, could I ask you a couple of questions?"

She shrugged. "Sure."

"What exactly did—does Matt do for a living?"

I ignored a derisive snort from Marcel.

"Um, he does computer things, puts programs on discs and stuff. And he's also kind of a salesman. He had boxes and crates of things coming to the apartment, and then he'd take them different places, and then he'd bring home some money. At first, I thought he was doing ebay, but I changed my mind, because he always got cash. You have to do credit cards on ebay, I think, and stuff."

I nodded sagely, though I had only a vague idea of how ebay worked. "When he left, did he take the computer with him?"

"No; I know because I thought about pawning it for the rent but was kind of scared to. I mean, if he came back, and it was gone, well—" Her face held such alarm, I regretted asking the question.

"I'm sorry. This is bringing back painful memories."

Yvonne rose from the sofa, picked up the box of candy and headed back to the candy machine. "Not really, Miss Prentice. I'm real glad to be home. Of course, it wasn't all bad. I mean, I felt kind of responsible for Matt after what we'd meant to each other. I mean, I worried that he didn't always eat right, y'know? That last day when he left in the morning, I wanted to make him a sandwich to take with, but he laughed and said no, he was on his way to pick up a lunchbox."

I blurted out my information as soon as he came on the line, "Dennis, I think I know the identity of the dead man on the lake."

"You do?" Police Sergeant Dennis O'Brien sounded amused. "Where did you get this information?"

I explained about the disappearance of Matt Ramsey and of Yvonne's involvement with him. "I don't think she had any idea what he was doing."

"Maybe you're right, but I think it's irrelevant now. His name isn't Matthew Ramsey," Dennis said. "We already know who he is, or rather, was. His real identity, that is."

"But how?"

"Amelia, what do you think? We just sit around eating doughnuts all day? We're in contact with law enforcement all over the country, all over the world, for that matter. How would you think we'd find out?"

"Fingerprints," I said, "of course." Another idea popped into my head. "And his computer?"

"I can neither confirm nor deny it," Dennis said, chuckling. "Did I use the correct grammar that time?"

"Yes, you did. So he was a criminal?"

"I can neither confirm nor—"

"All right, I can take a hint. But may I ask just one more question?"

In my mind's eye, I could see Dennis smiling. "You may ask, but I may not answer. You're married to a newsman now, remember?"

"You may know who he was, but who killed him?"

"That, Amelia, is a good question."

We left it at that. After I hung up, I realized that I had another question: Who, then, was the real Matt Ramsey, and where was he?

Chapter | Twenty-six

The morning of the sixth annual ice festival, the weather cooperated by dawning clear, sunny, and bitter cold. Gil and I rode into town together, bundled up to our eyebrows in layer upon insulated layer. Even so, for several miles our breaths came out in clouds until the car's heater was able to raise the interior temperature above freezing.

Over the past few weeks we had watched while all around town preparations for the big day had gradually taken shape. And now, for better or worse, it all came together in a huge community effort.

"I'm going to drive through town first, just to see the sights, then drop you at Chez Prentice," Gil informed me. "There'll be so much going on that this may be our only chance to look at it all.

"Well, here we are," he remarked, slowing at the intersection that marks our town's downtown area.

A huge banner, reaching from lamppost to lamppost, had been draped across the street, offering welcome in both English and French in deference to the many French-Canadian visitors. We followed the street over a bridge and along the river.

"Look out there," Gil said, nodding in the direction of the broad, white expanse that was Lake Champlain. "The ice fishing contest has already started."

The ice was dotted with tents similar to the one I'd seen at Shea's, oddly-shaped lean-tos, even a number of brave, hardy, and well-wrapped souls sitting out in the open on folding chairs, staring at their set-ups. Here and there I spotted the ten shanties that Bert and Etienne had built, looking for all the world like so many portable toilets.

I lowered the car window and squinted a the lake. "It looks like they sold some advertising, after all. Half of them have signs. I can't make out what they say, though. Wait a second! Gil, there's an ad for the newspaper on one of them!"

My husband shrugged. "What can I say? Etienne's a good salesman."

Speaking of portable toilets, we spotted half a dozen of them in the parking lot behind the public library. "I suppose they're necessary, but yuck. I hate to use those things!"

Gil leaned toward me and spoke out of the corner of his mouth, "This is highly secret and confidential, so keep it under your hat, but the restrooms at the Old Episcopal Church are open for the festival workers. I read it in the committee handout we printed." He handed me a small brochure.

The Old Episcopal Church was a small but impressive gray granite structure located just off the town square, built in a Gothic style, complete with an old-fashioned bell tower. In recent years its congregation had dwindled to a tenacious few, served by a visiting pastor on alternate Sundays. They were a loyal lot, however, and managed to keep things going.

Recently they had received a charitable grant from a historical foundation, and many badly needed improvements were being made. I filed the information for later use.

"Good to know."

Next we passed the high school football practice field, covered with a thick white blanket of snow. "Snow Bowl. Admission two dollars. Kickoff at 4 p.m.," Gil read on a large crudely lettered sign fastened to a light pole.

"Some of the boys from the high school organized it at the last minute," I told him. "They're going to play two quarters of touch football hip-deep in snow and give the proceeds to the food bank."

Gil chuckled. "Sounds like fun." He put on his blinker. "Let's take a look at the snow sculptures. I want to get a look at what they've been hiding behind those tarps all week."

We turned at the corner and drove along College Road. Gracing the front yard of each fraternity and sorority house was an entry in the sculpture contest. The variety was breathtaking. A full-color effigy of SpongeBob SquarePants frolicked next to an unpainted miniature Mount Rushmore. We saw our esteemed district attorney, Elm DeWitt, and three other members of the legal profession closely examining a handsome replica of the capitol building in Albany, complete with gilded dome.

"What're they doing?"

"Didn't you read the program? They're the judges for the snow sculpture contest."

The elementary school playground was on the left. "Look, they have things for the little children to do," I said. "There'll be a blanket toss and junior karaoke, and they'll get to meet all the high school mascots. Over there, they're setting up for the pancake fling. Mrs. Breen told me that the cafeteria ladies were going to stay late last night to make up hundreds of pancakes and put them in the school's big freezer. Here they come," I added, as recognized that estimable lady pushing a wheelbarrow laden high with foil-wrapped pans.

The bleachers along the college running track had been swept clear of snow, but the track itself was unplowed, with small flags indicating the route. Gil pointed to another banner.

Junior Snowshoe Races, 10 a.m. Sponsored by Shea's Quality Sporting Goods. Snowshoes provided.

"The paper interviewed Kevin Shea about this race," Gil said. "It's mainly for the elementary school kids. He said he wants to highlight the less well-known winter sports."

"And get his name in front of the voting public."

"Why you cynical minx, you!" Gil said with a twinkle. "Look, I'm going to be busy at the paper all morning. The big parade begins at noon. Why don't you come by the paper a little bit before then and we'll go up on the roof? It'll be the best place to watch it."

He pulled up to the curb in front of Chez Prentice, we exchanged a quick kiss, and I emerged from the car to encounter Alec, quivering with excitement.

"Alec, it's wonderful!" I exclaimed, getting my first look at Chez Prentice, Jr.

It was an accurate, three-dimensional version of Alec's sketch, fully colored and exuding whimsical charm with many humorous details, even including the porch swing with a kissing couple. I stepped off the walk to get a closer look, but Alec pulled me back. "Thanks, but 'tis no matter. You can look at that later." He all but shoved me up the walk and onto the porch. "I thought ye'd never get here," he said in a rough whisper. "Listen, they've parked around back. Most of them are there, I think."

"Who are?"

"Our suspects! They're in the parlor, all of them! I extended an invitation to a pre-festival coffee at the inn, and they all came! You've got a wonderful staff, Amelia, they flew into action, directly I called 'em at the crack of dawn this morning!"

"Suspects? Alec, what do you think you're doing?"

He was trembling with glee. "It's brilliant! We can investigate up close! Perhaps even get a breakthrough! Just like Hercule Poirot!"

"And you didn't see fit to tell me about this on the phone last night? Alec, this could be dangerous!"

Alec held up one finger. "Firrst, it only came to me in the wee hours, too late to call ye back." He held up a second finger. "And secondly; no, it's not dangerous. I invited the police in the person of Dennis O'Brien, and he's inside already, stuffing himself full of dainties!"

It was a *fait accompli*. I sighed. "All right, I'll join the party, but be careful, Alec."

I could hear cheerful conversation and laughter coming from the parlor as we entered. The tall pocket doors that divided the parlor from the entryway had been pulled half closed, and a small metal stand at the entrance held a card announcing, "Private Party," lest B&B guests be tempted to join the group. The red tapestry Victorian settee near the door held a large mound of coats.

"Alec, just how many did you invite?"

"Look out, I've got hot coffee!" Scarcely giving us a nod, Hester Swanson bustled past, carrying one of our heirloom sterling silver coffeepots swathed in a clean dish towel. She shouldered her way into the room, bawling warning all the way.

We laid our coats on the pile and joined the group inside.

"Hello, Amelia!" Dennis O'Brien was the first to greet me. "Long time no see! You did a great job on that thing out front." He waved his hand, and his coffee cup in the other hand rattled slightly.

"That was Vern and Alec's work. It is amazing, isn't it?" I added in a low voice, "Dennis, I need to speak to you about something." I thought I'd better warn him about what Alec had in mind.

"Sure, but don't forget, this is my day off. I had to really wangle to get it. Excuse me, but I need to top off this coffee." He edged toward the refreshment table. "Be right back."

I paused to survey the others in the room.

Mrs. Daye was chatting companionably with Fleur LaBombard and Judith Dee. Yvonne was with her father, looking out the front window, apparently admiring the snow sculpture.

Mayoral candidate Kevin Shea was the only member of the party not attempting to, in the words of Hardy Patchke, make nice. He stood glowering in front of the parlor fireplace, scowling into the merrily dancing flames.

Chuck Nathan was sitting grasshopper-like on a chair that was far too low for him. He set his coffee cup on a nearby table, unfolded himself to a standing position and approached Alec. "It's real nice of you to invite me to this shindig, Professor, no problem, but I got to get going. We're finishing up our float for the parade."

Alec nodded. "If you'll just linger only a few minutes more, please." He held out his hand. "Mrs. Swanson, it would seem Mr. Nathan here has a fondness for those lovely apricot confections. If you would be so kind?"

Hester smiled and nodded.

"Something smells delicious," someone said behind me.

I turned. Blakely Knight stood at the entrance. He moved smoothly inside, followed closely by Lily Burns. "I hope you folks don't mind, but I brought a date." He tossed a sidelong glance at Alec and placed Lily's hand in the crook of his arm.

Even from across the room, I could feel Alec take a long, deep breath. He applied a hearty smile to his hairy countenance and boomed, "Of course, of course! Please, enjoy the refreshments!"

From her place at Blakely's side, Lily gave me a strange look, part smug smile and part cringe. I smiled back vaguely and went to get myself a plate.

I had eaten a hearty breakfast, but I was starving again. Hester had managed to arrange quite a spread at a moment's notice, and she had pulled out Mother's best company party pieces to dress up the occasion. On a three-tiered plate were finger-sized egg salad and ham sandwiches; an arrangement of tiny crudités and olives; and on the bottom, toast points and a variety of razor-thin slices of cheese. The aforementioned apricot tarts shared a large platter with cranberry-filled cookies and chocolate-dipped shortbread fingers.

The handmade sweets, I knew, had been commandeered from Chez Prentice's commodious freezer and simply thawed. They were intended for just such an occasion as this. Well, not exactly like this.

I took one of the gold-rimmed dessert plates and a napkin and proceeded to load up. Since coffee was out of the question—it still made me gag—I asked Hester to fetch a glass of milk from the kitchen.

I glanced at my watch. It was almost time for the festival to open, and I knew that most of these people had places to go. With my plate of goodies in one hand, I made my way over to where Alec was explaining to Marcel how he had painted the Chez Prentice snow replica.

"It's getting late, Alec. These people need to leave. Why don't we just let them?" I whispered in his ear just before I popped an egg salad sandwich into my mouth, then one more for good measure. These were teensy sandwiches.

He seemed startled, then recovered himself. "Quite right, m'dear. The company was so pleasant, I almost forgot."

He moved quickly over to the pocket door and closed it, then cleared his throat. "Ladies and gentlemen, I want to thank you for coming this morning."

The room fell silent as most of the guests turned pleasantly smiling faces toward him.

What on earth was he going to do?

"However, we had another reason to gather you all together, and the charming Miss Amelia will now explain." He made a broad gesture toward where I stood chewing, and the collective gaze shifted accordingly.

I stood, paralyzed with surprise.

Alec had organized the tennis match, figuratively speaking, then tossed the ball in my court.

Why did I ever want a sidekick in the first place?

Chapter | Twenty-seven

"Um, mff," I began, chewing quickly and swallowing with difficulty.

A thought had just occurred to me, and it wasn't a pleasant one. In the fictional scenes Alec had mentioned, Hercule Poirot already knew who the guilty party was. I hadn't a clue, so to speak, and I was going to have to wing it. How did one go about getting a killer to confess?

I began again, "Well, yes." I set down my plate and milk glass on a nearby table and dusted off my hands. "That is, I am a great believer in communication and, er, dialogue among people, you know. That is, Alec and I are."

The looks I was getting now were puzzled, at best.

"What I mean to say is, I think we can all agree, I mean . . . "

A few confused frowns.

"Okay. Lately, there have been a number of really strange things going on."

"What d'you mean by that?" Chuck Nathan had put down his own plate and given me his full attention.

Kevin Shea added his two cents. "Yeah, what?"

Judith Dee looked puzzled. "I beg your pardon?"

"All right," I said carefully, and grabbed the first idea that popped into my head. I directed my gaze noncommittally toward a nearby chair arm. "Somebody sent some flowers—a flower, I mean; a single flower, that is—with a weird message." I didn't look up, but felt a stirring in the room. "It said, 'You've killed him.' Don't you think it's important to find out who killed whom?"

Police Sergeant Dennis O'Brien stepped forward. "Amelia, what are you doing?"

"That was private and personal!" Blakely Knight barked. I looked up and felt skewered by his scowl. "Who told you that?" He looked over at Chuck Nathan. "You?"

"What're you talking about? All I know is this gal," the florist pointed at Mrs. Daye, "orders one big honkin' lily to be sent to the high school, which is weird, all right, if that's what you're talking about."

Mrs. Daye's eyes widened.

"Amelia, what's this all about?" Dennis said.

"Oh, yeah, my Serry saw it all," Kevin Shea said. "She saw you and this, this, gigolo guy getting lovey-dovey in the teacher's room."

"What?" I said, appalled at the outright lie.

"What?" Lily said at the same time, going dead pale and backing away from Blakely.

"Gigolo?" Blakely Knight said in chorus with us.

The entire room erupted into confusion, with everyone talking at once.

"How do you get out of here? I'm leaving!" Kevin Shea shouted, slapping the closed pocket doors.

"I must say," Judith Dee commented mildly, "this is the strangest party."

Even the president of my fan club, Fleur LaBombard, approached me with a frown. "Are you accusin' us of something?"

Alec stood off to one side, shaking his head.

Don't look at me. You're the one responsible for this disaster, I said to him with my eyes.

"Stop!" A high-pitched scream cut through the din. "Stop this! It was me!"

The noise subsided, except for heavy sobs coming from Mrs. Daye, who collapsed into a chair.

Everyone instinctively formed a circle around her. Kevin Shea stopped attempting to leave and joined the group.

Dennis O'Brien stepped forward and knelt beside her. "What do you mean, Mrs. Daye?

What did you do?"

Tears streamed down the woman's cheeks. "My . . . my name's not Daye. It's really Knight." With a shaking hand, she pointed to Blakely. "Ask him. He's our son."

Blakely's hostility was palpable. "I'm no son of hers," he growled, "or his any more, for that matter. My own mother died two years ago—not that they cared."

"Oh, Blake, we tried to reach you when Harriet died. We did."

Dennis brought things back to the point. "What exactly did you do, Mrs., er, ma'am?"

"The flower—that stupid lily. I sent it to Blake. He wouldn't talk to me, kept hanging up on me, sending back my letters unopened. I thought if I jarred him a little bit, it would make him get curious, contact me or something." She started crying again. "But it didn't work! It just made trouble for all you nice people."

Dennis looked up at Blakely. "Is that right, Knight?"

Blakely frowned fiercely. "Not that I owe anybody an explanation, but yes, this is my stepmother who ran off with my dad twenty-nine years ago last Easter. And I guess she was the one who sent me that rotten flower."

"It—that—" Chuck Nathan sputtered.

"It's just a figure of speech," I hastened to reassure him. "It was a beautiful flower."

"You should know," Kevin Shea put in snidely.

Blakely ran a hand over his eyes. "I just gave the flower to Mrs. Dickensen on a whim. It didn't mean anything at all," he said with exasperation.

"But it did!" Blakely's stepmother finished using the handkerchief Dennis had given her and added, "He is dying, your father! Or he could soon! He's even got me planning his funeral! That's why I needed to talk to you."

Blakely went pale.

She continued, "He needs a kidney transplant right away, Blake. We need you to get tested. I'd do it myself, but I'm—I'm not a match."

Blakely turned and found a chair for himself. "Tested. To give him one of my—"

Mrs. Knight nodded. "That's right. I know it's a lot to ask."

Lily Burns piped up, "You bet it is! You've got a lot of nerve—"

"Shut up, Lily. You don't know anything about it!" Blakely

barked. He stood and came over to Mrs. Knight. "Look, you've got a room here, right? Why don't we go up there and talk about this."

The older woman nodded. She allowed herself to be assisted to her feet and escorted through the now-open door by Blakely and Dennis.

Silence fell on the room, then was broken by people fumbling with cups and saucers and mumbling about how it was time to leave.

Judith Dee put her hand gently on my arm. "It's very sad, isn't it? It gives one food for thought." She moved toward the door, nodding and murmuring, "Food for thought."

Chuck Nathan approached me. "I guess I should give you an apology too. I mean, about the other day out back with what's-his-name." He jerked his head in the direction of the rear of the house. "He called last night and said he agreed with me after all and wouldn't be putting any more ads on the sides of those fishing shanties." He plunged his hands in his pockets sheepishly. "I guess I get a little over-excited when it comes to the environment."

"I'm glad you two worked it all out. Etienne is a good fellow."

Good, but a bit devious. If I knew Marie's husband, he hadn't had any green epiphany; he'd just realized that the ads couldn't be read from the shore.

Kevin Shea disappeared right after Mrs. Knight left. The LaBombard contingent drifted out with courteous thanks. Thus abandoned, I began helping Hester to gather up the used cups and plates.

I was surprised when Lily Burns came alongside and began assisting me. In silence, we carried the remains of the feast into the kitchen.

Lily rinsed her hands and was drying them on a paper towel when she elected to say, "Look, I got the birthday present. It was lovely. You didn't have to do that."

I shrugged. "Old times' sake, I guess."

"Well, it was nice of you and I appreciate it." She tucked a stray blonde wisp back into place. "I've felt kind of bad about that quarrel we had."

"Me, too, Lily."

"And I want you to know that I'm prepared to forgive you."

"Forgive me?"

"Yes, I accept your apology. And I have something to tell you. I should've told you before, but—"

"What apology?" I felt icy. "I don't recall tendering an apology."

We looked at each other for a long moment.

"No, that's right, you didn't." She turned and walked crisply out of the room.

I sank into a kitchen chair and put my head down on the table, cradled in my arms.

"Amelia, I don't know what to say."

I looked up. Dennis O'Brien was standing over me with a look of such thunderous wrath, I leaned back in my chair.

He had his gloves under one arm and was buttoning his coat. "That was some stupid, idiotic stunt you and the professor pulled, and I ought to—" He clapped his lips shut and began pulling on his gloves. "I have to be somewhere right now, but this conversation isn't over, not by a long shot. Keep out of trouble until then or I will arrest you, and the chief will back me up!"

He spun around, nearly colliding with Alec, who was entering the kitchen. Dennis poked Alec in the chest with a gloved forefinger. "And that goes for you, too, pal!" And on that dramatic exit line, he left.

Alec sat down across from me. "Amelia, I accept full responsibility for this mess."

I looked over at him and sighed. It was simply impossible to stay mad with this man. Why on earth was it so easy to forgive Alec and so difficult to do the same for Lily Burns?

"No need, Alec. I went along with it. And perhaps some good did come of it all: Blakely and his stepmother are communicating now."

He pulled a checkbook from the copious pocket of his winter coat. "At least I can pay for the refreshments."

"At cost only, since I was partly responsible," I said, wearily waving my hand. "I'll have Marie send you a bill."

He replaced the checkbook and sighed. "It seemed like such a good idea."

"We should have remembered that neither of us is Hercule Poirot if indeed anyone ever was."

"Aye."

"But you know, I honestly thought that that flower had something to do with the murder on the lake."

Hester walked by, pushing an unplugged vacuum cleaner before her. "Amelia? There's somebody here to see you. I put him in Marie's office."

I hurried down the hall to Papa's old study, where I found Martin Rousseau clutching a watch cap and pacing. If it was possible, he looked even worse than when I had last seen him.

"Martin! How are—"

He grabbed my arm and said earnestly, "Miss Prentice! My boys! Have you seen 'em?"

"The boys? Oh, no. Are they gone? Are you sure?"

He scratched his jaw. "Oh, yeah, they are. I slept late this morning. When I got up, nobody was in the house. I hunted in the basement, even. They just snuck out."

"Can I be of help?"

"Just be on the lookout, okay? But keep it kind of quiet, y'know?" He quoted a phone number. "That's my cell. Just call me if you see either one of them. Tell me where they are, and I'll do the rest. If I can just get 'em back home before anybody notices . . . "

Given the boys' dramatic propensities, I had my doubts that Martin could accomplish this, but I jotted down the number on Marie's memo pad and put the paper in my pocket.

"You might be able to see everything a little better if you go up on the roof of the Sweet Shoppe building. You can take the stairs that go past the newspaper office."

I didn't suggest he consult Gil on the matter. The boys' defection was too tempting a news story.

We parted, wishing each other well. As I promised to watch for the boys, I felt a little guilty. I had purchased those corsages for them, hoping to cheer them a little. In retrospect, it was easy to see that I had only abetted their unauthorized plans to attend the festival.

It would truly be miraculous if they managed to escape the consequences of this particular breach of the rules. As I headed down the front steps of Chez Prentice, I sent up a prayer for this stressed father and his wayward boys, all the while scanning the passing crowd.

Jury Street was long and lined with large old homes built at the turn of the twentieth century. Some of the houses bore signs with Greek initials. The elaborate contest entries in their front yards told me Vern and Alec had stiff competition.

My favorite of the snow sculptures was a giant jewelry box the size of a large automobile, lying open with various brightly-colored jewels cascading out of it. The centerpiece was a necklace featuring a string of clear ice "diamonds," each as big as a man's head. An accompanying sign said, "Gamma Sorority, Gem of the Campus." So this was the Gamma house of song and story! I had seen the place many times, but had never really noticed it.

"Mrs. Dickensen!" I turned to see Melody Branch walking my way, followed by several of her sorority sisters. "Are you headed to the awards ceremony too?"

Why not? I thought. It would be as good a place as any too look for the Rousseau boys.

Melody took my arm and whispered in my ear, "Please don't breathe a word about our helping Vern. I'd be in trouble if it got out that my roommate and I worked on another sculpture!"

I nodded my compliance and changed the subject, asking about Melody's family, just as my own parents had done in ye olden days. She was the daughter of a dentist, and her mother kept the office. One brother, one sister.

She didn't seem to mind this gentle inquisition, but responded with questions of her own about Vern. I explained that his mother had died only about two years ago, he had no siblings, and his father, a retired Air Force sergeant, was a car salesman.

"There's a problem between them, I think," she said, "with the father, I mean, though he doesn't talk about it much."

"I think you may be right."

"We all have our secrets," she said cryptically, sighing, then brightened. "Here we are! Wow! Look at all that!"

Our staid, granite city hall had the giddy air of an over-dressed matron who has had a few too many cocktails. A slightly crooked welcoming banner, a twin of the one Gil and I had seen stretched over the street, spanned the roof of the portico. Two wide red carpets sprinkled with glitter ran up the broad front steps. The small light poles on either side of the stairs sported huge colorful jester's caps, and a podium bearing the city crest stood center stage.

Flanking the entrance were two impressive snow sculptures, a full-color one that recreated the nearby law library's life-size painting of the swashbuckling Samuel de Champlain and an all-white snowy depiction of the Lincoln memorial.

Melody and I found a place off to the left, where we could perch on a stone wall and see a little above the heads of the crowd. Just as the mayor and a handful of other local dignitaries strode up to the podium, someone stepped roughly between us. I teetered on the edge of the wall, but was caught around the waist by a strong arm.

"Hold on there!"

"Vern!" Melody said delightedly.

The young man in question wrapped his free arm around her and planted a quick kiss on top of her dark head. "Brr! It's cold. Get close and warm me up!"

The anxiety and a little of the anger that had haunted Vern for days was still in his eyes, but there was also a spark of pride. He nodded toward Melody.

"How do you like her?"

"She's lovely," I said sincerely, surprised that he would express himself so openly.

"Shh!" Melody cautioned. "They're starting!"

After the usual minor adjustments were made to the public address system, our distinguished District Attorney Elm DeWitt stepped up to the microphone and announced the awards, beginning with the smallest. One by one, the winner raised his gloved hand, polite applause was given, pictures were taken and one of the three costumed school mascots—a hornet, a wolf, and a bear—handed over a small, golden loving cup to the recipient.

I scanned the crowd for the missing boys, but had no luck.

As the fourth prize was awarded, Vern bent down and muttered, "Nothing so far. That means either we won big or we got nothing! The suspense is starting to get to me!"

Melody consoled him with a gentle smile and a comforting pat on the chest.

Third prize, second prize, then first prize was awarded. As this winner was handed his cup, Vern shrugged and turned around. "Ah, well. Better luck next year, eh? Come on, who's for hot chocolate? The Kiwanis Club's got a trailer across the street—"

At the same time he said these words, I heard Elm DeWitt declare in a loud voice, "And the Grand Prize Winner is . . . Chez Prentice!"

After a split second of disbelief, Melody screamed and jumped up and down. We raised our arms to be recognized and turned a confused Vern over to a huge human hornet, who led him through the crowd and up the red-carpeted steps.

As we watched happily, he accepted a large blue ribbon bearing the words, "Grand Prize Winner," which was meant to be placed on the sculpture along with a check for a presumably generous amount. Cameras flashed as the district attorney and the other judges shook Vern's hand.

Just before he left the platform, Vern leaned over to the microphone and said, "This really should go to the man behind the idea, Professor Alec Alexander, a true genius."

There was scattered applause and a bit of frowning discomfiture among the dignitaries, some of whom had openly found Alec's quest for the Lake Champlain monster to be an embarrassment. *Genius* was hardly the word they'd used to describe him.

The awards ceremony concluded. Vern descended the stairs, along with the hornet mascot and a reporter from the newspaper.

"Come on. We're going to the B&B to take pictures!"

Melody joined him and beckoned to me, but I smiled and shook my head. The chill between Vern and me wasn't just from the cold air, and besides, I had hunting to do.

The small, happy throng headed off in the direction of Jury Street. I watched them go, smiling. Melody seemed to be a sweet-natured and perceptive young woman, and I could tell Vern was fond of her. This relationship definitely had possibilities.

Not if he goes to jail, it won't.

Where had that thought come from? Obviously, my mind was voicing the fears that had dogged me for the past few days.

At this thought, I halted in my tracks, and someone bumped forcibly into me from behind. "Excuse me!" I turned to assure them that I was unhurt.

"Miss Prentice!" a child's voice rang out.

"It's Mrs. Dickensen, sweetie," Dorothy O'Brien corrected her daughter, "Remember the wedding you were in?" Meaghan had been my flower girl.

Dennis was justifiably proud of those he called his two girls. They made a most attractive mother-daughter pair, with their freckled cheeks pink from the cold and bright red curls peeking out from under identical colorful stocking caps.

Meaghan's mittened hand held a festival program. "We're going to the pancake fling. I'm gonna throw pancakes like they're frisbees. Daddy taught me how. Wanna come with us?"

Before I could accept or decline, Dorothy said, "I heard that Chez Prentice won the top prize. Congratulations!" She grinned.

"Con-go-lations!" Meaghan echoed.

"Thanks, but it was all the work of Vern and the professor. They're the ones who built the sculpture. Meaghan, dear, I'm afraid I can't come with you right now," I told the child.

Come to think of it, where had Alec gone? He would have been a lot of help in the search for the Rousseau boys.

Meaghan spent no time on regrets, only tugged at her mother's sleeve. "Come on, Mommy, we're going to be late!"

A frightful thought occurred to me. "Dorothy, where's Dennis? He said he had to be someplace right away." The image of Dennis encountering one or more of the Rousseau boys in this crowd made me shudder.

Dorothy rolled her eyes. "He promised to help with the snowshoe race. We get him back when he's finished there."

"Mommy! Come on!"

With an apologetic smile, Dorothy allowed herself to be pulled toward the elementary school.

"The snowshoe race," I repeated, consulted the tiny map on the festival brochure, and struck out in the proper direction. If I could head the boys off at the pass, so to speak, and get them to return home, perhaps I could keep circumstances from further ruining Dennis' day off.

The race's venue, the high school track, was located down a steep incline behind the main school building. Despite the salt and sand that had been lavished on the sidewalk, it was risky going until I arrived at the scene of the snowshoe race.

Half a block ahead of me, a stocky middle-aged man slid into a handily placed snowdrift. When he recovered, slapping snow off his coat and replacing his expensive hat, I recognized Kevin Shea, sponsor of the race. He looked around to see if anyone had seen the mishap, and I tactfully pretended to be pawing through my satchel. He made rapid progress after that, and by the time I reached the ticket stand, he was at the race's starting point, directing his employees to assist the young entrants with their footwear.

"Hi, Mrs. Dickensen!" The ticket-seller, Hardy Patchke, took my admission fee and filled me in on how the race was to work. "There's gonna be three heats, for the different age groups. If somebody doesn't have snowshoes, Shea's Sporting Goods'll loan out used ones." He handed me my change. "The first race is for eight- and nine-year-olds."

I hastened to the small metal bleachers along the track and climbed several levels in order to get a good view of the track. The seats were cold and a chill had soon numbed my hindquarters.

Rummaging in my bag, I found the tiny cell phone and pressed the appropriate buttons to call Alec.

"Hello, this is Alec Alexander. I'd be grateful if you'd leave a message."

I sighed with frustration and glanced around to see who might be listening, then, cupping my hands to keep out the ambient noise, I waited for the beep and said, "Alec, there have been complications. The two subjects are out. If you encounter either subject, please make sure they go home right away. I don't have to tell you what the consequences could be if they are, um, apprehended. Call me for more details, please."

I snapped the little phone shut and looked around again. Nobody had paid the slightest attention to me. They were all too busy cheering on their favorites.

I stared at the proceedings. It was hard to determine the identities of the various adults who occupied positions along the large oval track. There was a variety of heavy parkas, plaid woolen lumberjack coats, and dark overcoats, not to mention hats of every imaginable form: Russian-style ushankas with fur-lined flaps, whimsical long-tailed stocking caps, and one or two of those Alpine hats that always seemed to be adorned with shaving brushes.

At last I spotted the tallish hatless figure near the finish line, and when he characteristically lifted his hand to brush his hair back, I knew for sure it was Dennis. He never wore a hat, even in winter, trusting in the thickness of his dark blond hair to keep his head warm.

"Everyone to your places!" Kevin Shea announced through a bullhorn. "On your marks!" they chanted, and the crowd joined in, "Get set!" I looked over to see Brigid Shea with her hand held high in the air. "Go!"

A gunshot sent a jolt through the group. Cheers went up and the race was on.

I watched as Mrs. Shea thrust the small starting pistol into her purse and turned a painted-on smile to the crowd. If Kevin Shea was indeed elected mayor—and it was a distinct possibility—that would make Brigid First Lady of our town, not a thought that I relished. As if she sensed my negative thought waves, she whispered in her husband's ear, descended the stairs of the platform and disappeared into the crowd.

The young racers, mostly little boys, set off gamely, using a curious foot-lifting gait, aided by short, kid-length ski poles. These were not the snowshoes depicted in cartoons, which resemble tennis rackets.

Today's snowshoes were smaller, lighter, and scientifically designed to work with the walker's foot to move him swiftly over the surface of the snow. They ranged in price from $39.95 to $199 and could be obtained at a fantastic discount at Shea's Quality Sporting Goods if the customer produced a ticket stub. Or so Kevin Shea announced to the crowd with his bullhorn.

The adults stationed around the track, I soon learned, were there to help those who fell over and also to ensure against tussles among the participants. As the crowd shouted encouragement, I watched Dennis O'Brien pull apart two over-zealous racers and send them on their way.

Moments later, to my surprise, I spotted Brigid Shea at Dennis' elbow. Clearly annoyed at the interruption, he frowned and bent to hear something she spoke into his ear. He gestured into the distance; she nodded and melted into the crowd.

My seat was becoming unbearably cold, so I edged my way past the enthusiastic parents to the ground level. "How long does this event take?" I asked Hardy at the entrance.

He shrugged. "Mr. Shea told me to stay two hours."

"Will you be racing in the teen division?" I asked, and immediately regretted my words.

Hardy's usually cheerful face registered a second of chagrin. "Nope, my asthma, remember?"

"Of course." It must be frustrating for an active, enthusiastic boy to be sidelined in such a way, and I had made it worse with my tactlessness.

"Hey, it's okay. I'm making some money doing this, y'know."

"For your college fund, no doubt."

He grinned. "Nope, games for my Play Station. You leaving? Here." He grabbed my hand, pulled back part of my glove and stamped the skin with a Shea's logo. "You can come back in if you show this."

I feigned gratitude, but now that I was sure that Dennis and the Rousseau boys probably wouldn't be within fifty feet of one another for the next two hours, there was no need for me to sit shivering amid this cheering throng.

I bid Hardy farewell and headed back up the hill to continue my search for the runaways. And, incidentally, to find a restroom.

Chapter | Twenty-eight

I passed the movie-theatre parking lot, where the various bands had gathered. It would be the starting and ending point of the parade. The young band members, thickly bundled in their particular school band uniforms, looked cold, nonetheless.

They were tuning up with a variety of drumbeats, clarinet scales, and trumpet flourishes. It was a sound that had always given me a sense of pleased anticipation. I knew that they were looking forward to the moment they could get marching. Their breaths came out in clouds. I shivered for them and waved. A few waved back.

But right now I had something else on my mind. It was getting urgent now, the need to find a restroom. There were numerous bright orange portable toilets in three strategic spots around the downtown area, but the nausea that had become my constant companion warned me that I'd pay dearly if I didn't find a pristine, relatively scentless place to do my business.

"Well, the Old Episcopal it is," I muttered grimly and continued my walk, swimming upstream, as it were, against a tide of happy festival-goers lining up four deep along the sidewalk, waiting for the parade.

I'd never actually been in the restrooms at this church, but I had attended several ecumenical chapel services and had a sketchy knowledge of the floor plan.

As I went, a variety of different smells—funnel cake, flap-jacks with maple syrup, Italian meatball sandwiches—mingled with the chilly gusts and tempted my taste buds, but the rest of my body was insistent. I must get to a toilet, and soon!

When I crossed the memorial square in front of the church, the crowd had thinned a little, and I took a short cut, as I frequently did, through the adjacent old graveyard that dated back to before the Revolutionary War. This time, the names and dates had an added poignancy for me with small headstones lined up next to larger ones. Parents lost so many children in those days, mostly to disease. I paused and said a prayer. I was so very thankful that I lived in an age where my baby would be far less likely to suffer the fate of, say, little Matthew Revere Ramsey, dead at the age of only 12 days. "Suffer the little children," the stone read—

Matthew Ramsey?

This was important, I knew, but before I went to Alec—or to Dennis—with this information, I really, really had to go to the bathroom.

Hastily, and a little bit sheepishly—I wasn't really a festi-val volunteer, after all—I went up the steps of the church and through the heavy, carved wooden doors.

The granite-floored narthex was quiet as I entered and the doors to the sanctuary were closed and locked. I stomped a bit to shake the snow off my boots. The smell here was of candle wax and the faint moldy fragrance so common in old buildings. My steps echoed as I followed the hallway around to the left where a small sign indicated the bell tower, church offices and restrooms.

The door leading to the bell tower was next to the room marked "Ladies." With a sigh of relief, I pushed through the door.

A good deal of the church's renovation had been accomplished, but the restrooms had clearly been saved for last. Though the floors had been recently mopped and the room smelled of lemon cleaner, the sinks were old and stained, the light switch was the antique push button kind, and a large eyelet latch reinforced the shaky doorknob.

A woman was peering intently into the cracked mirror as she applied lipstick. An array of cosmetics occupied the small shelf over the sink. Brigid Shea scowled at my reflection in the mirror and snapped, "What're you doing here?"

"I—uh—using the restroom, like you." I said, and hurried into a stall furthest away. *Neither of us is a festival worker, Mrs. Shea*, I thought, *so we're both guilty of trespassing.*

The lock on the stall door was no longer there, but with some effort, I managed to persuade it to stand open only a few inches and afford the required privacy.

I had flushed the toilet and was making ready to emerge when I heard Brigid Shea say, "You aren't supposed to be in here!"

I opened my mouth to respond, but closed it when a male voice answered, "Don't you worry about that!"

"This is the ladies' room! What are you doing? Why did you lock the door?"

The man's voice was a half whisper, but I thought it sounded familiar. "I need to talk to you about what happened on the lake."

Brigid's voice wavered. "On the lake? Wh-what do you mean?"

"You know precisely what I mean. You came up with the idea of making the drop in that stupid tent and that gave the kid the idea he could stiff me."

There was cold menace in the man's voice, and cold fear in Brigid's. "S-stiff you? What are you talking about?"

Clutching my satchel to my chest, I backed into the back corner of the stall. Maybe he wouldn't notice that I was there. Maybe Brigid had forgotten.

"Cut the dumb act, Mrs. Shea. It's over. I'm closing down here and winding up unfinished business." He spoke her name with contempt.

"You're the contact? You?"

"You seem surprised." He chuckled, and in that moment, I suppressed a gasp.

I knew who it was.

Brigid began to chatter, "I—I had no idea. Matt never told me who it was. He just said it was somebody local. He's dead; Matt, I mean. It was in the papers."

"I knew it was you on that hill with binoculars. They flashed in the sun, you know." He laughed. "I must hand it to you, Mrs. Shea, you don't scare easily!"

"Was that you whispering on the phone?"

"What did you say to O'Brien back there?"

"What?"

"Were you telling him about the CDs, huh? Did you think they'd help you?"

"No, of course not. I—um—I just asked him if his daughter was in the snowshoe race." Her next words were a shout. "Hey! Get out of my purse! You can't have that! It's—" I heard grunting and heavy breathing and the sound of a blow. Brigid whimpered.

"This'll have to do," he said. "Come on, we're going someplace else, where we won't be disturbed."

"But that's—"

I heard another blow.

At that same moment, in the midst of a thick cloud of fear, something happened deep inside me. My hatred—and I could admit it now, it had been hatred—for Brigid Shea dissolved and was replaced by an intense pity and a desire to help her.

Please, I prayed, *please help her! Or show me how!*

The pipes gurgled in the wall behind me. Apparently, someone was using the men's room next door.

"Hey, is there anybody else in here?" Brigid's tormentor asked, and I heard his steps come closer.

Brigid's voice was barely a squeak. "No, nope, just me. Honest."

My eyes widened. Was the woman actually trying to protect me?

The outer door to the restroom rattled and a young girl's voice called, "Hey, no fair! The ladies' room's locked!"

Brigid gave a muffled whimper.

"Shhh!"

The three of us waited, listening, for several minutes.

"They're gone. Come on," he said finally, and I heard the latch being undone.

As soon as they're out the door, I'll run for help. Or use my cell phone to call 911.

At the same time I had the thought, a faint but lilting tune echoed throughout the high-ceilinged room:

> *Maxwellton's braes are bonnie*
> > *Where early fa's the dew*
> *And it's there that Annie Laurie*
> > *Gave me her promise true . . .*

Even as I retrieved the tiny telephone, opened and snapped it shut again, I heard the scrambling sound of footsteps.

The stall door swung open.

"Why, hello, Mrs. Dickensen," Blakely Knight said pleasantly, "Fancy meeting you here."

Chapter | Twenty-nine

"Blakely Knight, just exactly what is going on here?" I asked in my stern teacher voice.

He made a rather fearsome sight, with one arm wrapped tightly around Brigid's neck and the other holding a tiny pistol pressed into her cheek. A trickle of blood ran from her mouth and down her chin.

My attempt at playing the outraged authority didn't fool him for a second. "Come on, now, Amelia. You're an intelligent woman, and I would imagine that from what you just heard you've surmised exactly what's going on."

He let go of Brigid with a shove, and she staggered back a few paces but didn't fall. He then turned and relocked the restroom door.

Frowning pensively, he fingered the barrel of the pistol and murmured, "Change of plan."

Shakily, Brigid went over to the sink. Moving automatically, she dampened a paper towel and wiped the blood from her mouth. As if in a daze, she retrieved her purse from the floor beneath the sink and began quietly dropping cosmetics in it.

Stop that, I thought, *you're removing the clues that show you were here!*

Obviously, Brigid wasn't thinking strategically. I'd have to do the thinking for both of us.

All at once, Blakely seemed to make a decision. "Okay, I got it. Come on, you two." He grabbed Brigid by the elbow and rammed the gun against her side.

"We're leaving," he told me. "You go out there and see if anybody's out there. And Amelia, if you do or say anything out of line, I'll blow out her ribcage, right through her coat. Now, unlock the door and do exactly as I say."

With shaking hands, I complied and pulled the door open.

As I stepped into the dim and chilly hallway, I was surprised to see two figures twined tightly together, only a few feet away, standing next to the door to the bell tower. It was J.T. Rousseau and Crystal Gervais, exchanging a passionate kiss.

I couldn't help myself. "Really!" I exclaimed, reflexively, "Necking in a church!"

The two sprung apart, wide-eyed.

For the moment, I forgot that Blakely and Brigid were hiding behind the restroom door. I was in full angry teacher mode.

"J.T. Rousseau, you're in big trouble! Your father is looking all over town for you!" Fortunately, my senses returned suddenly. "In fact," I added with a deep breath and an unspoken prayer, "everybody is looking for you: Vern, Mrs. Dee, Mr. Berghauser, and even Mr. O'Secoor."

Grabbing Crystal's hand, J.T. looked abashed, then his eyes widened. "Even Mr. O'Secoor? Oh, gosh, Miss Prentice, thanks for telling me! C'mon, Crystal."

In a twinkling, they had left, and Blakely emerged with his hostage. Strangely, he didn't seem displeased with me. He even chuckled.

"Just can't stop being a teacher, can you, Amelia?"

I shouldn't have, but I couldn't help myself. I said, "No, but apparently you can."

His voice changed to a growl. "Turn left and go through that door. Get going, up the stairs. We're going to take a look at the bell tower."

To my surprise, the door to the bell tower opened easily. The doorknob was loose, and it was apparently impossible to lock. *They'd better do something about that broken lock,* I thought absently. *They could get sued. Attractive nuisance, they call it.* As I pulled open the door, a bitter cold breeze blew into our faces.

"Go on," Blakely urged, gesturing with the gun.

It was a small one, but I had seen small guns fired before and knew they could have relatively long range and do a good deal of damage.

The stairs in the bell tower proved to be the twisting Gothic type. Blakely paused for a moment, regarding them.

"Okay," he said, gesturing with the pistol, "up the stairs, and stay where I can see you at all times. You first, Amelia."

It was strange, mounting these stairs for the first time under these circumstances. I'd always wanted to go up here. How many times in my childhood had I heard the sound of the Old Episcopal Church bell, calling worshippers to services or tolling the hour? It had been a local joke when I was a girl that the Old Episcopal bell was usually two minutes early, or rather the bell ringer was. The bell didn't ring these days. The bell ringer had retired, the bell itself had been sent away for restoration, and the tower was waiting to be renovated.

I took the first few steps slowly, trying to think, well aware of the incongruity of the situation. If I had some kind of weapon, a piece of wood or a rock, perhaps I could hit Blakely with it as he rounded the curve. But he had threatened to shoot Brigid if I misbehaved, so I discarded the ambush idea.

Words were my strong suit. Perhaps talking would help matters.

"Blakely," I said, "what on earth do you think you're doing? You're jeopardizing your career, your life, even the life of your father."

Blakely snorted. "Yeah, right, my ever-loving dad. Where does he get off, expecting me to come to his rescue?"

"So you're not going to give him your kidney?" I brushed the cold stone walls with one hand. If I were to stumble backwards, could I cause Blakely to fall down the steps? The problem was Brigid, who was between us, shivering visibly as she climbed. And of course there was no guarantee I wouldn't injure myself in the fall as well.

"Oh, Lissy thinks I'm going to be tested. We had such a touching reunion back there. She even apologized, as if that made up for everything." His tone changed, hardened. "Not that it's any of your business. Keep moving!"

Brigid whimpered again. He must have prodded her, poor thing. It surprised me how protective I felt of this poor woman who had so infuriated me in the past.

We arrived at a landing halfway up the tower. Blakely, panting, said roughly, "Stop here." He leaned against the wall, breathing hard.

As we stood shivering, watching Blakely catch his breath, I asked, "Brigid, how on earth did you get involved in all this?"

Her answer was low, almost whispered. "I don't know. We needed money for the campaign, and Matt knew a way to make some. He was such a smart boy."

Blakely snapped, "Matt? Don't make me laugh! He was just the computer nerd, not the one taking all the chances."

A remnant of Brigid's feistiness seemed to return. "He made the discs, didn't he? And I saw that they got to you, didn't I?"

"Yeah, right. You were so subtle, keeping them right there in your store so that Rousseau kid thought they were music and offered to buy them from you. That was real smooth, Bridge, real smooth. Then you made it even worse by firing the kid."

"But I came up with another idea," she said. In a strange way, she seemed to want some modicum of credit for the outrageous scheme.

Blakely's voice was dripping venom. He gave Brigid a look of pure hatred and chanted, "Oh, right, making a drop, in a tent, on the lake in a converted lunchbox. Wow, how could I forget? Was it your idea or Matt's to keep the discs and sell them yourself?"

"But we didn't keep them! He left them in the tent! It was those two kids—they got the lunchbox."

"What?" He seemed genuinely confused. "What kids?"

"The two boys they arrested," Brigid said desperately, "they stole the lunchbox! I saw them do it!"

All color seemed to drain from Blakely's face. "Somebody stole—then Matt—"

Now Brigid's face registered contempt. "He told you the truth, and you killed him."

Chapter | Thirty

As Blakely and I stood staring mutely at Brigid, my mind was racing. Was this my chance to escape?

I analyzed my options: I would have to step, or leap, over Brigid to go back down the stairs, a risky undertaking at best. And I surmised that there was no real exit at the top of the tower, so running up the stairs wouldn't do me any good. All I could do was bide my time and pray that J.T. had contacted the police by now. Or would he?

Blakely's moment of hesitation had passed. "Come on!" he barked. "Get going, you two!" He gestured upward with the gun.

Slowly Brigid regained her footing, her purse still dangling from her crooked elbow as if she was on her way to go grocery shopping. It was a remarkable transformation. She was once again the arrogant Mrs. Shea, future mayor's wife. Her shoulders straightened and with her free hand, she took hold of the railing and took a step.

We resumed climbing.

I had faced death once before, and when it seemed imminent, I had accepted my fate, secure in my faith and willing to concede that my life had come to an end.

This time was different. It was no longer just me. It was Gil and the little person I carried within me. This time, I was going to fight in whatever way I could.

Years ago, as teenagers, Lily and I had discussed self-defense. She had read an article.

"It's simple," she'd said, "You just kick 'em where it hurts the most." We giggled, a little embarrassed at our ribaldry. Now I considered the possibility.

If Blakely was determined to kill me, I would resist with everything that was in me. In the meantime, however, I decided to try to reason with him.

"Blakely, you can't possibly get away with, um, harming us. You'll be caught immediately. Why not just leave us here and make your escape now, while you can?"

He actually chuckled. "Nice try, Amelia, but you forget that nobody has seen me here. I made sure of that. And you got rid of those kids for me, thank you very much."

We reached the top step and stepped though an open door into a small, hexagonal room, with windows on every side. The windows had no glass in them, only angled wooden slats, through which we could hear the sounds of a crowd cheering.

The parade must have begun, I thought, *but I don't hear the music.*

The wood of the slats was rotten with age. Some sagged; some were gone altogether. Cold gusts blew between them, refrigerating the room. As I had expected, there was no bell in the tower, just the old wooden yoke where one had hung and a small hole in the floor where the pull rope had reached down to the bottom floor.

"Over there, Amelia." Blakely gestured with the gun across the room, some ten feet away, while he took tight hold of Brigid's elbow.

The room was empty; there was no place to hide. I obeyed, praying inwardly, *Give me an opening, a chance, anything.*

"Here's how it's going down," Blakely said in a conversational voice. "Everybody in town knows you two women hate each other. You got in an argument up here in the tower, and Brigid shot you. Come over here, Brigid." He jerked her to his side and tried to force her hand around the gun.

"No!" Brigid yelled, struggling, "No way I'm shooting a pregnant woman. D'you think I want to go to hell? Do it yourself!"

"Pregnant?" Blakely looked utterly dumbfounded.

"How did you know?" I demanded at the same moment.

Brigid backed away from Blakely while she answered me. "Are you kidding? It's all over school that you barfed on the principal's desk. You signed up for childbirth classes. One of the Gervais girls saw you. And—"

"Interesting, even tragic," Blakely interrupted sharply, once again asserting himself, "but not relevant to the matter at hand. Never mind, Brigid, I'll do it. My plan still holds. Your fingerprints are all over this gun and mine, as you can see, are not." He indicated his leather-gloved hands.

"So long, Amelia," he said suddenly, and fired straight at me from across the room. I hadn't time to react at all. I barely had time to close my eyes as the report echoed against the stone walls.

I flinched, but felt no pain. Another shot rang out. I flinched again, but again, nothing.

Blakely's expression registered utter astonishment. "What's wrong with this gun—Arghhhh!" There was a crashing sound, and splinters of wood flew through the air. A hand and sturdy arm, coming from outside the tower, had punched through the rotten slats and had a grip on Blakely's hand.

As Brigid and I watched, Blakely and the anonymous hand struggled for possession of the gun.

A split second later, exchanging significant glances, we two women realized that our chance had come, and Brigid hastened forward to enthusiastically administer Lily Burns's version of self-defense.

Chapter | Thirty-one

"We've got to stop meeting like this. Hold still, iss-May—but you're married now, aren't you? It's not iss-May any more, is it?" My former student Toby House wrapped a blood pressure cuff around my upper arm and began pumping it up. "Be quiet, please."

He looked at his watch. Even when using the playful pig Latin I had introduced to my classes, Toby, a paramedic, was all business with regard to matters medical.

We were in an ambulance parked in front of the Old Episcopal Church, Brigid Shea and I. The groaning and incapacitated Blakely Knight had been whisked away—under guard—to the hospital in another one.

Brigid winced as another paramedic treated her swollen split lip and bruised cheek. "Ouch!" she said as he dabbed on antiseptic with a gauze pad. "What Blakely said up there was all bull, you know."

"Really?" I didn't believe her.

Toby gave me a stern look. I was sitting on one of the two ambulance cots, and he was holding my wrist, taking my pulse.

"Totally. He's nuts—you can see that. The way he treated us? You know, you weren't in very much danger, but I was."

She sat still as the paramedic finished with a butterfly bandage at the end of her mouth, pressed a cold pack to her cheek, and moved away.

"What do you mean?" I asked and was again shushed by Toby.

"He used my starter's pistol, the idiot. It's usually really dangerous only up close. Like that guy—the one on TV? He was just fooling around, holding it to his head, and it killed him. Stuff comes out of the gun, even if it's not loaded with bullets, and it can get you if you're close enough. But you were all the way across the room. Blakely must not know much about guns."

I remembered that night at the Lion's Roar and Blakely's casual answer to Gil's question: *I'm afraid I'm not much for the great outdoors; hunting, fishing, none of that.*

Toby took off the cuff. "You're okay. You didn't sustain any trauma, but you need to see Dr. Stout to check out the little guy, just to be on the safe side, okay?"

I'd told him of the pregnancy. It was apparently a matter of public knowledge, anyway.

He patted my shoulder. "'Appy-Hay 'aby-Bay."

Toby was one of my all-time favorite students, but don't tell anyone.

"Thank you, 'oby-Tay."

He turned to Brigid. "Mrs. Shea, you sit here and keep that cold pack on your face while we let the painkiller kick in, okay?"

She nodded. He climbed out of the ambulance and began to consult with the other paramedic.

I had another question for her. "Why didn't you tell him I was there, back in the restroom?"

"I figured you'd go for help."

"Oh."

Abruptly, Brigid put down the ice pack, retrieved her purse, and announced to me, "I'm feeling much better now. I need to get going."

As she climbed down out of the ambulance, Police Sergeant Dennis O'Brien met her. "Mrs. Shea, we have some questions for you," he said firmly. "Please come along." He turned a stern look at me and raised his voice slightly. "And I'll want to talk to you, too, Mrs. Dickensen."

"All right, Sergeant," I said meekly. Poor Dennis, despite all my efforts we'd ruined his day off.

I sat there, amid the hubbub of the crowd, thinking about what had happened.

You answered my prayer, didn't you? You really did.

I couldn't think of strong enough words to express my gratitude. I closed my eyes.

"That was pretty cool, signaling me with the French like that," J.T. Rousseau said softly as he and Crystal Gervais crept into the ambulance, glancing over their shoulders. "You were right about it coming in handy!"

"Thanks, J.T.," I said. "And thank you for what you did. But you took a terrible risk, climbing the church tower. Why didn't you just go to the police?"

The two young people exchanged glances. "Are you kidding? Think they'd believe me? They were having a cow down on the ground while I was climbing. The cops were waiting at the bottom to arrest me when all of a sudden they heard those shots. Everybody ran upstairs and forgot about me—for now. We don't want to miss that dance tonight, so we gotta run. *Au revoir!*" The two disappeared around the corner of the ambulance.

"Wait, you're going to be—" I began, and sighed. There would be repercussions, no doubt, but it would probably all come out in the wash, as Martin Rousseau had said.

I exited the ambulance, feeling quite brave and sane and was re-buttoning my coat when I was suddenly engulfed in an embrace.

"Amelia! Oh, thank God! What happened?" Before I could answer, Gil hugged me tight again. "Oh, never mind, you can tell me later. Oh, if anything had happened to you!"

We looked into each other's eyes. I crumpled in his arms and began to sob.

Gil knew the routine. He let me go on until I was a hic-coughing, nose-running mess. Then, proffering a handkerchief, he guided me over to Mann's Drugstore, just down the street. He deposited me in a booth at the snack bar, ordered hot chocolate and a toasted cheese sandwich, took my hand across the table and held it tenderly.

"Got to keep your strength up. After all, you're eating for two."

My nose was stopped up. "You doh?" I asked.

He nodded. "Um, hm."

"But how?"

He sighed. "Honey, I'm a newsman. Don't you think I know the symptoms? Don't you think I hear the local gossip?"

He beckoned me closer. "I'll bet I know something you don't: The rumor is that ours was a shotgun wedding!" He laughed heartily, and I joined him after a fashion, as I dabbed the last of the tears from my cheeks. Gil added, "Seriously, I wanted to let you tell me in your own time."

I stroked his hand and smiled. I whispered, "Gil, we're going to have a baby."

He grinned. "I doh."

I made quotation marks with my fingers. "What about, 'Here's to things staying just the way they are,' cross your heart and hope to spit?"

He made the same gesture and quoted, "I have learned, in whatsoever state I am, therewith to be content."

"That's from Philippians. Gil, you've been reading the Bible!" He had only recently begun going to church with me.

He shrugged. "Don't make a big deal out of it. It just seemed appropriate."

"What about, 'no fuss, no muss, no crying and messy diapers'?"

"Hey, I knew that was what you needed to hear at the time. But that diaper stuff comes with the territory doesn't it? In life, you take the stinky with the sweet." He sighed. "You know, it is kind of miraculous. I feel like one of those old geezers in the Bible, having a kid at my age."

"You're hardly a geezer."

'That's not what Vern's going to say."

"Will he ever forgive us for turning in the lunchbox?"

Gil reached across the table, grabbed the pickle from my plate and took a bite. "Sure, eventually. Besides, what's to forgive? We did the right thing."

"He says it has something to do with respect."

He signaled for the check. "Yeah, well, that's a two-way street, you know, but enough about Vern." He looked at his watch. "Do you feel up to watching a parade?"

The ice festival parade was delayed only a half-hour and it did our community proud. To my surprise, there was very little to indicate that a crime had taken place in the vicinity, only some yellow police tape at the entrance to the church and a police car parked in front. We could see this from our vantage point, cuddled close together on the roof of the newspaper building, three stories above the ground. Judging by the cheery mood of the crowd, word of the showdown in the church tower hadn't spread very far yet.

Marching with youthful enthusiasm were three high school bands and one from the college, the aforementioned assortment of costumed team mascots, some ingeniously designed floats and open cars, showcasing female festival royalty waving gloved hands at their subjects. The Flowers by Nathan float featured banks of multicolored mums and the Maple Syrup Queen.

"Look who's coming." Gil pointed in the direction of yet another open car festooned with decorations and a sign saying, "Grand Prize Snow Sculpture."

In the car rode Vern and Alec, waving merrily. Alec happened to look up, spotted us above them and reached in his pocket. Vern looked up, too, and gave a vague wave in our direction, before returning his attention to the crowd.

In a matter of seconds, the now-familiar theme of "Bonnie Annie Laurie" played in my coat pocket. I answered it.

"Where've ye been?" Alec asked accusingly, "I got your message and tried to call." I could hear the stereo rattle of drums echoing in the background.

"I know you did. I was busy at the time."

Even at a distance, I could make out Alec's stern expression. "Please try not allow distractions to make your eye stray from the goal. Need I remind you, Amelia, of the seriousness of our mission?"

I laughed. "No, you needn't remind me, Alec but as I said in the phone message, there've been a number of developments. Just enjoy the parade. I'll fill you in later."

Alec gave me a puzzled look as he was carried past us in the parade car. "Will do," he said into the telephone and hung up.

Chapter | Thirty-two

Gil and I didn't go to the ice dance. We had too much to talk about, too much planning to do, so we headed home.

"Have you thought about any names?" Gil asked as we drove.

"A little. It's a rather awe-inspiring task, giving someone a name that he'll carry for a lifetime."

"When you put it that way, yeah. But I already came up with some."

"You have?"

Gil grinned. "Margaret Bourke White Dickensen if it's a girl and Edward R. Morrow Dickensen if it's a boy."

I laughed. "I see a theme forming, but I'm not sure I can go along with it."

"Oh, really? Tell me you haven't thought about something from literature, like Charles Dickens or Scarlett O' Hara or maybe Edgar Allen Dickensen. Am I right; huh, am I?"

I was spared further kidding by the buzz of Gil's cell phone.

"Dickensen. Yes, she's with me. We're headed home. Oh, you did?" Gil glanced over at me. "She's pretty worn out. How about tomorrow at the B&B? All right, she'll be there." He snapped the phone shut. "You are to meet Dennis at Chez Prentice right after lunch tomorrow, no ifs, ands or buts."

"Oh, I forgot all about him!"

"They say you get a little soft in the head when you're pregnant."

I answered that with a good, juicy Bronx cheer, a conversational tool that Lily Burns had taught me years ago.

Dennis ran his fingers through his hair for the fourth time. "And that's everything you know? Absolutely everything?"

His tone was annoying. "Yes, Dennis, I haven't held anything back. Now I have a few questions for you."

We were in the office at Chez Prentice with a plate of Hester's oatmeal raisin cookies between us. Dennis had only partially consumed a cup of coffee, and I had just drained my glass of milk. The environment was cozy, even if the subject wasn't.

Dennis certainly lacked his usual congeniality. He snapped his memo pad shut, clicked his pen, and pocketed them both. He took another sip of his coffee.

"I can't promise I'll be able to answer, but fire away."

"What happens to J.T. and Dustin?"

Dennis sighed. "Amelia, things are very, very complicated."

My mouth dropped open. "You mean they're still suspects?"

"I'm afraid so. The DA thinks they may have been part of the CD scheme with Matthew Ramsey."

"But he fired on them! You found Matt's gun in the tent. Wouldn't that prove they weren't in on it if they found the bullet?"

"Maybe, maybe not, but Amelia, there's no evidence of a bullet. We searched the car."

"But what about Blakely? I just told you what happened, what he said!"

"Both Knight and Mrs. Shea have lawyered up. We don't have a lot of evidence that implicates them in this CD thing."

"It's just my word against theirs," I said resignedly.

Dennis sounded slightly more sympathetic. "That's right, but cheer up. Knight's definitely going to be indicted for kidnapping and maybe attempted murder."

"And Vern?"

"Since he's cooperating and agreed to testify about how he got that lunchbox, he's pretty much in the clear."

I took a deep breath. "Well, that's a relief, at least. Thanks, Dennis."

He stood, and I did, too. He pulled on his coat and I walked him to the front door.

"Don't go throwing any more suspect brunches, please," he told me with a hint of his old twinkle.

He reached for the doorknob, but suddenly, I remembered another thing.

"Dennis, yesterday as I was walking through the Old Episcopal graveyard, I found something strange." I told him about seeing the tombstone of little Matthew Revere Ramsey and concluded by saying, "He died in 1781, at the age of 12 days."

Dennis nodded. "A stolen identity; makes sense. It was his stock in trade. So this dead man is the one calling himself Matthew Ramsey, after all, as well as being—well, a certain rather important name that came up on our AFIS search. We'll have to talk to the girlfriend, maybe get her to ID the body. We may be calling in Homeland Security on this."

He jotted Yvonne's name and her parents' address in his notebook. "Thanks, Amelia."

I leaned against the door for some time after Dennis left. *Poor Yvonne. Her nightmare with Matt isn't quite over yet.* It was a blessing that she had her parents for support.

Though Gil and I had tried to keep this Sunday as normal as possible by attending church and having lunch in town, things still seemed out of joint.

Vern was still rooming at the B&B and keeping his distance, Lily was still on the outs with me, I hadn't seen the professor since the parade, and with all the new information coming out about the crime on the lake, Gil was swamped at the newspaper.

I wandered into the kitchen in search of company. "May I help you with that?" I asked Hester. She was sorting and folding clean towels on the kitchen table.

"Sure thing. Sit here and do the washcloths. You look kind of dragged out, if you don't mind my saying so. Of course, it's easy to understand, what with the baby and this church tower thing and all."

I pulled several cloths from the overloaded laundry basket. "I guess so."

Hester's face brightened. "Say, d'you want to hear some-thing?"

I gazed at her warily and put a folded washcloth on the stack. "Maybe."

"Mrs. Daye checked out this morning, and—"

"That poor woman! Blakely was a wretch to lead her on like that."

"Sure he was, but listen: Somebody else volunteered to be tested!"

"For the kidney? Really? Who?"

She folded another towel into thirds vertically, then in half and half again. "Don't you mean whom? I mean the grammar and all?" She plopped it on the stack of towels.

I shook my head and laughed for the first time that day. "No, Hester, who is correct in this case."

She rose and gathered the tower of towels into her arms. "Well, if you're sure. Excuse me, I gotta get these upstairs. I'll be heading home as soon as I'm done." She moved toward the hall.

"But Hester, who was it?"

She stopped and turned around. "Oh, yeah. I don't know. This Mrs. Daye, Knight, whatever; she didn't say."

I was folding the last washcloth when I head the front door open and the professor's voice say, "Come on, now. Don't be a ninny. You promised you'd do this."

I hurried into the drafty hallway. "Alec? And, um, Lily?" This was a real surprise.

Lily Burns was carrying some kind of luggage and seemed hesitant to meet my gaze.

Alec nudged her with his elbow. "Go on, dear, tell her."

"Tell me what?"

Abruptly, Lily put the case she was carrying in my arms. "Here. Be careful there; hold it level. He's skittish in that thing. Hates it, actually." Her tone was sullen.

"He?"

I took a closer look at the case. There was a little window in the side and small round holes in the top.

"Sam? Is that you?" I hurried over to a table in the front sitting room, set the case down carefully and stroked the cat's soft fur through one of the holes with my finger. "Oh, Lily, you found him! How can I thank you?"

Alec said again, "Go on, dear, tell her."

Lily heaved a huge sigh. "I didn't find him, Amelia. I mean, I did find him, but it was in December, right after you left on your honeymoon."

I sat down, frowning. I was having trouble processing this information.

"He came to me, Amelia. He turned up on my back doorstep one night, shivering and hungry. You were out of town, so of course, I took him in."

"Of course," I repeated vaguely. Something was nagging at my memory: a tuft of gray.

"Well, I was going to tell you about him when I, you know, called you that time, but we argued and, well, I—didn't." She clamped her mouth closed and her pretty face took on that stubborn look with which I was so familiar, "and it was Sam I was wrestling with, while we were on the phone, not Blakely."

"So Sam's been with you all this time?"

Sam made a chirruping sound in his throat, his version of pleading. He wanted to be released.

Lily looked away, her expression petulant.

Alec cocked his head and folded his arms. He gave her an articulate stare from under his bushy eyebrows and Lily shrugged.

"Yes, he has. And he's been really happy, too. I took him to the vet and put him on a diet and got him a scratching tree and gave him the run of my house. He's in the best health of his life; the vet says so. I've got all his supplies at the house, and I'll get them to you tomorrow." She shot a questioning glance at Alec, who arched an eyebrow at her. "And . . . and I'm . . . I'm sorry, Amelia. I deceived you."

Alec put in, "And?"

Sam began frantically scratching the inside of the case. He was trying to tunnel his way out.

Lily sighed. "I sort of . . . stole your cat. Alec brought me here to, um, confess and ask your forgiveness." She gave a short, sharp nod as a child does at the end of a recitation.

Alec stepped forward and wrapped an arm around her shoulders. "I told her you were a forgiving woman, Amelia," he said with a warm smile.

I stood and reached out my arms. "Of course I forgive you, Lily."

Lily accepted my hug and returned it listlessly. "Thanks. Well, bye." She bent down and gently tapped the cat carrier, which had begun bouncing on the tabletop. "Goodbye, Sam."

She headed out of the room and toward the exit with Alec close behind her.

From within the cat carrier, Sam began a plaintive, high-pitched moan.

"Lily, wait!" I called.

She paused in the foyer and I caught up with her. I put my hand on her shoulder. She didn't meet my eyes, but she didn't shake off my grip either.

"You love that crazy old cat, don't you? You always have."

"Well, yes, I am fond of him."

"Well then, Lily, I think he ought to stay with you. I don't know why I didn't think of it before. He loves you. He proved it by leaving my house and coming to you."

I was laying it on a little thick, rather like the sour cream Lily had often given Sam when she thought I wasn't looking. And even when she knew I was. That, plus his old cat door had been boarded over at Chez Prentice.

I went on, "Pretty soon I'll be too busy to devote very much time to a pet."

"You will?" Lily smiled a little.

I hadn't prepared any graceful announcement phrase, so I just blurted it out. "Gil and I are having a baby!"

Alec's face lit up like a Hollywood marquee. "I knew it was something like that! That glow!" He gave me a gentle bear hug.

"Oh, I see. You need the room." Lily's reaction was considerably more reserved. "Well, if you really need somewhere for Sam to stay, I guess I can help you out." She headed for the front parlor. "I'll just go get him."

As she left the room, Alec leaned down and whispered, "So very kind of you, Amelia. She was terrified, poor mite, that you'd be furious with her. Thought perhaps you'd call the police on her, silly lass."

"Alec," I whispered back, "are you two an item again?"

He twinkled down at me. "Looks that way, since I understand that—among other considerations—Mr. Blakely Knight can't stand cats!" He opened the Chez Prentice front door as Lily emerged from the parlor carrying Sam. "Ready, my dear?"

As they left, I thought I heard Alec whistling "Love Lifted Me" faintly between his teeth.

Chapter | Thirty-Three

I had expected things to seem a little strange at school on Monday, and I was right. Though I had no outward physial signs of my adventures, the gossip mill had been on overdrive, and it was widely speculated that not only had I been involved with some sort of altercation in the Old Episcopal bell tower, but I was pregnant and probably "had" to get married. I knew this, because I once again eavesdropped in the girls' restroom.

But I wasn't Cruel Gossip's only victim.

"That Serry Shea," Micki Davenport told Brenda Bordeau, "she's always been so full of herself. Says her dad's gonna be mayor? I don't think so!"

Brenda chimed in, to the sound of running water. "Yeah, her mother's going to jail. Did ya hear that?"

Giggling, they left the room, leaving me to emerge from the stall, muttering, "Kick her while she's down, would you?"

Again, my protective instincts had emerged and dispelled the well-buried resentments I'd carried with me. I glanced at the ceiling and smiled.

Are you working on me, Lord? Is that it?

I was surprised. I hadn't realized how very much I'd despised Brigid and her daughter until I stopped despising them. The class bell rang. I whispered a quick prayer for them and plunged into the class-changing melee.

As I called the roll for the next class, Serendipity entered, late. I glanced at her, then looked again. If someone had taken the old Serendipity, plunged her into a large washing machine, then into a capacious dryer, the result might have looked much as this girl did: pale blonde hair, tangled and matted flat, eye makeup smudged, and no lipstick at all. Her tight pullover had a stain on the shoulder and her jeans were at least a size too big and badly wrinkled.

She slumped into her chair with an insolent air, and for a moment she seemed her old, defiant self. But when she looked me in the eye and registered no expression at all, only vagueness, I knew something was terribly wrong with Serry.

Instead of pointing out her tardiness as I might have done the week before, I simply made note of her presence and began class.

Today the first order of business was the discussion of the short homework essays to be entitled My Vision of the Future. It had stemmed from a magazine article published some seventy years ago that predicted that by the year 2000 there would be helicopters on every roof and a form of humanity that evolved into huge, bodiless heads, because of increased brain activity. We had all laughed at the incongruity of it, and I thought it would to fun for the students to make their own speculations on the coming century.

I was right. There was a lively and sometimes hilarious discussion. Hardy Patchke's essay suggested that in a hundred years man would have an overdeveloped thumb from multiple decades of texting; Lew Epstein liked the idea of time travel and Micki Davenport predicted that mothers would be able to give birth to baby girls especially bred to already have lipstick and eyeliner, which elicited laughs and a few catcalls.

Serendipity didn't participate. She didn't even react to the discussion. A few minutes before the end of class, as the essay papers were being collected, she abruptly excused herself and left the room, head down and hair obscuring her face. I caught a quick glimpse of her expression and made no objection to her leaving.

As the classes changed, I remained at my desk and shuffled through the various papers, putting them in alphabetical order. To my surprise, I found a paper by Serendipity Shea among them.

"My Vision of the Future," she wrote in her long, back-slanted hand, "isn't what I thought it would be before. My world was wonderful. It was full of fun and love and happiness . . . " She went on in this same vein for several paragraphs, then ended with, "But I have no future now. My life is over."

Serendipity was extremely depressed. I put the essay aside to give to the school counselor. Normally I'd call the child's parents, but under the circumstances . . .

In my break period I checked with Olive in the school office. Elise Turner, our part-time school counselor was at a conference at the local college until late afternoon. I explained that I had important information about a student.

"Put it in her box," Olive ordered, with her eyes glued as usual to the computer screen, "I'll make sure she gets it."

330 | E. E. Kennedy

It was the best I could do under the circumstances. I wrote a short cover note, put the essay in an envelope, and headed for the teacher's work room.

As I entered, I saw Judith Dee extracting notes from her message box. *Does the woman* live *in this room?* I thought, but smiled my greeting, found Elise's box and deposited the envelope.

I was about to leave when Judith said, "Oh, Amelia, I'll be out of school all next week."

That wasn't earth-shaking news. Judith only worked mornings, anyway. I paid merely polite attention to her. I was foraging in my satchel for another packet of peanut butter crackers. The bouts with nausea were becoming more manageable if I just kept something on my stomach at all times.

"I hope there's nothing wrong," I said, more as a courtesy than in true concern.

She smiled at me beatifically. "Oh, no, not at all. Just a series of tests. I'm healthy as a horse, thank heaven. They checked me out thoroughly after that situation last year. I'm fine. It's just tests."

"But a whole week—" The light dawned. "Judith, are you being tested to donate a kidney?"

"How did you know? Oh, but you had Felicity staying at your house, didn't you? She must have told you."

"Well—"

She sidled closer and spoke in a whisper, though there was no one else in the room. "I knew him, you know? Blakely's father. Quite well, in fact." She pulled on a chain that extended down inside her neckline and extracted a dime-sized, heart-shaped locket.

She opened it. The two hearts contained tiny black-and white photos of two different young men. Judith pointed to the one on the left. "That's him."

I didn't correct her: That's he was admittedly pretty clumsy.

"He looks a lot like Blakely," I remarked, squinting.

"And that's Will Dee, my husband," she said, indicating the other picture of a balding, pleasant-faced young man.

She sighed. "I miss them both." She dropped the locket back into her blouse. "I suppose it's why I had such a soft spot for Blakely." She gathered up her purse and papers. "You know, Amelia, I came into a little money recently—an elderly relative died—and I've wondered what it is I should do with it all. Now I know. I can use it for my traveling expenses to Ohio, should I be chosen."

"It's an admirable thing to do—to be willing to do, Judith," I said.

She waved away my admiration modestly. "Aw, no, not really." She tilted her head and looked at me, straight on. "You know, if I'd had the chance to do this for my husband Will, I would have in a heartbeat." Her face pinched a little. "So now, I do have the chance to do this for my first love, and it's a privilege." She tightened her mouth, straightened her back, and smiled at me. "A true privilege."

She headed out the door and said, almost gaily, "Say a prayer that I'm a match!"

Chapter | Thirty-four

"I'm trying again, Amelia," Alec said as we drove along the snowy country road to my house late that afternoon. "Preparations." With a backward nod, he indicated two large sacks of groceries in the back seat. "Friday night I'm fixing her a steak dinner with all the trimmings and popping the question once more."

"At your place?"

Alec lived just a few miles down the road from us, also on the lakeshore, in a sixties-style brick ranch house that retained all its eccentric, outdated features, much like Alec. "Have you shown it to her?"

"Nope. Not until now." He smiled. "Might as well let her see the real me, warts and all."

"That's probably a good plan." I laid a hand on his arm. "But Alec, don't get your hopes up. Lily's, well—"

"Never fear, dear lady, I have no illusions about her, not any more. She's a quixotic little thing with a short attention span, prone to wander, but I do love her." He began to quietly whistle a snatch of "Come Thou Fount of Every Blessing,"

Prone to wander, Lord I feel it . . .

Alec turned into our driveway. "Well, here we are."

"Thanks for the lift, Alec."

"No bother. And don't fret. The lad'll come round eventually."

Vern was still staying at the B&B and avoiding Gil and me like the plague. It was why I had to get a ride home from Alec.

"I do hope so."

Only a few minutes later, the front door opened and Vern came striding in. I rose from my spot on the sofa where I was enjoying my second peanut-butter-sandwich-and-milk snack of the day.

"Vern, hello."

"Mmm," he answered with a curt nod. In three long steps, he was in the kitchen, where he located several large black garbage bags. Then he brushed past me into his room.

I followed. "Vern," I began, "we need to talk."

He pulled open a dresser drawer full of underwear and dumped it unceremoniously into one of the bags. "No need. Everything's fine. I just made a decision, that's all."

"Decision?"

This didn't have a good sound. I felt a little sick, so I sat on the edge of his bed.

He located a pair of sneakers under his bed and dropped them into the bag. "Yep. You know, I've been mooching off you and Gil for too long. It's time I did a little growing up, went out on my own." He pulled a poster of the periodic table from the wall, rolled it up, and fastened it with a rubber band from his pocket.

"But where are you going?" I asked his back as he wound an extension cord around his arm.

"The dorm. I got a buddy whose roommate dropped out. I can stay rent free for the rest of the semester, then figure out what to do from there."

"Well," I said weakly, "if that's what you want to do."

He paused in his packing. "It's what I want to do." He gave me a small smile. "Don't look like that, Amelia. I don't hate you."

"You—you don't?"

"Well, maybe just a little bit, but it's all going to turn out for the best." He waved a long arm dramatically in the air. "You'll have this room for little what's his name, and I'll be going out into the great big world to face my future. Congratulations, by the way. Alec told me."

"Thanks." I remembered something. "Wait just a minute." I left the room and returned carrying the Wile-E-Coyote tie.

"Thanks," he said, his tone a little more gentle. He rolled it up and stuck it in a side pocket.

All at once, I felt a strange vibration on my upper thigh. "Vern? Something's happening."

I looked down at my leg. The vibration had stopped. Then it started again: *Bzzzzz.*

"What on earth?"

"Here." With an exasperated sigh, Vern reached into the patch pocket on my oversized sweater and extracted my cell phone. "You must have set it on vibrate." He flipped it open and handed it to me.

It was probably Gil, I thought. "Hello?"

I heard a breath, then a kind of squeak. Was this some kind of obscene phone call?

The words came out in a whisper and a gulp. "My life . . . is over. I hope you're happy."

"What? Who is this?"

A little louder this time, "My life is over. Aren't you glad?"

"Serendipity? Where are you?"

Vern leaned forward, frowning, a question on his face. I held up a restraining hand.

Serendipity spoke again. "I'm far, far away, where you'll never find me." The voice seemed to fade away, then returned. "Never, never, never . . . find me . . . "

I put my hand over the receiver and whispered, "Serendipity's in some kind of trouble. We've got to find her. Can't the police locate her cell phone or something?"

He shook his head. "Takes too long," he whispered. He pointed to his ear. "Let me listen."

We held the receiver between our two heads.

"Serry? Why did you call me?"

"My mother calls me Serry. Don't call me that. My . . . jailbird mother calls me that—" A honking blast, rather like an extremely loud car horn, sounded twice in the background.

Vern gestured to me to keep her talking.

"I'm sorry, Serendipity. I didn't mean to. Where did you say you were?"

We could hear the blast again. It sounded familiar.

Vern frowned and mouthed, "Ferryboat?"

"Where?" I mouthed back.

"Somewhere far away. Somewhere cooold. Somewhere high, high . . . " She launched into a sing-song. "I can see for miles and miles and miles . . . "

Vern snapped his fingers. "Hogan's Cliff," he mouthed.

I nodded. It was a precarious, scenic overlook well within earshot of the ferryboat horn. If she wasn't there, she had to be somewhere nearby.

"But why did you call me, Serendipity?" I asked carefully.

As I continued to talk on the cell phone, Vern took my arm, led me down the hall and helped me on with my coat.

"Serendipity? Why did you call me?" I repeated, concerned by the silence on the other end.

Vern led me out into the cold. There was only one car in the driveway: the Rousseaus' battered VW. He ignored my questioning expression and insistently urged me into the passenger seat.

Serendipity answered me at last. "Because . . . because-because-because . . . I wanted to make you happy, Miss Prentice."

"Happy? You want to make me happy?"

I tried reflecting her statement back to her. I'd taken a counseling course in college. Now was as good a time as any to try out the technique since I couldn't think of anything else to say.

She gave a mirthless laugh. "It's the only chance I'll ever have to make you happy, Miss Prentice. And I really do want to make you happy."

I pretended not to hear the sarcasm. "I appreciate that. But why do you want to make me happy?"

By this time, we were careening down the icy country road, heading toward the ferryboat dock. Contrary to what one might think, the ferryboat ran through most of the winter, since the crossing location was where the water seldom froze over.

"What if . . . what if-what if-what if . . . you never had to mess with me again?"

"Mess with you?"

"Well, yeah! You know, never having Serendipity Shea to pick on again." She laughed.

"You'd like that, wouldn't ya?"

Vern was on his own cell phone, calling the police and trying to drive at the same time. It made for some narrow misses on the slippery road.

"No," I said. "I like having you in my class."

"Oh, get real! Don't lie to me! You're always on my case! You hate me!"

Not any more. "That's not true. I like smart people. I like the challenge of—"

"Smart? You think I'm *smart?*"

We made the turn onto the road marked Hobson's Cliff Scenic Overlook. It was a little-known spot, a favorite among professional photographers, a beautiful place with a small parking lot and a totally inadequate barrier dividing the solid ground from the overhanging rock that thrust outward, hanging at least two hundred feet above the lake surface.

"You certainly are smart. You have loads of, um, intellectual potential."

In the little phone, I heard her say, "Hah, guys don't like girls who're smart."

Slowly Vern drove the bright purple VW along the narrow gravel road through the woods to the lake.

"I don't know what you're talking about. Why, look at my husband. He'd never marry a woman who wasn't smart."

I turned to Vern and put a warning finger to my lips. We didn't want to startle the girl.

"I heard a different story, Miss Prentice. I heard—"

Sharply, I said, "Do you believe common gossip, Serendipity Shea?"

There was a long pause.

As I waited for the girl's reply, I frantically chastised myself. *Why, oh, why did you let this girl get to you at a time like this?*

The sound of Serendipity's voice made my heart resume beating. "No, I don't. I hate gossip! Do you know what they're saying about my mom? What they're saying about me?" She gave a little sob. "They used to be my friends!" She began crying in earnest now.

Her father's car, a snazzy red sports number, stood alone in the parking lot. She was too young for a driver's license, but that infraction wasn't important now.

And there she was, sitting with her back turned to us at the very tip of the forbidden ledge, hunched over and swaying a little in the bitter wind.

We parked the VW and closed the doors silently. I headed toward the small, forlorn figure. Vern tried to join me, but I vigorously gestured him back.

"No!" he whispered, "Stay back! Wait for the police!"

"Serendipity?" I asked gently on the telephone, "May I come talk to you?"

"You can't find—" She turned around, wobbling a little, and I gasped, but she retained her seat on the edge of the cliff. She stared blankly at me.

Glancing back over my shoulder, I was relieved to see that Vern had found a hiding place behind the VW. I held out my free hand, palm up, in friendly supplication.

"May I join you?" I said on the phone, then, taking a chance, I clicked the phone shut and dropped it in my coat pocket. "Please?" I called.

She closed her own phone, turned her back on me, but shrugged, so I took that as assent.

How to do this? Dear Lord, please help me!

Slowly, slowly, I stepped over the low chain that marked the cliff's edge and got down on my hands and knees. Moving even more slowly, I made my way along the narrow outcropping until I was directly behind the girl.

"Serendipity? Can we talk?"

I suppressed a highly inappropriate giggle. I'd quoted comedienne Joan Rivers just then.

The wind blew my hair across my eyes, and I brushed it back with one hand. This unthinking gesture nearly caused me to lose my balance, and I swayed a little myself, but recovered. "It is cold up here, isn't it?" I shouted with a friendly laugh.

Serendipity pulled her coat tighter about her and said nothing.

There was no room to sit beside her, so I addressed the back of her head as her pale hair whipped around in the sharp, bitter wind. "This is a pretty tough time for you right now, isn't it?" I said at the top of my voice.

She nodded and said something I couldn't hear.

"What did you say? Please come back here so we can talk."

She yelled over her shoulder. "I said, that's right!"

What to do? Shortly, the police would arrive and try to extract the girl from this precarious perch, using their own methods. I doubted that any good would come of that.

I decided to lay my cards on the table. "Serendipity, please come back with me! It's dangerous here, and I don't want you to get hurt!"

Abruptly, she turned around and shouted in my face, "I already am hurt!"

"I know, dear," I shouted back, "I know you are. Come on." I beckoned carefully with one hand.

She looked down at it, pursed her lips and nodded.

Then, very slowly, very gently, we crawled back toward solid ground until we reached the chain. I helped her over.

We sat right down in a snowdrift. She put her head on my shoulder and began to sob.

"Mom's going to jail. She's pleading guilty! She's telling everything she knows so she'll get a better sentence. What am I going to do?"

Even as I rocked her, stroked her hair and fished in my coat pocket for a tissue, something in the back of my mind said, *If this it true, then perhaps J.T. and Dustin are cleared! Oh, thank you, Lord!*

"My life is over," she said, blowing her nose.

I decided to try some tough love. "Who are you and what did you do with Serendipity Shea?"

That got her attention. "What?"

I was surely winging it now. "Where's the Serendipity who, uh, led every fashion trend at the high school? Where's the Serendipity who . . .who . . . " I groped about in my memory for another one of her attributes, " . . . whose, um, will and personality were so strong that nobody ever dared call her Dippy, not even in grade school?"

Her eyes widened. "That's true. How did you know?" She blew her nose.

"Teachers hear things." I stroked back her tousled hair. "You're stronger than you think, Serendipity. And no question, you're smart. You know exactly what you're doing in my class, don't you?" I was remembering her crumpling the test paper.

She looked down at the tissue in her hands, sniffed, and hiccoughed. "It is kind of fun pulling your chain sometimes."

From the corner of my eye, I could see a police car entering the parking lot. Vern approached it and began talking to the officers, gesturing in our direction.

I said, "You know, I looked it up. Serendipity means a fortunate surprise." I'd paraphrased Webster somewhat, but no matter. "You could surprise a lot of people by going back to school and being the Serendipity we all know." I added, "With one big exception, of course."

"I know." She rolled her eyes. "You want me to study."

"Why not? That would really surprise everybody, wouldn't it?"

She gave me the tiniest smile. "I guess so."

"And I'll be there to help you any time you need it. I promise."

She shrugged. It was hard to know if I had reached her, but at least she was safely off the ledge.

Vern approached hesitantly, with a female police officer close behind.

I said, "Now, Serendipity, Surprise Girl, you need to let the police officer take you home. I want you to go back and start helping your dad through this mess. He needs you."

"I didn't think about that," she admitted.

"Well, he does. And your mother does, too, believe it or not. And remember, I'll be praying for you."

She nodded. With astonishing meekness, Serendipity allowed herself to be led over to the police car.

The male police officer approached us. "Could you folks meet us back at the station to answer a few questions?"

"Sure," said Vern. He winked at me. "*Déjà vu*, ain't it?"

"Sir?"

"Just a little joke, officer," I said, sighing happily.

Vern had winked! Surely that meant he had forgiven me?

As we headed to the VW, the officer said, "Uh, oh. Looks like you folks have a flat there. Here, I'll help you change it."

As the officer and Vern opened the VW's front trunk, I asked, "Why are you driving this car, anyway, Vern?"

"Martin loaned it to me this morning when I went to visit the guys. Ironically, mine has a flat tire too. I should've expected something like this. This car's a real piece of junk."

They began to unfasten the spare tire from its moorings. As they pulled it out, something tiny and metallic bounced off the side of the fender and into the snow.

"I'll get it." The officer dug the thing out with his gloved hands and held it up. "What d'you know?" he said, "It's a bullet!"

Hester's Version of Michigan Sauce

North Country natives may recognize the reference to Michigans in *Death Dangles A Participle*. Hester Swanson, who worked for many years at the college cafeteria, came up with this version and dictated it to Amelia. She makes no claims of authenticity, but says, "It surely tastes like what I remember!"

3 lbs finely ground beef, sautéed and well-drained
10 tsp chili powder
14 oz. can Hunt's tomato sauce (or less)
Scant ¼ cup Frank's or other good hot sauce (Not Tabasco! Even less if your kids will be eating it.)
3 tsp garlic powder
3 tsp onion powder
2 tsp black pepper
3 tsp ground cumin

Make sure the beef is cooked into tiny particles. (Hester uses a pastry cutter to achieve this, chopping the ground beef even more before cooking.) Mixture should ultimately be just barely moistened, so add the tomato sauce very sparingly. Blend all ingredients well before cooking. Cook for two hours, stirring frequently. Results are best if you use non-direct heat, such as a crock pot or double boiler.

There is some controversy about using tomato sauce. Some say there should no tomato in this sauce, but this recipe turns out a very authentic-tasting result. It makes enough to top a whole lot of hot dogs! (At least 25.)

This is best (in Gil's opinion) if served over a good-quality, steamed hot dog in a bun, topped by a thin line of yellow mustard and sprinkled with coarsely chopped sweet onions. To quote Gil Dickensen, "Ambrosia!"

MURDER
IN THE PAST TENSE

Miss Prentice Cozy Mystery Series

Book 3

By | E. E. Kennedy

Coming September 2014

Elkhart, Indiana
46514 USA

Chapter | One

I wish to state at the outset that, until the day in question, I—Amelia Prentice Dickensen—had never in my life bought a supermarket tabloid.

That's not to say I never sneaked the occasional surreptitious glance at a lurid headline as I unloaded my grocery cart. And it's also true that I'd once become so desperate that I actually encouraged one of my more recalcitrant English students to read them, just so he read something. Still, as literature, I understand that if you use a little vinegar, they're great for cleaning windows.

But on that particular evening, as I placed a sack of overpriced seedless red grapes on the conveyor belt and let my eyes drift absently over the rack of colorful papers, magazines, and thin paperback cookbooks, my attention was snagged by a familiar face. Not just a famous one, but an actual, familiar, I-know-that-person face.

My heart made an audible thump. I read the caption: "Charlotte with third husband, Danny diNicco, on their honeymoon. Last year, the theatrical producer was found brutally murdered in his Manhattan office."

Surely it wasn't who I thought it was. But how could there be more than one? I looked again.

There he was, grinning into the camera with that wide, sensuous mouth, his hand carelessly draped over Charlotte's shoulders, some long-ago breeze lifting the dark wave that always dipped just above his forehead. It was a small color picture, printed on cheap newsprint, but those glittering black eyes with the long, black lashes were unmistakable.

I pulled the paper from its metal stand and skimmed the front page. Apparently the murder of an erstwhile husband was just another event in the colorful life of character actress Charlotte Yates who, in the face of overwhelming misfortune, kept picking up the pieces of her life and carrying on, her pointed little chin held high and famous squawking voice ever ready to entrance her audience.

There was a picture of Charlotte with Husband Number One (an acting teacher), from whom she was divorced; and with Husbands Number Two (a stockbroker) and Number Four (a rock musician), who had shuffled off this mortal coil due to motorcycle accident and drug overdose, respectively. More details and photos would be forthcoming on page eight.

Fascinating as that was, it wasn't Charlotte Yates who interested me. It was her third husband.

"Amelia?" said Gil, "Are you going to buy that, or what?"

I looked up. Apparently all our groceries had been checked, bagged and paid for by my spouse while I was doing my reading. "I'm buying it." I fished a few dollars from my pocket and tendered them to the clerk, who, I noted with embarrassment, was one of my students, though I hadn't seen her in a long time.

"That's a good issue, Miss Prentice," said Kim Mallard, smiling conspiratorially, "Especially that spinach diet." She leaned forward, her eyes on my expanding middle. "How're you feeling? Any more morning sickness?"

Everybody knew everything in a small town. "No, I'm over that now. Just tired all the time. Thanks for asking."

The girl sighed. "I hear you! Between swollen ankles and trips to the ladies room all day, I'm exhausted!"

That's when I realized that her loose smock covered the same condition as mine. "Oh, my," I said.

Kim, by my figuring, was seventeen.

She waved a hand airily. "Oh, it's okay. Brian 'n me're getting married as soon as the baby's born and I can fit into a wedding dress!" She glanced over her shoulder and pointed to a magazine rack. "Hand me that *Modern Wedding*, would'ja?"

When I complied, she eagerly turned to a large full-color illustration of a thin, ethereal-looking young woman in an elaborate, stark-white wedding gown. "That's it!" She tapped the page with an overlong fingernail decorated with a silver peace sign and turned a glowing smile at me. "Got it on layaway at Formal Dreams over at the Mall."

"It's lovely, Kim."

"This magazine costs fifteen bucks. Better put it away." Guiltily, she slapped the huge magazine shut and allowed me to replace it. "Of course, it all depends on Brian getting a job at that new foundry." She looked at me speculatively. "I'm seven and a half months. How far along are you?"

"Eight and a half." I glanced over my shoulder at the line forming behind me, and then at Gil's back as he strode out of the store, pushing the cart. "I guess I'd better be going. Good to see you, Kim. Take care of yourself."

Waving goodbye, I folded my tabloid under one arm and scurried after my husband, who was once again exhibiting the signs of his besetting ailment.

Rather than agoraphobia—fear of the marketplace—Gil suffers from what I call Fear of Shopping. Accurate statistics are hard to come by, but I have it on good authority that approximately half the male population of this country is afflicted. I discovered this terrible secret on our honeymoon, but like the valiant comedienne, Charlotte Yates, I had decided to bravely get on with my life, embracing the good with the bad.

Making this job far easier was Gil's solid, manly physique and head of thick, semi-silvery hair. Not to mention an IQ roughly the same number as the price of a loaf of multi-grain bread and a smile that—well, considering my condition, you can guess the rest. My students certainly did.

As I approached our car where Gil was opening the trunk, I spotted another familiar figure; this time, a live one. "Vern! Hello!" I called, waving at the tall blond young man who was carrying a six-pack of cola and taking long strides away from the store. Without a glance my way, he continued walking and quickly was well out of earshot.

I sighed. "I think he heard me. Apparently, he's still not speaking to us."

Gil moved aside a case of bottled water and an emergency snow shovel to make room for the groceries. "And you're surprised?"

"Well, I thought after everything died down, maybe."

We lifted the groceries into the trunk.

Gil said, "Honey, you're underestimating the grudge-carrying power of my side of the family. That kid may never speak to us again."

"But we did the right thing!"

"I know that, and you know that, but well . . . " Gil shrugged, slammed the trunk door and grabbed the folded tabloid I was carrying. "Since when have you taken to reading those?" he asked teasingly. He was trying to change the subject and cheer me up.

He read the headlines aloud: "Aliens Endorse Academy Award Winner for President,' 'Medium Martinka Yeka Boldly Predicts American Idol Winner.' "

With a sad glance in the direction of our disappearing nephew, I said, "Since today. There's somebody I know in it. Or rather, somebody I once knew."

"You know that psychic woman? How do I get an exclusive?"

Gil held tabloids in even lower regard than I did. It was a matter of professional pride. He was, after all, editor of our town's only real newspaper, *The Press-Advertiser*, which was struggling mightily in these hard times.

"What does she predict about us?" Gil slid behind the wheel and turned the ignition key. He grabbed my hand and pulled it to his lips. "Will it last?"

I looked down at my round tummy and smiled, sending up a quick but fervent prayer of thanksgiving, "It better."

I picked up my copy of *Worldwide Buzz* and turned to page eight. Impatiently, I skimmed the illustrated retrospective of Charlotte Yates' career from her humble beginnings as a rubber-faced extra in a roller skating movie to her recent best supporting actress Oscar for a Tennessee Williams remake.

There were just the barest facts about Danny diNicco. He'd met Charlotte in the mid-nineties on a movie set where they were both bit players. The marriage lasted a little more than a year and produced no children, but their split was apparently amicable. After the divorce, Danny had become a theatrical entrepreneur, owning and managing a string of dinner theatres and dance clubs across New York, Pennsylvania, and New Jersey.

To my frustration, after having imparted these newsy tidbits, the reporter dropped the subject of Danny and moved on to Husband Number Four.

The next mention of Danny was under a small photo at the bottom of the page. The picture was in black-and-white, a grainy, angled shot of an ordinary office desk, topped by a pen in a holder, a computer monitor, a keyboard, and a large blotter. This orderly still life was freely spattered with ominous black stains.

I read the caption: "Scene of the Crime: Danny diNicco's lifeless body was found in this Manhattan office last January, shot twice in the head, execution style. Police are said to have no leads in the case."

"What's the matter?" said Gil.

"Huh?" I looked up.

"You made a funny noise."

"I did? What kind of noise?"

"I don't know. A kind of a groan; sort of high-pitched. A feminine kind of a groan. What's wrong?"

"I don't know if I should tell you."

"Why not?"

"It's about an old crush of mine. Are you the jealous type?"

Gil smiled his irresistible smile. "What do you think?"

So I told him. It had all been a long time ago, but once I got into telling about it, Gil remembered.

He'd been there . . .